The Spence Women

Other Books

All Ways A Woman
a celebration of women
their thoughts, their loves,
their lives, their dreams
and desires.

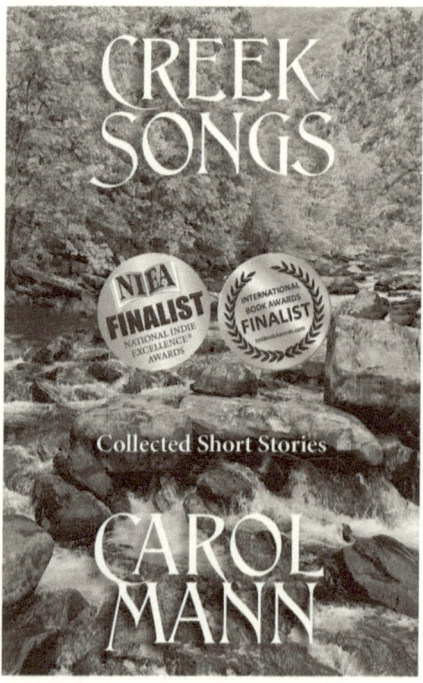

Creek Songs
Collected short stories. Each
story is a drama of a unique
life, as diverse as rocks in the
the creek near Carol's house.

The Spence Women

Carol Mann

Published posthumously with permission from the author.

AquaZebra Book Publishing - Cathedral City, CA

Mann, Carol
The Spence Women

1st edition

Library of Congress Control Number: 2025901438
ISBN 978-1-954604-15-5 (paperback)

Published by

AquaZebra™
Book Publishing

Cathedral City, California
www.aquazebra.com

Lynn Jones Green, Editor
Cover photo by Steve Harvey on Unsplash

Cover/interior design

AquaZebra™
Web, Book & Print Design

Mark E. Anderson
www.aquazebra.com

For my sister Donna

"And then many will fall away and betray one another and hate one another."

—Matthew 24:10

rologue

Pearl Spence

When I was little, old-timers would say to me, "A penny saved is a penny earned," and, "Life's a bumpy road." The first one taught me to watch my money. The second one helped me know when one of life's bumps had arrived. Sometimes it was just a pothole that jiggled me a little. Other times I fell into a sizable crater that near buried me.

But I figured somethin' out. You might just as well hunker down 'cause you only got but one road. And, so far, praise the Lord, I've stayed on mine for eighty-two years.

My road began in Ozark country near Salem, Missouri, where I grew up and married Hank Spence. That road took us out west to California. When my husband died in a freeway crash, I felt like I'd hit a sign tellin' me the road had ended. But I had a little girl to raise, and she kept me movin' forward, puttin' one foot in front of t'other.

There's still plenty of pavement stretchin' ahead today for my daughter, Audrey, my granddaughter, Maegan, and me. I call us the Spence women. Most of the time, we've steered around surprises in our path. Until a simple birthday card spun us onto a gravel shoulder, into a guard rail, and nearly off a cliff.

Chapter One

Pearl Spence

January 2010—Beaumont Valley, California

Some folks think birthdays are just another trip around the sun. Others think they're big hoop-de-doos. Me? I'm kind of an in-betweener. And as a grandma? One thing for sure: A grandma don't forget a granddaughter's birthday. Ever. 'Specially if she's only got one grandbaby, like me. That sweet girl, Maegan, is all grown up now and lives way off in Los Angeles, but that don't matter. I send her a birthday card every year. But this one time, well, things got a little bumpy.

Back in 2007 when Maegan's thirtieth birthday come 'round in November, I bought a card at the local Hallmark store. It had her favorite flower on the front, a yellow rose. The words inside was real nice, too. So I signed it like always: Love, from Gramma Pearl.

You should know that me, Audrey, and Maegan have had to make plenty of choices along the way, the kind we hoped was good ones. They're also the kind of choices that can backfire—most families have made some of those decisions a time or two, I guess. I hoped what I chose to do wouldn't come back and smack me in the face. But I couldn't stop myself. I had a secret just plain burnin' in my heart.

So, I put a little note in her birthday card 'bout what had been buried inside me since she was born. The words reared up and jumped out like a spring from an ol' mattress. Oh, my stars, those words near tore me and the girls apart.

What nobody knew was that Audrey and me signed lawyer's papers right after Maegan was born. We didn't want to. The terms was hard, but we signed 'cause it was best for my little granddaughter. And, like we promised in those papers, we told nobody nothin'. Folks know a Spence woman keeps her word.

But I felt the time had come to tell. Keep a secret too long and it begins to swell up like a carbuncle. I'd seen unhappiness ooze from this one for too long.

My heart ached for Maegan like poor Abraham's did when God told him to sacrifice his son, Isaac. Maegan done nothin' wrong, but she'd suffered unhappiness. Least I could do was unlock the secret. The burden just plain weighed me down.

I wasn't sure what Maegan would think when she read my note. She might get madder than a wet hen. Fact is, she's been mad at her mother for years, and I sure didn't want her mad at me. But I felt the girl had the right to know, and she'd figure out what to do 'bout it. Maegan's real smart.

That was two years ago.

Chapter Two

Maegan Spence

January 2008—Los Angeles, California

Maegan nestled against the pillows of a brown couch, comfortable in jeans and a sweatshirt, her long slender legs curled beneath her, light easing into the living room of her one-bedroom apartment from a table lamp's soft glow. Beside her on the sofa cushion lay a birthday card with the image of a solitary yellow rose and the words "For a Granddaughter's Special Day." Maegan twisted and untwisted a strand of her thick auburn hair, a frown on her brow.

She glanced up at her best friend, Jennifer, thankful she was there. They'd met at law school on their first day and had become each other's cheerleaders as classes and professors grew more difficult. Tonight, Maegan needed her cheerleader friend.

"Is that the card you mentioned?" Jennifer nodded toward it. Seated across from Maegan on a large, overstuffed hassock, she pushed up her sweater sleeves and scooped a handful of popcorn from a bowl sitting on the coffee table between them. She ate the kernels, one by one, brushing salty residue from her grey slacks.

"Yes, it's the birthday card I received back in November." Maegan picked up the card with her left hand. "And then with all the holidays, I laid it aside for a while. It's from my grandmother, Pearl. I wanted you to read the note folded inside. I'm still contemplating the information, how to approach it. It's something you know I've been dealing with for years. I'd appreciate your input."

Jennifer took a cocktail napkin from the table and wiped her fingers.

Maegan looked at the card, running the fingers of her right hand gently over its surface. "Pearl wrote to say, 'It's time.'"

"Time for what?" Jennifer opened a small red purse beside her, removed wire-framed glasses, and put them on. She pushed her long blond hair behind her ears.

Maegan rubbed her chin. "Time to tell."

"Tell what, my friend?"

"About my family."

A smile spread across Jennifer's face. "Oh, Maegan, that's something you've wanted for so long."

Maegan nodded. "My grandmother's eighty, and, evidently, the past has haunted her for a long time. The handwriting's a little hard to read." She offered the card and its note to her friend.

Jennifer took the card, admiring its image and words. "Nice," she said as she opened the card and removed the note written on a piece of lined paper. She began to read it aloud.

Maegan honey,
    Soon after you was born, your mother and me got a letter to go to the Bank of America over on 6th Street. The bank officer said if we signed some fancy papers, I'd get money every month, deposited in a special account to help raise you.

When you reached twenty-one, the money would come to you for the rest of your life. We had to promise not to tell anyone and never try to find your father—or the money would stop. We figured the agreement was better for you than going after a man who'd run off.

I don't know how the bank found us, but it's time to tell you what I know.

Your father's name is Roger Hemmings, Jr. In 1977, he was going to Arizona State University over in Phoenix. He wanted to be a lawyer. He came to Palm Springs on spring break.

The papers we signed come from First Republic Bank of Arizona. I saw a signature on those papers—Roger Hemmings, Sr. I also glimpsed a business card stapled to the folder. Never forgot. Jensen, Hemmings and Hargitay, Esquire, Attorneys at Law. Couldn't read the address except for Phoenix, Arizona.

I hope this helps.

Love,

Gramma Pearl

"Wow! This *is* big." Jennifer removed her glasses and dropped them on the table. "I know it's something you've wanted forever, but . . ."

"But what?"

"According to this note, if you find your father and contact him, you break the agreement. That's money for life—gone!" Jennifer shook her head. "That's a big price tag."

Maegan looked away. Right now, as a newer attorney, she needed that money—not only for herself, but for her grandmother. She sent Pearl money every month.

"There's something else." Jennifer paused, slipped the note into the card, and placed it on the coffee table. "You already know my own father walked out one day, only to reappear nine years later. He wasn't a nice man. Not a happy reunion. It hurt. A lot. I wouldn't want to see you get hurt like that. Not again."

"Thanks, Jen. I get it. My father appears to be an absent deadbeat with money." Part of her ached to know her father, now identified as Roger Hemmings, Jr. What did he look like? What kind of man was he? The other part of her wanted to confront the man for what he'd done.

"Maegan, you've dealt very well with not having a father."

"I suppose, on the outside." Maegan hesitated. "But on the inside, it's always been a problem . . . an ache, if you will."

Jennifer waved her hand. "We all carry baggage. Sometimes it's best left in the suitcase."

"Maybe I want to unpack mine." Maegan wondered if her friend understood her feeling of loss. The way you could both love and hate someone you'd never met.

"A lot of people grow up without their fathers." Jennifer folded her arms.

Maegan recognized the argumentative, lawyerly tone. "Jen, most of those people probably know who their fathers are or were. You do. I don't. I've just now learned. With the names and information Pearl gave me, I'm going to do a background check. Then I'll ask one of our firm's investigators to dig deeper."

Jennifer unfolded her arms, shaking her head. "Don't use in-house investigators. You know how gossip spreads through our lofty law offices. The lawyers at Hawthorne, Sharp and Whitelaw like to talk. So does the staff."

"I know, I know," Maegan nodded. "Old Man Whitelaw is a strait-laced church deacon, holier than Moses."

"My point exactly. If he found out, he could get a wild hair and make things tough on you."

"Do you really think being an illegitimate child would be an issue in today's world? Besides, they'd be afraid of a discrimination or harassment suit. Bad for the firm's image."

"Discrimination can be subtle," Jennifer replied. "Meetings that exclude you, cases not awarded, invitations not received, credit not given, a gradual slipping from the loop—and you couldn't prove a thing."

Maegan's face flushed. "Point taken."

Jennifer played with a large silver ring on the index finger of her right hand. "You could hire an independent investigator, but if things go wrong?" She stood and walked to the window, peering into the night.

Maegan felt Jennifer's body language; however, this was her life, her decision. She picked up the note, held it in her hand, as if weighing the message, feeling its real weight travel through her. True, she'd be risking her future and Pearl's if she lost the money. But she didn't plan to be a struggling attorney all her career. Wasn't it also true she'd be cheating herself if she didn't try to find the man?

Jennifer turned from the window. "You know, your life is going great. You've worked hard. You're starting to make money. You have income from that special account every month."

"Money's a poor substitute for a father."

Jennifer replied quickly. "Ah, I'd think about that statement. Just because he's related brings no promises. You have no idea what kind of a man he is."

"I doubt he's on the FBI's Most Wanted list." Maegan felt her stomach tighten, heard the bite in her voice. Jennifer always pushed her point.

"Maybe not," her friend replied. "But he could be an abuser or a drunk. He's obviously selfish and thoughtless."

"We don't know that." Maegan shook her head. "My parents were young kids."

Jennifer raised an eyebrow. "I think it was a case of irresponsible cold feet."

Silence. Maegan smoothed her jeans. The burden felt heavier than ever. Why had Pearl given her this information now?

"Well, you know how I feel." Jennifer turned from the window, returned her glasses to her purse, and reached for a black shawl draped on the arm of the couch. "As they say, a little devil's advocacy never hurts. Hope you find an answer. Better hop on that computer. I'm leaving, girlfriend, before I say anything more."

Maegan walked Jennifer to the door. "I'll call you later, Jen."

She closed the door slowly, knowing she had to make up her mind. Too much time and energy had been spent on this issue over the past years.

Restless, she kicked off her shoes. The carpet felt soft under her feet as she walked to the window. Light from streetlamps painted shadows on the surrounding old brick buildings. Red, yellow, blue and green neon signs lit up businesses and restaurants. Tip Top Cleaners. Elite Hair Salon. Mort's Deli. Wong's Produce Mart. The scene usually pleased her. But not tonight. She felt disconnected from it. Disconnected—like her life.

She opened the sliding door, stepped onto the balcony to the aroma of Filippi's Pizza and the honk of a horn at the intersection. A couple dressed in black stood by the curb in conversation, surrounded by the nighttime activity on Hillhurst and Franklin Streets in the Los Feliz

District, a crossroads where the funky old collided with the glitzy new of Los Angeles.

Maegan placed her hands on the railing, her life also at a crossroads. What should she do? Make contact? Not make contact? She kneaded the back of her neck, feeling the tightness. The evening's noises began to rub on her nerves, pushing her back into the living room, face to face with an open manila folder on her desk—an air pollution case. She should work, but she couldn't make herself focus. With a sigh, she closed the sliding door.

The apartment, always her refuge, now felt like a cage. She dropped onto the couch, laid back her head, and stared at the ceiling. After a few deep breaths, she took the card and note from the coffee table and put it on the lamp table beside her next to a small wooden box, a gift from her grandmother. A carved roadrunner standing on the lid would serve as a reminder of the desert where she grew up, Pearl had said. She placed the box in her lap. It hadn't been opened for a while. She grasped the roadrunner in her fingertips and opened the lid.

Nestled in a corner, her grandfather's wedding band—the grandfather she never knew, killed in a big-rig trucking accident on Interstate 10. A good man, she was told. Maegan held the band between her fingers. She thought of the men in her mother Audrey's life. Roger Hemmings who left, never to return, and after him, Dixson Dupre, who never left but should have. She rotated the ring on her little finger, then settled it back in the box.

Various photographs of her family drew her attention next. One of Pearl, a big smile on her face and an apron wrapped around her ample figure, leaning against a wooden picnic table with a bowl of apples ready to be cut for one of her famous pies. Another photo, this one of

Maegan's half-brother, Winston, the would-be jazz musician, holding a guitar. Yet another of her mother, Audrey, smiling, her long dark hair in a ponytail, taken at Maegan's high school graduation. There were no pictures of her other stepbrother, Neville, or of her stepfather, Dixson.

A shiny penny for good luck peeked from under the photos, turning Maegan's thoughts to money. Should she risk losing the special account? Would she be successful enough to take care of her grandmother without it? She wanted to be able to afford in-home care or a good, assisted-living facility for Pearl when the time came.

She closed the lid and placed the box back on the lamp table.

Maegan leaned forward, head in her hands. She'd never know what life might have been if Roger Hemmings had stayed with her mother, Audrey. Maybe better, maybe worse. More money, probably; not so much struggle. One thing she did know: Pearl had been the person who held a little girl's life together, who guided a teenager to adulthood. She had been the one to protect her, center her values, build her character, teach her loyalty. Give her unconditional love.

She thought of her grandmother's words: "Remember, honey, the glass of life fills with what you put in it."

A solution broke through her maze of uncertainty, a strategy she could live with *and* protect her emotions and her finances at the same time. The big question of why he had left and never returned wouldn't be answered. But knowing why wouldn't change what happened. But she could know who and where he was. She'd be satisfied with that.

Jennifer answered on the second ring.

Maegan didn't give her a chance to speak. "I need your help. I want you to hire an independent investigator to find Roger Hemmings. That will keep me and my name removed from anyone nosing around. If anyone inquires, act like it's for a current case you're working on. Be discreet. I won't try to meet him."

"Whew! You're a wise girl. This can be done on the downlow." Jennifer paused. "I have an outside person I can trust that I've used on occasion. Glad you're not angry with me. After I left, I thought maybe I'd said too much."

"I just want to know," Maegan replied. "I'm beginning my own research right now."

"Good luck, girlfriend. I'll get started on my end." Jennifer hung up.

Maegan went to her desk, shoved aside the pollution case file and opened her laptop. First, she logged into *Accurint* for address history on Roger Hemmings, Jr., Phoenix, Arizona. Next, she logged into *AutoTrackXP* for the most current information on Roger Hemmings. She was, as an attorney, no stranger to search engines.

She'd made her decision.

Chapter Three

Pearl Spencer

January 2010—Beaumont Valley, California

When my daughter Audrey was a senior at Beaumont Valley High, she asked to go to Palm Springs for spring break like all her friends. That would've been back in March 1977.

I rolled my eyes and said, "No." I knew what spring break could be like with its drinkin' and carryin' on.

She got scratchy and whiney as a puppy in a box, scared she'd spend all her days in Beaumont Valley. "I don't have a life," she'd say, a big pout on her face.

I'd say, "Nope. Just not a good idea."

We fussed and fussed. But I thought on it, how she'd be graduatin' soon. To make her happy, maybe I could let her go.

Sure do wish I'd thought about it more because I blame myself for what happened. I knew Palm Springs got wild with kids in town from all over. Trust me, I'd talked to her about boys, but she was like an innocent little bird let free from its cage. In my heart, I knew I'd protected her too much after her daddy died, but I thought she'd be stronger. I could have used my Hank's thoughts on a Palm Springs trip.

When Audrey was five, my husband was killed on Interstate 10 near the town of Whitewater. Trucker fell asleep at the wheel of a transport truck and hit my man's pick-up. Audrey cried and cried about the loss of her papa. I had to cry when I was alone so I wouldn't upset her. From then on, I worked real hard every day on my pie business to support us and keep Audrey in school. Eventually, I had a little shop—Pearl's Place.

I was always busy with the shop. I'd cook and taste, cook and taste. How I got so fat.

You could smell those pies for miles around. Cherry. Apple. Blueberry. Then I added a breakfast and lunch menu. Made a chili that'd bring tears to your eyes. Audrey grew up with the shop and worked at it on weekends, sometimes during the week after school. Everybody said she was the prettiest girl in Beaumont Valley.

Well, I had a change of heart, sorry to say. I let her go to Palm Springs and a few months after that trip, she started actin' peculiar. Moody. She'd cry at the drop of a hat. Didn't want to go nowhere, be with nobody. Didn't want to talk. One day I sat her down. Told her we'd sit right where we was until she told me her troubles. It didn't take long to figure out the girl had got herself pregnant. My blood rushed through me like an outta-control train, like a frantic engineer grabbin' at one control, then another. Who was I mad at? Who did I blame? Her? The boy? Me?

Then I got real sad. This wasn't what I wanted for my daughter. But when that baby was born? My, oh my! I loved that sweet little thing to pieces. Audrey named her Maegan after our Scotch-Irish ancestors. Little red-haired Maegan Spence, the sweetest thing I'd ever seen. My heart filled with love, big like the mornin' sun risin' over the mountains. She had velvet skin. Soft auburn curls. Brown eyes'd turn a person to melted butter.

But the wheel of time don't go backward. What really makes me so sad? Neither of them girls—Audrey or Maegan— had a father. One died. One run off. Just wasn't right.

Well, after I'd written that note in Maegan's birthday card, she called me. You know, about her daddy and that special bank account. She asked me why I'd decided to tell her. I said she'd wanted to know and had the right to know. It was time to make her own decisions. It would be wrong for me to take what I knew to the grave.

Chapter Four

Jennifer Bevins

April 2008—Los Angeles, California

Jennifer relaxed under the lighting of vintage chandeliers, sitting at a table for two in the Water Grill, one of the best seafood restaurants in Los Angeles according to the *Los Angeles Times*. True to its name, a gentle flow of water undulated down a copper wall, the soft, rain-like sound a welcome contrast after a busy, noise-filled day. She pondered the fresh seafood list, decided on Alaskan halibut, and put the menu aside just as her friend arrived.

"Hi, girlfriend," Maegan said. She slid into the chair across from Jennifer's, her brown eyes extra bright, auburn hair framing the blush of her cheeks.

"Well, your team winning that air pollution case certainly makes you sparkle." Jennifer watched her friend place her purse and a computer case on the floor beside her.

Maegan smiled, a soft dimple forming in her right cheek. "We left nothing but ashes."

"Congratulations."

"Thanks, Jen. Should be worthy of a small bonus." She paused.

"I've got more big news."

"What's more exciting than a win and a bonus, even a small one?"

Maegan put her elbows on the table, leaned forward, rested her chin on her clasped hands. "I'm going."

"Going where?" Jennifer reached for her water glass.

"I wrote Roger Hemmings a letter. Told him I was his daughter. That I would like to meet him."

"You what?" Jennifer's hand hit the glass. She grabbed it before water spilled all over the table.

"He asked where," Maegan continued. "I suggested we start at the beginning. In Palm Springs where he and my mother met. We're meeting at the Hyatt."

"Damn it, Maegan." Jennifer pursed her lips, shaking her head. "We decided on a plan, *your* plan. No contact with him, just me gathering information."

"Jen, I realized I couldn't live with that. I need to find out what made him leave us. In person." Maegan smoothed a napkin into her lap, picked up a menu.

"Hemmings abandoned you." Jennifer paused. "You know he's in a wheelchair."

"Yes. You told me. Your investigator found that out. I also saw a picture of him online. Probably age or disease related." Maegan put the menu down. "I could have just gone ahead and met him and not told you."

"Maybe you should have." Jennifer crossed her arms. "The special bank account?"

"I have my grandmother's blessing."

"You sure don't have the blessings of your stepfather, Dixson, or Neville, that oldest son of his." Jennifer leaned forward, forearms on the table. "They've always coveted that money. They've often threatened you harm while trying to get at it. If that money stops, they'll never believe you aren't receiving it anymore. They'll think you're lying."

Maegan nodded, tapping the fingers of her right hand on the menu. "A possible problem."

"A *possible* problem?" Jennifer huffed. "You told me yourself they sometimes sell drugs in the Coachella Valley, working out of a downtown Palm Springs casino. You might run into them."

Maegan shook her head. "Not according to Pearl. Neville's down around San Diego, near the Mexican border. Dixson and my mother live somewhere in San Bernardino."

"Why not meet Hemmings in Phoenix where he lives?"

"It'll be okay, Jen. Dixson and Neville shouldn't be a problem. As far as they know, I'm in Los Angeles."

"Dixson tried to *rape* you!" Jennifer felt her friend's silence.

Maegan slowly rubbed her palms on the tablecloth. "That was fifteen years ago."

"Yes, okay. What about Jack?" Jennifer pressed. "You're in a relationship that's working. At least, that's what you've said. Does he know what you're doing?"

"He doesn't need to know. We *were* in a relationship. We've parted ways."

"When?" Jennifer asked.

"In early February. Happy Valentine's Day to me." Maegan laughed quietly.

"Sorry. I didn't know. How come you didn't tell me?"

"Life got busy, and I buried myself in work," Maegan said, playing with her napkin. "To sum it up, Jack said my life was too crowded."

"What's that supposed to mean? You're going to tell me all about it over a good martini, but not now." Jennifer paused. "Where was I? Ah, yes, your sweet brother, Neville—sarcasm intended. When his father went to jail after the attempted rape, he threatened you."

"I still keep restraining orders on both him and Dixson."

Jennifer shook her head. "Pieces of paper, on a good day."

Maegan reached across the table and touched her friend's hand. "Look, Jen. This is my journey. Please don't tell anyone. Okay?"

Jennifer pulled away. "For God's sake. I thought you'd finally dealt with your baggage."

"And I thought you'd be more understanding," Maegan snapped back.

"I'm going to the ladies' room." Jennifer managed to push the chair back on the plush carpet and stood. Her napkin slipped to the floor. She stepped on it as she made her way to the restroom.

Her scowling face stared back at her from a large gold-framed mirror in the ladies' room as she thought of the time wasted getting information on Hemmings. That was supposed to be the deal—information only. Maegan behaved like an uncooperative client, asking for advice, deciding on a plan, and then doing the opposite. Impulsive. Stubborn.

The beginnings of a dull headache throbbed behind her eyes. She dug a silver pillbox from her purse, removed two aspirin and dry-gulped them. They lingered on her tongue and in her throat, their bitterness making her grimace. She swallowed several times.

Why was she getting so upset? Maegan could do what she liked. She rubbed her forehead. But these men—Roger Hemmings, Dixson Dupre, his son Neville Dupre. There were too many chances for things to go wrong.

Oh, Maegan, what are you getting into?

Chapter Five

Pearl Spence

March 1977—Beaumont Valley, California

Well, obviously, I got my Audrey to Palm Springs.

One day an idea buzzed into my head, and I phoned my brother, Seb. No one called him by his Christian name, Sebastian, except our daddy, and he was a long time dead. Seb lived in Palm Springs. Ran a souvenir shop. Sold T-shirts, postcards . . . stuff for tourists.

Anyway, with spring break almost here, I figured it was gonna be a long week of listenin' to Audrey complain and sass. Maybe she could work for her uncle. She'd make money, have a safe place to stay, meet people. Then come home and be nicer after all that bad talk about the trip in the first place. But when I talked to that brother of mine, he wasn't so nice. We had us a conversation.

"No way," Seb sputtered. "I'm no sitter. The town'll be full of tourists and college kids and shenanigans. My own boys had their share of spring break troubles a few years ago. Beer. Girls. Fightin'. Brawlin'. A pretty girl like your Audrey? Boys'll be all over her like one of your hot pie crusts. She's better off in Beaumont Valley."

"You mean she can't work for you?" I pressed. "Help you out for a week? You're always complainin' about wantin' someone workin' for you who you can trust."

"The day's not the problem, Pearl, and you know it. It's the night. College kids in town from all over. Parties until the sun comes up. Chasin' the girls. And all that action brings out the town toughs. They roam around lookin' for easy marks, fat wallets. Nothin' but trouble."

"That's no problem," I reasoned. "We'll just set down some rules for Audrey. You keep her with you and your wife."

"Listen, Pearl. I've got business day and night. I can't be totin' a girl around. And you know Sharon works all the time sellin' Avon."

I could feel the heat stokin' in my gut. "You mean there's no time to be with my Audrey? *Your* niece? Take her to the movies, show her a few sights so she gets Palm Springs out of her system?"

"That's it."

I got real mad, like a trussed-up turkey. "You sure have a short memory, brother. Family helps family."

"What're you talkin' about?" Seb said, all innocent.

"Old Uncle Jake took you in for a while after our daddy died because Mama'd had enough of your big britches mouth and your runnin' around. You mean you forgot that?"

"That's a long time ago, Pearl," he said.

I kept tossin' wood on the fire I was buildin'. "You told me Uncle Jake straightened your ass out good. Probably kept you out of jail."

"That's not the same, Pearl, and you know it. Different for boys."

Then I pulled out the big guns. "Well, I also remember the time I lent you a little money. It was a stretch to find any extra after Hank got killed. Also kept your boys with me for a time. They was little then.

All that so you and Sharon could get that store in Palm Springs. The way I see it, you owe me."

"Goddammit, Pearl!" Seb was breathin' hard. "You're like a dog grabbin' a man's leg. Your bite hangs on tight."

"Is that a 'yes'?"

So you know I got my way, and you know I wish I hadn't.

Chapter Six

Audrey Spence

Spring Break 1977—Palm Springs, California

Sunlight glared through the plate glass window of The Desert Tee, her uncle's souvenir shop in downtown Palm Springs. Audrey stopped folding tie-dyed T-shirts and watched three what looked like college kids in front of the store. A shirtless boy held an open bottle of beer over a girl's head, pretending to pour it. Another girl in short-shorts took their picture. She wondered where they got the money to come to Palm Springs at spring break. It must be nice to have rich parents. Nobody she knew was rich . . . or went to college. They'd probably just laugh at her.

The trio moved down the street. Audrey straightened the pile of folded shirts on the display table. She hated being stuck in the shop, but it was better than rotting in Beaumont Valley. Besides, Uncle Seb paid her more than her mother did. At least for a week she escaped being bored to death. Palm Springs felt alive, noisy, crowded, bright with color, even if she did have to watch from the sidelines.

"That's the Way I Like It" played softly from an old Motorola radio on a shelf behind the cash register. Shirts, jeans, and hats crowded shelves and tables. Vests and jackets hung on hangers from sagging clothes rods. Beads and cheap belts dangled from chrome display hooks. Shot glasses, plates, ashtrays emblazoned with "Souvenir of Palm Springs" lined the shelves. Audrey watched three women fumble through a rack of postcards and then buy three. She groaned after they left. The cards needed to be straightened. Again.

Audrey thought her uncle might be up to something when he worked at night. She'd found a box in the stockroom of small bags containing what looked like herbs. Like what her mother used in her cooking. She was pretty sure they weren't herbs, but she didn't dare tell Pearl. Her mother'd yank her home. Audrey'd never gotten high, but she'd seen kids use weed at parties.

Pearl said Uncle Seb was known to have his finger in more than one under-the-counter pie. Uncle Seb said he kept his eyes open for business opportunities, nothing too shady or serious, just extra cash in the pocket. Audrey'd keep his secret.

She wandered the shop, pretending she could have anything she wanted. She tried on a suede leather vest with long fringe, the most expensive thing in the store, thinking about a husband who could do more than fix cars or drive big rigs or work in a feed store. The thought of selling pies and chili the rest of her life made her want to run far away. Maybe to Miami. She'd helped in that old pie shop ever since she was little, working there after school and on weekends. And here she was now, clerking for her uncle. When would she have some fun?

Two blond-haired girls walked by the shop, carrying swanky I. Magnin shopping bags from that expensive department store up the street, their long hair swinging back and forth, matching the rhythm of their hips. They crossed the street to join a sunburned boy with a tennis racket case hanging from his shoulder. He moved in between them, his arms around their waists. They swung their butts in rhythm, laughing. Snobby tourist kids with money to spend. Audrey jammed the vest back on the hanger.

In the cheap wall mirror, sunlight caught the shine of her long black hair, parted in the middle. Faded jeans hugged her bottom. The boys said it was a cute bottom, two melons bouncing. They also liked the bumps that teased through her turquoise, orange, and yellow tee. According to her mother, her skin was like expensive white peaches. Smooth with a nice glow. And she had spirit like her Scotch-Irish ancestors.

That was all very nice, but when would she have a real boyfriend? When would she have a life? Her mother had to stop watching her so close. She stepped nearer the mirror to check her lipstick.

"I like what I see, too." A boy, at least six feet tall, had entered the store and now approached her, grinning. He had to be in college. His T-shirt and khaki shorts looked clean. White socks topped his blue and white Adidas. She felt his confidence, felt herself wilt.

"W-w-what?"

He brushed back his reddish-blond hair. "I like what I see, too."

Audrey felt herself blush.

"Do you have one of these in an extra-large?" He pointed to a pile of T-shirts with Palm Springs printed on the front.

"I think so. Sometimes they get mixed up." Audrey fingered through several stacks and found one.

A boy in a maroon and gold Arizona State University jersey leaned into the shop's doorway. His wide frame, his muscular shoulders and arms, filled the opening. "Hey, Roger. Meet you in the next block at The Palms Bar." He turned and left.

"Okay!" the boy called Roger yelled back and turned again to Audrey. "What do I owe you?"

"Two dollars. Includes the tax." She waited while he pulled money from his jeans. He had long, slender fingers, nice hands, not callused with dirty nails. Her palms turned sweaty.

"Where does everybody go for fun?" He leaned on the counter.

"I don't know. I don't live in Palm Springs." She pressed a key on the old cash register and the money drawer clanged open. She put the cash in with the other singles and closed the drawer. As she looked up, he was smiling at her. Her girlfriends would call his eyes "flirty." She wished for something clever to say, but her mind went blank. A boy this handsome had never given her a look like that. She felt warm all over. Back home the boys weren't smooth. Dave Hawkins always groped her. It made her feel dirty.

"Come on, you must know of some place," Roger insisted.

She pointed to a stack of flyers on the counter. "There's a new disco called Zelda's, not far from here."

Roger read the flyer. "Yeah, sounds pretty cool, like what I'm looking for."

Audrey smoothed her palms on her thighs, the denim comforting against the excitement rising in her. She wanted him to stay in the shop, but he'd soon leave to join his friends, find some college girls to party with. She wondered what it was like to really party. Not that she didn't have fun with her friends. But this would be different. *He* was different. And she liked that. Her heart raced.

"We just got here yesterday. Here for five days and then back to ASU to finish the semester." He held up the flyer featuring a black and white picture of people on a packed dance floor, a large neon sign on the wall proclaiming "Zelda's," and a line at the bottom of the page that read, "Where Strangers Become Friends."

"You ever been there?" he asked.

"No." She shook her head. "You need to be careful after dark, with all the tourists in town. Be careful of your wallet."

"It seems okay around here to me."

"It is, in the daylight."

"Guess I'll have to be sure I stay with my buddies." He smiled. "Are you in college?"

"Start in the fall," she lied.

"Then you're almost a college freshman."

"Yeah, I suppose," she answered. He didn't need to know that after she graduated in June, she'd be at the pie shop full-time.

Roger glanced at the flyer again. "How about going to the disco with me? It'll be the first time for both of us."

She started to say, "Oh, no, my mother would never let me go to a disco with a stranger." But then she realized her mother would never know. Neither would her uncle if she was careful. "I guess I could," she replied.

"Great. I'll meet you here at eight." He turned to go but stopped. "You know, I don't even know your name. I'm Roger."

"I know. I'm Audrey."

He started to the door again. She called after him, "Roger, not here. I'll meet you in front of The Palms Bar down the street. At eight."

Uncle Seb was late. He always came in at seven to handle the night customers. It was twenty minutes to eight. She wouldn't have time to fix her make-up or change her clothes. Why was he so late? Roger might come to the shop to get her. Then everyone would know her special secret—she'd met a boy.

By 7:55, she could barely stand the cheapskate tourists rummaging through the piles of T-shirts. Her head ached. She felt like screaming or crying. A chance to go out with a handsome college boy might never happen again.

Uncle Seb walked through the door at 8:25 p.m.

"Evenin', Audrey. Glad to see you're busy. Had some business problems." He held a box under his arm, the same kind of box she had seen in the stockroom. The one she thought contained small bags of marijuana.

"Can I leave now?" she asked, a slight tension in her voice.

"You goin' someplace?" Uncle Seb raised his eyebrows.

"Remember the girl from the donut shop I met when I got you some chocolate creams?" She had her story ready. "I'm going over to her house."

"Where's she live?"

"Around the block from her father's shop."

"I know where it is." Uncle Seb held up his index finger at her. "One. Be back here no later than eleven." He added another finger. "Two. Don't be late. It's no time for you to be out alone. Goddamn hooligans run wild."

"But I'm eighteen and . . ."

Her uncle leveled a frown at her. "Audrey, you got your watch on? I know this town. You don't. Eleven."

Audrey didn't answer. She ran from the shop, past stores and bars and clubs bustling with night trade. Past neon signs, loud voices, louder music. Through the heavy scents of restaurant food, perfume, and body odor. She wove her way into the crowd, the party atmosphere wrapping her in its cocoon.

She slowed her pace near The Palms Bar, not wanting to look anxious. Out front, kids stood drinking beer, laughing, flirting. Sounds of live music erupted into the street. She'd never been here, but knew it was a spring break hangout.

It had to be at least 8:35. Roger had probably found someone else to take to Zelda's. Or else he'd just gone with his friend and would meet a new girl or lots of girls at the disco. But *maybe* he was inside. She entered, elbowing through the group. Smoke burned her eyes. Dancers shook their hips to a drumming beat.

She pulled at her tee, making sure it was tucked in. Her mouth felt dry. Smoke stung the back of her throat as she looked for Roger, hoping his reddish-blond hair and his tall frame would stand out. Nervous energy ebbed away, the search consuming her. She didn't see him.

"Hey, remember me?" Audrey turned toward the loud voice. "Buy you a beer?"

Roger's friend, still in the ASU shirt, shoved his way over. His large hand gripped a bottle of Budweiser by the neck.

"Is Roger here?"

"Hell, no. He's playin' tennis. Come on, have a beer." He put his arm around her shoulders.

Audrey tried to pull away.

"Stuck-up, huh?" He tightened his grip.

She shook her head, ducked under his arm, and ran back through the crowd. Out on the street, she wiped tears and smoke from her eyes.

The only thing she could do was go back to the shop and make up a story about a change of plans.

The street bustled, even busier than before. Audrey moved in her own world of hurt, disappointment, and anger—at herself for being so gullible. Maybe her mother was right. Boys, no matter how nice they seemed . . . she'd hoped Roger might be different.

"Hey, Audrey."

She walked faster. Was that stupid friend of Roger's coming after her?

"Hey, Audrey. Wait."

She felt a hand on her arm. She shrugged it off and moved faster.

"Audrey, it's me, Roger."

She stopped and whirled around. "What do you want?"

"Hey, hey, sorry I'm late," he said as he put his hands up. "I played tennis. I ran back to the hotel to shower. I told my friend Rick—the one who stuck his head in the tee shop when you and I were talking—I told him to watch for you just in case the match went too long. To tell you I might be late, but I'd be there. Did he see you? Tell you? Did he wait with you?"

"He's a real jerk."

"Oh, okay. Got it." Roger rolled his eyes. "He can be, especially after too much beer. I apologize for anything he said or did. And, like I said, I apologize for being late. I thought I had it covered."

As they drew nearer Uncle Seb's, Audrey felt a pang of sadness. "I have to go now. I'll go the rest of the way to the store by myself."

Roger took her by the hand. "Can't we just cross the street here like everyone's doing, avoid the shop, and go to Zelda's? Forget what happened? I like you. I *think* you like me."

Audrey looked down at the sidewalk, not sure of what to do. She wanted to be with him. After a moment, she said, "All right. I guess I could."

They drifted into the maze of people crossing the street and moving toward the disco. Audrey had never seen so many kids having fun. Roger continued to hold her hand. She couldn't believe she was with such a good-looking boy. But her uncle's warning spoiled everything. If she didn't obey him, he might send her back to Beaumont Valley right away.

They entered Zelda's, its huge dance floor packed with spring break partiers. Brilliant lights flashed pink, blue, red. A huge disco ball hung from the ceiling, rotating, illuminating the glistening foreheads of the dancers. "Turn the Beat Around" blared from the large speakers on the DJ's stand. She and Roger moved onto the floor and danced until she felt breathless.

Her watch pulled at her glance, a magnet on her arm. She couldn't dismiss it. At ten minutes to eleven she grabbed Roger's arm.

"I need to go back to my uncle's. Right now!" She shouted above the noise.

"What?" Roger drew her close.

"I have to go!"

"But the place is just getting going."

She edged off the dance floor. "I have to, Roger. I'll be in a lot of trouble with my uncle if I don't. The shop closes at eleven. He and my aunt live in an apartment behind the store. I'll be locked out."

She waited for him to make fun of her, call her a square, a mama's girl.

"I want to see you again. What are you doing tomorrow?"

"What?" *He wants to see me again.* "I work tomorrow. You can't hang around the shop. My uncle won't like it."

"Where can we meet when you're done?"

Audrey thought a moment. "There's a little coffee shop across from The Palms Bar. It's called Sandy's. It's always busy and always open. We could go there."

"I'll see you there tomorrow night." Roger squeezed her hand. "Same time?"

"Yes."

The two ran from Zelda's toward Seb's shop. Roger stopped at the corner. She ran toward the door and opened it just as Seb strolled from behind the counter, preparing to lock up.

"Cuttin' it pretty close, Audrey. How was your friend?"

"Oh, fine," she replied, hoping that was the only question. "We just hung out and watched TV."

Audrey met Roger at Sandy's the next night and the next—always on the pretense of getting Uncle Seb a piece of pie to go. They never had much time. They sat side by side in a back booth, their talk softening to whispers to gentle kisses to hands moving. Audrey couldn't remember being so happy. She had a boyfriend at last.

On the night before Roger had to fly home, they planned to meet by the fountain in Hardy Park. Finally, they'd be alone, away from everyone. Audrey'd tell her uncle she was going with her girlfriend to a movie.

Chapter Seven

Audrey Spence

Spring Break 1977—Palm Springs, California

Audrey wore her jeans with daisies on the back pockets and a new yellow tee.

"You're lookin' pretty tonight. Plannin' on goin' to your girl-friend's again?" Uncle Seb asked, looking around the shop crowded with tourists.

Audrey nodded. "We're going over to The Plaza to see "*A Star Is Born*" She hoped for no more questions.

"Well, I need you here for a while. Too busy for me to handle by myself."

"But the movie starts soon and . . ." She stopped. She didn't want her uncle getting curious.

Audrey rang sales, bagged T-shirts, and answered endless questions. She kept glancing at the clock. What should she do? Roger'd think she wasn't coming. She felt sick to her stomach.

By 8:30, she hated Uncle Seb for making her stay.

Her uncle's best friend Marcus Burton walked in. Audrey leaned across a table of blue jeans toward him.

"Could you stay and help?"

"What?" He waved at Seb. "Speak up, girl."

"Could you work for me now, here? I need to meet my girlfriend. For a movie." She knew he sometimes helped with the store and other endeavors.

Marcus came around the table, looking her up and down. "Sure pretty and sure excited over meetin' a girlfriend." He smirked.

"We're going to the movies."

"Ain't a good idea, runnin' off."

"Please."

"I don't know, little lady." Marcus settled his gaze on her, followed by what seemed a long, thinking pause, one that Audrey thought would never end. "All right. Just watch out for the boys. I know how they think. Young once myself, you know."

Audrey told Uncle Seb that Marcus would stay and help. Before her uncle could tell her no, she was out and running to Hardy Park.

The fountain sat between a band pavilion and a palm grotto. She ran along the fine gravel walkway, small stones edging into her sandals, hurting the soles of her feet. At last, she saw him, sitting in shadows cast by small white lights strung in the surrounding trees. He sat on a mosaic wall, his elbows on his knees, staring at the ground. He stood and started to walk in the opposite direction.

"Roger! Wait!"

He turned. "Hey! I thought you'd changed your mind and weren't coming."

She hurried to him. "My uncle made me stay but I got his friend to work in my place."

Roger put his arms around her. She felt safe.

Two young men approached, slinking along the edge of the gravel path, leering at Audrey. One wore a faded red tank top hanging over dirty jeans. Scrawny and tall, he slouched, his chest looking like it had collapsed. Dirty blond hair brushed the sides of his neck, hung in his eyes. He put his hands behind his head, shoved his hips forward and back. With Adam's apple bobbing, he grunted, "Oh yeah, oh yeah, baby, uh, uh."

The other, pudgy, soft, in cut-off khakis and torn blue T-shirt, danced from side to side, clapping to a singsong, "Oh, man, she's hot. Oh, yeah, man, yeah." His ponytail swung back and forth, hitting the sides of his face.

The deadbeats sidled by, eyeing them both.

Roger kept his arms around her, pulling her to him. He leaned down and whispered, "Let Redshirt and Super Freak go by."

Audrey leaned her head into Roger's chest and buried a giggle as the two passed.

"Hippie jerks," Roger laughed, just loud enough for Audrey's ears. "They're probably high."

He led her to a wooden bench sheltered by several Queen palms. She wished they were in a beautiful place, like the endless Hawaiian beach on the travel poster in her high school library. Feeling shy, she looked down at her hands, fingers entwined. He slipped his arm around her, stroking her face and neck, kissing her on the lips.

She returned the kiss. "I was afraid you'd be gone."

"Sh-h-h. I'm here."

His next kiss pressed harder, forcing her lips apart. His tongue explored hers. Audrey liked the sensation, the heat between her legs.

"God, there must be someplace we can go. Someplace private." Roger glanced about at a hedge of bougainvillea bushes, a stately saguaro ruling over a cactus garden, trees surrounded by grass, tennis courts in the distance. "Maybe there." He pointed to a grouping of five large, ornamental boulders with thick oleanders growing behind them. Huge palm fronds rustled above.

He took her hand and guided her behind the boulders until they were in what appeared to be a secluded chamber. The place hid them from any people who might pass by. He pulled her down beside him.

Roger said, "This okay? No one can see us here."

Audrey looked at the boulders in front, the overgrown bushes behind, the sandy desert dirt. Cigarette butts and an occasional beer can poked out from the base of the bushes, letting them know they were not the first to find the hiding place. She nodded.

Soft light from a park lamp near the gravel walk filtered into the space. Roger spread his sweatshirt on the ground and pulled her down beside him, kissing her on the lips, the neck. His hand explored her breasts and moved down her body. He fumbled with the button on her jeans.

She pulled his hand away.

"This is special, Audrey; you're special."

He pressed against her, kissing her. She turned away.

"Don't you want me, Audrey?"

"Oh, Roger, I . . ." A thought stopped her. Maybe he wouldn't see her anymore if she didn't do what he wanted.

"Don't stop me, please," he whispered into her neck. "I won't hurt you."

Desire stopped the warning voice in her head—Pearl's voice. She held her breath as he undid her jeans and unzipped his. She helped to pull their clothing out of the way, felt the push of his erection between her legs. He pulled her to him, his hand moving his penis to entry, to thrust. She arched into him, despite the initial pain. She began to move with him, holding him. It no longer hurt but gave her pleasure. Moving, moving until Roger gasped.

Afterward, they pulled on their clothes, Audrey not noticing a trace of blood between her legs. They lay together afterward, holding each other.

"I wish I didn't have to leave tomorrow," Roger whispered. "I've so much I want to say."

"Sh-h-h. Don't talk." Audrey curled into him, wishing he could stay forever. She'd waited so long to meet someone like him.

He raised himself on his elbow and looked down at her. "I want you to come see me. In Phoenix. I'll come back to see you in the summer. Get a job near you until fall."

She shook her head. "My mother will never let me do that. Besides, I'd never have enough money."

"I'll send you the money. Let me know when you can come."

"What about your parents?" she asked.

"Don't worry about them. Half the time they don't even know I exist. They travel a lot. My father's a big deal attorney. Besides, I have my own pad with some friends. I'll need your address and a phone number."

She found a pen in her purse and, in the sketchy light from the park lamp, jotted down Pearl's address and phone number on a napkin from Sandy's.

"I fly out early afternoon tomorrow." He pulled her up to stand. They straightened their clothes. "I'll come by the store in the morning."

"I don't know. My uncle . . . he's the one who usually opens the shop every morning."

"Audrey, I have to meet him sometime."

"Oh, Audre-e-e-ey, I have ta meet him someti-i-iime." A high, singsong voice rang out, a distorted echo. Pony-tailed Super Freak edged into the space from between the bushes and a boulder, leering at Audrey, rubbing his crotch. "That was a pretty good show."

Roger pushed Audrey behind him.

Redshirt clambered in, following his buddy. "Gimme your money, pretty boy."

Roger spat out, "Fuck you!"

Redshirt moved in on Roger while Super Freak grabbed Audrey and restrained her. Before Roger could make a retaliatory move, Redshirt karate-chopped him at the juncture of his shoulder and neck. Roger dropped to his knees, breathing heavily, rubbing his wound. The tough pushed him over, stepped on his arm, and, with deft fingers, stripped him of his wallet.

Ripping the wallet open, Redshirt smirked. "My, my! Seventy-five fuckin' bucks. Our lucky night."

Roger scrambled to his feet. The punk punched him in the stomach. He doubled over.

"Stop it." Audrey pulled free from Super Freak and grabbed at Red Shirt's tank top. It ripped. "You've got his money."

The tough swung around and slapped her. She felt the scratch of oleander branches as she fell.

"You're next," Redshirt snarled at Roger.

Roger lunged at him.

Super Freak came to life. "Dumb move, college boy."

Suddenly, the two punks descended on Roger.

"Audrey! Run!" Roger yelled. "Get out of here."

She backed away, watching them punch Roger in the face and ribs. Crying, she ran from behind the boulders to get help. A gray-haired man using a cane, a newspaper under his arm, strolled from the park toward a bus stop.

She stammered, "Help! I need help. They're beating my boyfriend."

The man shook his head, pointed with his newspaper. "You better run across the street. Get someone in the convenience mart to call the police."

Audrey stepped into the busy street. A driver in a blue Mazda pickup blew his horn, yelled through his open window, "Watch where you're goin'." She jumped back, ran along the sidewalk toward the corner.

A man approached with a bandana tied around his forehead. His thick, muscular chest spanned against his T-shirt, "Vic Tanny's Gym" printed on the front of it. She grabbed his muscled arm.

"Please help me. They're beating my boyfriend. Over in the park."

"Get the cops," the man said, stepping by her.

"Please." She pulled on his arm.

The man stopped as Audrey blurted out how they had been attacked. She turned and started to run, retracing her steps. The man fell in beside her. When they arrived at the scene, no one was there.

The man put his hands on his hips, looked around. "You know where the police station is? Better go report it."

Audrey nodded and thanked the man. But instead, she ran to her uncle's shop. When she arrived, only Marcus was there.

"Someone chasin' you?" he asked.

She shook her head.

"You sure?" he asked, surprised at her panicked expression.

"I just wanted to get home. It's dark."

Before Marcus could say more, he was distracted by someone calling his name from the shop's entrance. Soon he was standing out on the sidewalk talking to a buddy. The shop was empty.

Audrey grabbed the phone book. She looked in the front at the important listings like she'd been taught in health class. Under hospitals she found the number for Desert Regional Hospital. She called the hospital, but no Roger Hemmings had been admitted to the emergency room. She wanted to call again fifteen minutes later, but Marcus was back in the shop.

"I forgot something at my friend's," she said to Marcus as she stepped toward the front door. She'd use a pay phone down the block.

Marcus shook his head, moving quickly to block her path. "Your uncle'd kill me if I let you go out now. Whatever's wrong can wait 'til mornin'."

She spent a sleepless night, worried Roger had been injured, filled with dread that she might have to make a statement to the police. Everyone would know about her special boyfriend, her special secret.

Chapter Eight

Roger Hemmings

Spring Break 1977—Palm Springs, California

Roger remembered telling Audrey to run. Now he lay face down, hearing words. The voices sounded far away, jumbled.

"Shit, man. The girl took off." A deep voice.

"You got kinda rough." Another voice, this one whiney.

"I want the fuckin' spaz to remember us."

His mind cleared as he heard the two toughs shuffling around him, a woman's high-pitched laugh and music somewhere off in the distance. Roger's head pounded like someone was beating Jamaican steel drums inside his temples. He felt hands in his pockets, ripping, pulling.

"Come on, man. Fuck it. We got the seventy-five bucks."

"Yeah, okay. We need to get outta here."

Roger slowly focused through a tangle of thoughts. *Are they gone? Audrey. Is she safe?*

He moved—heard a groan, realized it was his own.

Concentrate, man.

A burning in his back and ribs. His sides ached. He hauled himself to his knees, shook his head. With his good hand he touched his face, a bleeding lip, a puffed cheek, a tender eye.

Moonlight wove abstract forms around him. Tall, slender palms in the secluded grove hovered over him. His last night with Audrey, ruined. He pushed to his feet, dizzy. He rubbed his eyes, tried to erase the image of the two druggies.

He'd yelled at her to run. Was she safe?

He told himself to move. The bastards must haunt the large park, looking for lovers, tourists, victims to taunt and rob—or worse. He'd fought, lashing with his fists, his feet. He didn't want to be a headline in a Palm Springs newspaper: "Man Mugged in Hardy Park." Or something uglier. Staying alive was something he'd never thought much about. He was twenty years old. Life would go on forever.

That was before tonight.

Roger forced himself to walk, limping like Quasimodo, the impact racking his body. He had to get back to his hotel and his friends. They'd help him, clean him up. His strides became faster, longer.

What would his father say? His old man hadn't wanted him to go to Palm Springs in the first place. "Head for Bermuda," his father had said. "That's where my crowd went for fun. Beautiful girls. Sow some oats, as they say. And use protection. Always."

But ultimately no protection existed for anything that had happened tonight and now he only hoped Audrey had gotten away. He'd known her a mere five days. But she was more than a spring break fling, he knew that much. His mother always said he was a kid who knew what he wanted. And when he turned seventeen, his mother had told him he'd know when he met the right girl.

Audrey was the right girl. She made him feel like he could accomplish anything. He had to see her and tell her how he felt. He didn't have much time before he had to return to Phoenix.

Gradually he broke into a trot of sorts, exited the park, and headed for his hotel. A man leaving the Desert Coyote Café took a drag on a cigarette and called to him, "Hey, man, you okay? Want some help?"

Roger shook his head and kept running. He knew what he wanted.

Chapter Nine

Audrey Spence

Spring Break 1977—Palm Springs, California

The next morning, right after Uncle Seb had opened the shop and left, leaving Audrey alone, Roger called.

"Oh, Roger, are you alright?" she asked, her voice breathless.

"Yes," he replied. "I managed to get back to the hotel. My friends helped me. Some bruises. Soreness. Black eye. But I'm lucky. No broken bones."

Audrey held back tears. "Did you call the police?"

"No. I called my father. He didn't want any police involvement. My flight's been changed. I fly out in an hour." Roger's voice grew softer. "I won't get to see you before I leave."

Disappointment pulsed through her. She managed to whisper, "Be safe."

He promised to call from Phoenix as soon as he landed. He promised to send money for her to come.

The remainder of her day crawled by. He didn't call.

The next day he didn't call. Nor the next.

Audrey cried herself to sleep.

Sunday afternoon, Uncle Seb said, "All right, Audrey, your mother will be here later to pick you up. Time to tell me what's goin' on. You're one sad young lady." He looked at her over the silver wire rims of his glasses. Aunt Sharon stood by her husband, joining them before leaving for an Avon party. She folded her arms and waited.

"Nothing," Audrey replied, studying the floor.

"This is more than nothin'," Uncle Seb prodded. "Your mouth looks like an upside-down horseshoe."

Audrey turned away. Uncle Seb swung her around.

"Now, Seb, mind your temper." Aunt Sharon laid her hand on his arm.

"This a boy?" Simon frowned at his niece. "You got a boyfriend? Marcus told me a few things."

Audrey choked back tears, nodding.

"Where is he? I never seen no boy around here."

Aunt Sharon joined in the interrogation. "Were you meeting him when you told us you were with your girlfriend?"

Audrey nodded and slowly told the story, apologizing for her lies. Her aunt and uncle looked at each other.

"Just how foolish you been, girl?" Uncle Seb sputtered.

Audrey ran to the backroom, crying. Everything was falling to pieces.

After time alone for as long as she dared, she emerged. She avoided her uncle and waited on customers. Her aunt was gone.

Pearl arrived late that afternoon to take her home.

Chapter Ten

Pearl Spence

January 2010—Beaumont Valley, California

Where I got such a forlorn, crazy idea to send my girl Audrey to Palm Springs, I'll never know. She fell in love with the first boy who paid her mind.

Seb told me she'd worked real good. Not sassy or nothin'. He said what happened was his fault, said he should have paid more attention where she went after work. Audrey had told him she was going to visit her new girlfriend from the donut shop; said they were going to the movies. All sorts of things. That's what she said, but he never checked.

How my Audrey lied. After she come home, she acted sort of peculiar. Told me she'd met a boy. I thought it was a case of the puppy love mopes. Weeks later, when she told me she'd missed her monthly, I knew the truth.

In my kitchen by myself, I cried. I'd tried to do the right thing to make my girl happy. But I couldn't stop thinkin' it was my fault. My own fault. I prayed for help.

God held me by the shoulders. "Pearl, the past is done. You take good care of Audrey, and you take good care of that new baby when it comes."

"Lord, we struggle now," I said. "What will I do with another child?"

"Pearl, you know you're going to love your only grandchild, as soon as you lay eyes on that baby." God cocked his head. "And you know I always take care of you."

"I know, but . . ."

"You heard me, Pearl."

"I'll do my best," I said.

But then I bothered Him with more sadness. "The neighbor ladies look at my Audrey and cluck their tongues sayin', 'Tsk, tsk.' The men look at her and poke their elbows in each other's fat bellies. They think I don't see, but I do. Her school friends don't come around much."

"Never you mind, Pearl," He said. "Just do the best for your family."

But I couldn't help blamin' myself. Made the nighttime hard. I kept prayin'.

"It's not easy, Lord," I murmured. "I just don't understand why this had to happen."

If the Almighty had a plan, He sure was keepin' it to Himself. What was we supposed to learn? Love each other and take care of each other, I guess.

Chapter Eleven

Maegan Spence

May 2008—Palm Springs, California

Roger Hemming's matter-of-fact tone stung. "I've changed my mind," he said. "I've decided against our meeting. We each have our lives well established. Nothing of merit will be accomplished."

Maegan gripped her cell phone. After finally finding her father, this was how it would end? The angry, hurt little girl inside her wanted to scream. She tried to keep her voice steady. "That's a hateful thing to say. I'm your daughter. You wrote you'd meet with me wherever and whenever."

"I repeat. I've changed my mind. I've done my duty for years. A rather lengthy financial record attests to that," he insisted.

"No one ever asked for money," she replied. A tightness rose in Maegan's throat.

"That 'never asked for money,'" came her father's reply, "bought you a first-class education and a way out of Beaumont Valley."

"Yes." Maegan closed her eyes, tears burning her lids. "And I'm grateful. But I have a right to know your reasons."

"Do you? That's my decision."

"You owe me something money can never buy. That *decision* shaped and governed my life," she said, trying to control the tremor in her voice. "Why did you choose to never acknowledge me until I forced the situation?"

Silence.

She took a deep breath, her next sentences steady and deliberate. "If you don't meet with me, I'll fly to Phoenix, contact your wife, walk into your law firm, and introduce myself to the other senior partners as your lovechild, your bastard daughter. While I have a feeling Hollywood types and liberals in Los Angeles wouldn't find this news particularly disturbing, I believe the people in your conservative, elite Arizona law firm might."

"What?" he asked.

"You heard my every word."

"How did you find me?" Her father's voice sounded strained.

"I told you in my letter. A private investigator traced you. It seems you are rather prominent." She paused, adding an edge to her voice. "I'm a lawyer in Los Angeles, a result of that 'first-class education' you bought me. Ironic, isn't it? The lawyer daughter you paid to train has tracked you down."

"Where are you?"

"What do you mean, where am I? I'm at the Hyatt Hotel in Palm Springs, the place and date we agreed on. It's near where you met my mother and a long way from Beaumont Valley where I grew up with my grandmother, Pearl."

Roger Hemmings took his time answering. "All right. I'll fly out as planned. I'll call tomorrow morning with the time of my arrival."

After the call ended, she sobbed.

The telephone conversation with her father had made sleep impossible, his matter of fact, austere voice grating against years of painful, unanswered questions. Maegan shoved the light coverlet to the foot of the bed with her legs and pushed herself up, turning her body until she slumped on the edge of the bed, her sheer nightgown twisted around her. Restless tossing had left her exhausted. She massaged her temples.

With a deep, aching sigh, she forced herself up from the bed, suddenly wanting fresh air. She opened the room's sliding glass door and stepped onto a small balcony. Warm, desert wind swept against her, molding the filmy nightgown to her tall, slender frame, outlining her breasts, hips, and thighs while strands of auburn hair brushed across her face. Like fingers tapping unhappy reminders, palm fronds rapped on the roof of her third-floor room. Beyond, the San Jacinto Mountains reached into the struggling dawn, jagged and unforgiving.

When she was young, the wind would stir feelings of restlessness coiled deep inside her. Those same feelings now spiraled again, tighter than she'd ever experienced. She hoped the meeting with her father would release them and give her peace.

She still didn't understand what drove her. Instinct? Obsession? A sick compulsion? She knew one thing: No one liked to be ignored and neglected. Or worse, abandoned. She put her head down, her mind a whorl of thoughts, her fingers wrapping around the balcony railing until they hurt.

Maegan stepped back into the room, closing the sliding door. She cradled the silver-cased cell phone in her hand and curled onto the bed to wait. He was to call with his time of arrival. With the endless night now behind her, the clock face glared at her: 6:00 a.m.

She dozed. Seven o'clock. She lay awake. Eight o'clock.

Her cell phone erupted with the theme song from *Sex and the City*. She jerked upright, grabbing it. "Hello?" Maegan held her breath.

A pause, then his brisk voice. "Miss Spence? Maegan? I can't get away as planned for a morning arrival. More like late afternoon. I'll be in touch after my business meeting."

"I'll expect your call." Maegan swallowed the lump in her throat. "Goodbye."

No response. She tapped the red circle to end the call that had already been ended.

A tangled mass of relief and anger pushed her into a black hole. She hauled out of bed and stood. Unexpected nausea coupled with vertigo forced her back down. After several deep breaths, she again stood, more steady, able to walk around the room, able to think.

She again stifled hurt and resentment, never sure what emotions might breach the psychological dam. Or when.

Before he'd arrive, she'd visit Beaumont Valley and the church of her youth to ask for strength and wisdom and give thanks for this meeting, no matter the outcome. She closed her eyes, remembering the peace she'd felt when her grandmother took her by the hand to walk down the chapel lane. She would return to that lane, that chapel.

She settled back, recalling the note scribbled in her thirtieth birthday card. Prior to that, Pearl had been close-mouthed when asked questions. She'd always said, "I have an agreement to keep. The time'll come."

Maegan thought about her family. Dixson's prison time for attempting to rape her. Audrey's betrayal, choosing Dixson over her. The two of them now living together in a double-wide somewhere in San Bernardino. Dixson's sons. The eldest, Neville, always jealous of her and that special bank account, selling stolen property and drugs—from San Bernardino to Blythe to San Diego, including Palm Springs, with Dixson heavily involved in his son's enterprises. Youngest Winston, the musician, trying to stay away from the family "business." Neville bullying him, trying to force him. Pearl's goodness.

She'd be watchful in case any of her "family" might surface in Palm Springs. A part of her wanted a showdown. Another part said, "Be done with them."

Chapter Twelve

Pearl Spence

November 1977—Beaumont Valley, California

I worried about Audrey as her time got closer. Would my little girl be okay, first baby and all? That boy Roger should have been beside her all through her carryin' time. Thanks be to God, I was there for her. That day she started actin' all wild-eyed, cryin', "Oh, Mama, something's happening," I called my neighbor. I'd asked him a while back if he could help us when the time came. He rushed her and me to the hospital in Redlands.

We helped Audrey into a crowded emergency room. She glanced around and grabbed at my arm. Near us, a man held a blood-stained handkerchief to the side of his head. Meanwhile, a woman cradled a whimpering boy in her arms. I could taste the Lysol antiseptic smell hangin' in the air. Made my nose curl.

I squeezed Audrey's hand. "It'll be okay, honey. It'll be okay," I said, trying to convince her and myself as we made our way toward the admittin' desk.

I told the nurse behind the counter about Audrey, who was lookin' a bit frantic. The woman picked up a phone right quick and pointed to a wheelchair. Before my neighbor and I could settle my girl into it, two young men appeared in hospital greens and transferred her to a gurney. According to their name tags, they was nurses.

All at once, two hospital staff, stethoscopes flyin', their faces tense, rushed by, ran down a hall, and through double doors. The nurse said something about a car accident. Scared my girl even more.

An attendant whisked Audrey away. "We'll take good care of her," he said over his shoulder. And they did.

Audrey had a hard time. Twelve hours passed until they induced labor, then a few days before she was back home. She didn't show no interest in her baby. She could only think about that boy, about how her heart had been broken. I thought by now she'd finally be good and mad at him. Several weeks later, while baby Maegan slept, I asked Audrey about him, hopin' she could tell me and not be a mess of tears. Maybe help her get the pain out.

"What's he like, honey?"

She looked at the kitchen floor, the worn green linoleum, and sighed. "Oh, Mom. He's tall. Thick, reddish, blond hair. Big blue eyes. Strong hands with long, tapered fingers. Clean fingernails. He touches me so gently." She closed her eyes and swallowed.

Oh, no, I thought. Here come the water works again. Why did I ask? It's not goin' to bring him back. "That's okay, we'll talk about somethin' else."

Audrey took a deep breath. Seemed like she wanted to tell me more.

"Mom, he smiles, and a big dimple comes on his cheek, just like mine. His teeth are so white and even. He told me he had orthodontia."

"What's that?" I asked.

Audrey pointed to her front teeth. "To make them straight."

"Like that boy Billy Jensen who had a crush on you in eighth grade?"

She shook her head. "Don't put that awful Billy in the same sentence with Roger."

My, she was struck hard by Cupid.

"How did Roger treat you?" I asked.

"So nice. We met every night at a little coffee shop called Sandy's. We talked and made plans."

I cocked my head. "What kind of plans?"

My girl looked off in the distance. "I was going to visit him in Phoenix and then . . ."

"You what?" The words come out kinda harsh.

Audrey bit her lip, stopped talkin'. I wanted to kick myself for openin' my mouth. "I'm sorry, honey. Didn't mean to go actin' like no judge."

She looked at me. I nodded for her to go on.

"We never ran out of things to say. It was only on the last night that . . ." She stopped.

I knew what happened that night. Even if that boy was a good boy, he did the wrong thing. I wish my Audrey'd been stronger. After all she told me, I couldn't figure why he never called or wrote neither. He knew Uncle Seb's store and had my phone number and address written down on a napkin from that Sandy's place.

"Audrey, why do you think he hasn't called or written?"

"I don't know, Mama. I just can't believe he's that big a liar. Maybe his father wouldn't let him. Maybe he didn't have the money."

I couldn't say what I thought to Audrey. That he was a no-good party boy. It'd start a big fracas. But I could say it to God when I was alone. "He was just a boy who saw a pretty girl and then he was just like any man."

"Now, Pearl," God said, "there are more good men than bad. You weren't there. Young love can be very true and very pure. Open your heart."

"I don't wanna be cross, Lord, but he had all sorts of time to do somethin'."

"Patience, Pearl. Forgive. You have a granddaughter, beautiful and healthy."

I said nothin' else. But deep down I wanted to strike that boy dead. Then I realized what a hateful thought that was. Maybe God could just make him miserable. Put a curse on him, nothin' real bad; somethin' like the all-over-itches or boils on his backside. Then I laughed at my silliness.

A few days later somethin' strange happened. I got a letter from a bank about money for little Maegan. What money and who from? How'd they find me?

Chapter Thirteen

Maegan Spence

May 2008—Palm Springs, California

After her father's phone call, Maegan prepared to leave, dressing in cropped pants, a camisole top and sandals. She stuffed a sun hat and keys into her shoulder tote and headed to the elevator, with plenty of time to drive to Beaumont Valley.

A café mocha from the lobby's coffee kiosk in her hand, she took the elevator to the underground garage and walked to her white BMW. It needed a wash. She'd tend to that later. The garage appeared deserted except for three people walking toward the elevator and several couples at their cars.

Maegan always felt ill at ease in parking structures, above or below the ground. Too many nooks and crannies for muggings or worse. As she approached her vehicle, she heard a loud rumbling noise, like heavy trucks rolling in to make deliveries.

An older couple was in a run-walk, the man pulling the woman by the hand, headed toward the garage exit ramp. The rumbling noise grew louder, now almost a roar. Three teenagers ran by, one scream-ing. Maegan turned to her right and gasped. The rear cement wall of the subterranean parking garage undulated in a horizontal, wave-like motion. For a moment she watched the rolling oscillation of the wall, fascinated. Then the thought, *Oh, my God, an earthquake!*

She ran toward the garage exit, terrified of being buried under jagged steel beams and tons of broken concrete, hugging her shoulder tote to her side, car keys in one hand and coffee in the other. Fear roiled in her stomach, the quake the most intense she'd ever experienced. As she ran up the garage exit incline, she realized the quake's loud roar had stopped, replaced by the sound of her shoes hitting the cement and the rush of her breathing. She scurried out into the sunshine. The shaking and cacophony had stopped. Was it over?

A balding man, mid-fifties, extra pounds spanning his Bermuda shorts and yellow golf shirt, ran up from the garage. "Are you alright?" he called.

"I think so," Maegan replied, catching her breath. "That was fright-ening!" She looked down. Splashes of café mocha formed Rorschach-like stains on her camisole top. Her coffee cup was gone.

"Never know when one of these things is going to strike." The man pulled a handkerchief from his pocket to blot his forehead, watching her wipe at her clothes. "I saw a cup fly out of your hand."

She shook her head. "I didn't even know that happened."

He seemed ready to say more, but her trip to Beaumont Valley had been delayed long enough. She had to change her clothes.

"I'm in a bit of a rush. Have a good day and stay safe," she said and hurried into the hotel lobby where tourists stood in groups, their gestures wide, their voices loud. She caught snatches of conversation.

"Boy, that was a real shaker."

"Almost knocked me down in the shower."

"I'll never come to California again."

She found the stairs up to her floor, refusing to board an elevator. When she reached her room, she quickly changed her soiled camisole for a tank top, and then left the hotel and drove toward Interstate 10 and Beaumont Valley.

Was the earthquake a bad omen? Enough shaken moments, physical and mental, had occurred in her lifetime. She hadn't needed more. She slipped Rod Stewart's *Great American Songbook* CD into the player, letting the sounds of "Embraceable You" help her relax.

Jack slipped into her thoughts. She pushed them away.

The sky, with its endless canvas of gold, white, and blue, reminded her of Navajo artist R.C. Gorman, who captured the desert skies as no other. Even the air smelled clean, unlike the smog-filled atmosphere of Los Angeles. The earthquake trauma faded. She looked forward to a moment of peace at the little church she and her grandmother used to frequent.

A glance in her rearview mirror revealed a line of traffic behind her, all heading west through the San Gorgonio Pass toward the Pacific Ocean and cooler weather. She took the Beaumont Valley exit and eased onto the streets of the small town, driving past where Pearl's Place used to be. After her grandmother had sold the pie shop, she moved to the outskirts of town and didn't travel much anymore.

Maegan felt a pang of regret. How quickly time had passed. She vowed to visit Pearl on her way back to Los Angeles after meeting her father. For now, her presence in town had to remain a secret.

As she drove toward Cherry Valley Presbyterian Chapel, she stopped for a red light. A gray Ford Taurus pulled beside her. The driver looked vaguely familiar.

The white clapboard chapel with its copper-roofed steeple nestled among the remains of an apple orchard. A small cemetery lay on the left. She and Pearl had walked among the gravestones, reading the dates, sensing the people of the valley—the apple farmers, railroad workers, cherry orchard owners. To the right, a construction site. Expansion of the church. Maegan felt sorry to see the coming change that would alter the structure she once knew so well. She parked next to a large pickup truck.

She swallowed and reached in her tote for a tissue. Sadness settled over her as she exited the BMW and walked to the chapel door, only to find it locked. In years past, it had always remained open.

A construction worker approached. "Help you, lady?" he asked politely.

"I'd like to visit the chapel. Do you have a key?"

"Nope. Only open on Sundays while construction on the new church is goin' on."

Maegan couldn't hide her disappointment.

The man smiled. "Let me check with the foreman," he offered.

Construction noise ceased as the crew broke for lunch. Soon a burly, bearlike man with a gape-toothed smile and "Foreman" stenciled on his construction helmet opened the chapel door for her and returned to his fellow workers gathered for lunch.

Once inside, she sat in the same pew she and her grandmother had used each Sunday. Quiet filled her ears. A feeling of peace wrapped around her, that feeling of well-being she treasured and remembered.

The void inside her would soon end. She would meet the *who* and learn the *why*. And then what? Forgive her father, whatever his story, no matter the outcome? But she struggled with the idea. *How do you forgive?* Pearl had taught her to seek God before doing anything big and important. At this moment, meeting her father loomed the biggest and most important event of her life. That was why she'd felt compelled to come to the chapel. She prayed, sensing the strength around her. She listened.

Minutes passed. The weight of anger and hurt seemed to lift from her shoulders. Could she keep them off and feel real forgiveness, not empty words once she left the church? She opened her eyes, feeling ready—or so she hoped. Slowly, she left the pew and walked to the door.

Outside, the wind had picked up, the temperature cooler than when she arrived. Strong winds made Maegan hug herself as she hurried to her car.

She turned the key in the ignition. Nothing happened. *Damn it.* She pumped the accelerator. Nothing. Shit, shit, shit. She clicked the ignition on and off. Still nothing. *Now what?* She waited a moment and tried again. A red icon lit on the dashboard. She fumbled through the glove compartment for the manual, flipping to the page showing icons and their meaning. The battery.

She dug in her tote for her wallet and cell phone. She found the wallet containing the auto club card amid a jumble of cosmetics, Kleenex, a water bottle, a business card case, and a box of raisins. But no phone. In all the earthquake confusion and quick changing of clothes, she must have left it back in the hotel room after she'd checked messages one last time.

What if her father called before she could get back to her room? He might not call again. He might think she'd given up, not gutsy enough to play hardball if she had to. How could she have been so careless? She had to get back.

Somebody on-site must have had a phone. She ran toward the construction shack where the same burly, bearlike man who'd opened the church doors for her stood talking with two workers, a soiled roll of building plans unfurled between his hands.

She asked the little group, "Can I borrow someone's phone to call the auto club? My car won't start. The battery."

"Just a moment, miss. Are we clear?" the foreman asked his workers, rolling up the plans. The two men nodded and walked away. To Maegan he said, "I've got jumpers in my pick-up. Get you started in no time, way before Ed Hazelton gets here from the Standard station on the other side of town."

The foreman pulled his truck in front of the car, opened both hoods, hooked up the jumper cables, and soon her vehicle's engine purred.

"Keep it running, let it charge up. Get it checked when you get back home."

As she drove from the church parking lot, a gray Taurus pulled in behind her. She adjusted her rearview mirror. This time there was no guessing. The driver was the man from the hotel parking garage, the one who talked to her right after the earthquake. Her lawyer's antenna alerted. Too much coincidence. She made a hard right into the parking lot of a strip mall and parked, engine running. She locked the doors. He followed and pulled in beside her.

Maegan lowered her passenger side window halfway. His window lowered. Their car engines idled.

"What do you want?" she yelled.

The man answered, "I'm supposed to keep an eye on you."

"What do you mean, 'keep an eye on me'? Who do you work for?"

"I'll come around and talk to you." The man started to open his door.

"Stay where you are. I can hear just fine. Answer my question."

The man cleared his throat. "A Jennifer Bevins. My instructions are to keep you, Maegan Spence, in my sights until you leave the desert. Make sure no one hurts you. That you're safe."

Jennifer had hired him. Maegan was stunned. No one was going to hurt her.

"What's your name?" she asked.

"Caleb Marley. I'm a private investigator."

"I don't need any help. Stay out of my way." Maegan pressed the button to close the window.

"Miss Spence, wait."

She lifted her finger from the button.

"I'll be happy to follow you back to the hotel, in case your car acts up."

"Why did you identify yourself to me?"

"Thought it might be comforting," Marley replied.

"Suit yourself." She closed the window. Comforting? Hardly. Who was supposed to hurt her? She wasn't going to be hurt physically. Emotionally? A possibility. Jennifer was way off base. Well, he might as well earn his money, she thought. She had to get back. She'd never forgive herself if she missed Roger Hemmings's call, even though she had other options. She wanted this meeting with as little rancor as possible.

Marley stayed behind her on the return trip. As she turned into the parking facility at the hotel, he nodded at her and drove off. Back in the room for only moments, she heard her familiar ringtone. Mercifully, the phone lay on the bedside stand where she'd left it. She grabbed her cell, tapped the small green circle.

"Maegan?"

"Yes," she replied.

"I'll arrive tomorrow morning," her father said. "I'll meet you in the lobby at 10:00 a.m.," and he ended the call.

Maegan settled into her room for another sleepless night.

Chapter Fourteen

Pearl Spence

January 2010—Beaumont Valley, California

When Maegan was born, my girl Audrey said God cheated her. Twice. He took her man away *and* cursed her with a child.

"How could the Lord have cheated you?" I asked. "He gave you Maegan, the sweetest little girl ever come along."

"Mama, if God really loved me, I'd have Roger, too."

The worst part? She wouldn't touch the baby. When Maegan cried, she walked away. Said for me to feed her or hold her. Said the diaper was all stinky. Held her nose. She didn't know the clean, sweet smell of her little girl after a bath, her soft skin. My daughter sulked and cried.

I made sure we attended church every Sunday, thinkin' maybe God would touch her. But the girl just didn't want her baby. Nothin' seemed to work.

Then a thought nudged a door open into my troubles. *Pearl, how could you be so stupid? It's the "baby blues."* So I talked nice to her, hugged her when she cried, held my tongue when she sassed, tried to teach her how to care for Maegan. But I began to feel my Audrey might be troubled by something deeper than I could dig at. What was I goin' to do?

I decided to take her to see a friend of my husband's. The two men used to drive for the same big-rig truckin' company. My husband always claimed Rupert Arenas to be level-headed and wise, someone to spend time with over a meal at a truck stop. We'd gone to see the man several times before when my husband was havin' a problem with another trucker. "Rupert'll know what to do," he'd said. And he did.

I thought maybe Rupert might have some ideas this time, too. Worth a try. God has always looked out for us, and I thank the Lord for that, but maybe Audrey and me needed someone to tell our troubles to. You know, just someone to talk to.

Rupert lived way out in the desert on the Morongo Reservation. His father had been a shaman and had taught him the ways of his people. Our bein' Presbyterian didn't seem to be enough for this problem, and I was runnin' out of ideas. I called Rupert, explained what was goin' on, and asked if he could help. Said to come on out. Audrey threw a hissy-fit, said there was nothin' the matter with her, and she wouldn't go. But after I said her daddy would want her to be happy and she sure wasn't happy now, she pulled on clean jeans and a blouse and away we went, her whinin' the whole trip.

Travelin' from Beaumont Valley to Anza is one trip I'm not gonna forget anytime soon. We left little Maegan with my neighbor who knew what was goin' on. My old four-door Honda overheated goin' up the mountain, and Audrey's anger steamed right along with it. Had to pull over to the side of the road, give the car a chance to cool down. Good thing I had a big plastic jug of water with me to add to the radiator so we could get underway again. But Audrey sure didn't cool down.

Seemed like forever before we got to Rupert's place and turned off the paved road, only to have a sandy cloud start billowin' around the car as we bumped our way up the long gravel driveway. The dust come in the open car windows. We rolled 'em up fast. Audrey coughed. I wiped at my eyes. My, it was hot. Felt the sweat roll down between my bosoms, my back stick to the vinyl seat. Audrey did nothin' but complain about the dust and the bumps and the heat.

Rupert appeared from around the corner of his doublewide and waved, lookin' at us from under a big black Stetson, his skin all brown, leathery, and full of wrinkles. He still had his great big grin, except his blue and brown plaid shirt stretched over a rounder belly than I remembered. The faded red bandana tied around his neck made his jaw look square and strong. A big scruffy dog, black as night, followed him, barking at us. Didn't look too friendly.

"Pipe down, Kyekit." Rupert said over his shoulder. The animal stopped barkin', came up beside him.

"Hi, Pearl. Hello, Audrey," he said, leanin' in, his forearms hangin' through the open window. A small leather pouch hung around his neck. Looked new compared to the rest of him.

"Go ahead and park over there."

He pulled away from the window and pointed to a spot between a rusted oil barrel and a round domed out-building covered in palm fronds and brush. A worn piece of burlap covered the doorway.

I drove over to where he pointed, opened the car door, and got out. Kyekit gave me a sniff. He looked at his master who motioned him away with the back of his hand. The dog wandered to the trailer's front door and laid down. My Audrey just sat, not movin', her seat belt still strapped.

I leaned in and whispered, "He's happy to see you. Get out." I heard a loud sigh. I slammed my door.

Rupert had known Audrey since she was little; sometimes she even called him uncle. The girl took her sweet old time, she did, gettin' out of the car, then closing the door. In my mind, I counted to ten. She was bein' rude to our friend.

Rupert seemed unbothered by the way Audrey was actin'. He also didn't waste any time. "Audrey, I understand you got some troubles."

The girl shot me a look full of sharp knives. She shrugged her shoulders, said nothin'.

"Cat got your tongue?" I said. "Rupert's talkin' to you, Audrey." She shuffled her foot in the sand.

Rupert walked on past her toward the outbuilding. "Why don't you two come on into the *kish* with me." He pulled the burlap open and held it aside for us.

I pushed Audrey ahead of me as we bent over to get through the low doorway. Rupert followed. The light inside was dim, shadows hangin' everywhere. A charcoal-black fire pit, bordered by stones, sat in the middle of the lodge, a hole in the roof above it. The smoke smell clung to the fronds, brush, and burlap. Tule mats covered the earth floor, and snake rattles hung on the poles holding up the roof. An old wooden chair sat shoved over to one side.

"Audrey, sit with me here." He reached for her hand.

Audrey pulled away. I started to say somethin', but Rupert shook his head.

"It's okay, Pearl," he said. "Just sit with me, Audrey."

He sat down cross-legged beside the fire pit and put his Stetson on the floor next to him, his thick gray hair pulled back in a ponytail.

Audrey looked at the door. I braced myself. Was she gonna run out? But then, takin' her sweet ol' time, she sat cross-legged on the floor in front of him.

"Pearl," he said, "you can sit over there on that chair." I did. He musta sensed that if I sat on the floor, I wouldn't be able to get up.

Rupert skooched forward a little closer to Audrey and extended his hands, palms up. "May I hold your hands?" he asked. My daughter hesitated. Then, like in slow motion, she set each of her hands in his. He held them, smilin'. In a kind voice, he said, "Audrey, I'm going to talk to the spirits. You won't understand what I'm saying. My language is ancient, as are my people's ways. But everything you hear me say or see me do is for you."

He bowed his head, eyes closed and said nothing. I could hear his deep, steady breathin'. Audrey looked at me, her angry scowl replaced by a wonderin', wide-eyed look. For the first time, I realized she might be scared. I mouthed, "It's okay, honey." Inside my heart, I hoped it was.

We bowed our heads. Minutes passed without a sound.

Rupert raised his chin. He chanted his ancient language in a soft sing-song voice, high pitched, then low. High. Then low. Gentle. Soothin'. Made everythin' seem like the world had stopped its ruckus and we could hear ourselves. The chantin' stopped. He began to speak his prayers. I felt the bad air we come in with drop away.

Slow-motion-like, he took his hands from Audrey's and untied the bandana from around his neck. He spread it between them, smoothin' out the wrinkles. Next, he pulled the pouch cord over his head and put the little sack on the bandana. He loosened the cord, turned the sack upside down and, gentle-like, shook out two small vials, three large pumpkin seeds, and a miniature toy horse with a spotted rump. Looked to be made of plastic. He arranged them on the faded material.

I scratched at my ear, wonderin' what this was all about.

"Audrey," he said in a hushed voice. "We know sadness and hurt are with you now, but they are only visiting. When you no longer make them comfortable, they will leave. Before you, I place special spirits. They will help you."

"Earth." He shook one of the small vials. In it, loose dirt shifted back and forth. He placed it back on the bandanna.

"Water." With a slow motion, holding the second vial between his thumb and index finger, he tipped it back and forth, the liquid movin' from side to side. He settled it back on the cloth.

Last, he separated the seeds with equal space between them on the faded scarf, tapping his index finger on each one as he said, "Seeds."

He stayed silent, looking at the items, before he spoke again. "Earth, water, seed. We are their stewards. We must treat them with care and respect. Mixed with sun and air, they are the source of all life. Precious life. Yours. Mine. Pearl's. Your child's."

He held the miniature horse between his fingertips. "The beautiful and noble Appaloosa. Strong. Spirited . . . as you must be, Audrey, for yourself and your child. As I know you are."

He picked up each item ever so careful, put them back in the pouch, then pulled the leather tie tight and took Audrey's hand. He placed the little sack in her palm.

"I made this pouch and collected what's inside just for you, Audrey. Remember the world's blessings. Keep them close."

Audrey glanced at the pouch, dropped it on the bandana and stood. She hurried toward the doorway but stopped. She turned. I could see tears in her eyes She rushed back to quick grab up the pouch. With it clutched in her hand, she run out.

I started to haul myself off the chair to catch her, but Rupert shook his head.

"Pearl," Rupert said. "Be patient. Your daughter is young and has much to think about. You and Audrey return whenever you want. You're always welcome. I'll add a bead in her name to my 'chanting beads' and keep her in my heart."

I got myself up. Audrey and me drove home in silence.

Sad thing is, I didn't see no difference in Audrey.

"Stop trying to drag me to church . . . and I won't go to Rupert's again. Just let me alone."

At night I still heard her cryin'. I wondered if she'd thrown the pouch in the garbage, but I noticed she kept it on her dresser by a little wooden cross given to her in Sunday School back when she was confirmed. I went to the Presbyterian church ev'ry Sunday and Wednesday. I sat in the front pew. I prayed. Audrey wouldn't come with me. She stayed with Maegan. She knew what to do . . . if she'd just do it.

But I'm convinced that the Lord and Reverend William Moore at the Presbyterian church and Rupert Arenas out in Morongo country and Audrey stayin' with Maegan while I went to church all made somethin' wonderful happen. Audrey started hangin' nearby when I was tendin' Maegan. I minded my business, pretendin' I didn't notice her. I didn't want no fuss-ups. One day she said, "Mama, I'll do that."

My heart thrilled. Over time, Audrey began talkin' more about her baby, less about the baby's daddy. Maegan became her little star. "Look, Mama, she drank all her bottle. Look, Mama, she's got the cutest dimples when she smiles."

At night I got on my knees, thankin' God for helpin' my girl. I even prayed all the sad stuff wrenched from Audrey would make mischief for the boy who gave her so much hurt. God caught on to my doin's because He shook me by the shoulders and whispered in my ear, "Forgive that boy, Pearl." I heard Him, but . . .

When Maegan grew a bit, I took her to church and then to Sunday School. Keep the world's evilness from her anyway I could. I wanted her to be strong, like our Scotch-Irish ancestors. Audrey come along— sometimes. She was doin' better.

Chapter Fifteen

Maegan Spence

May 2008—Palm Springs, California

The sun disappeared behind nearby rugged mountains, leaving its heat behind. With nighttime settling around her, Maegan slipped into a pensive mood. She drummed her fingers on the arm of the metal chaise lounge where she tried to rest, still dressed in her cropped pants and camisole top from the morning's trip to Beaumont Valley.

She'd returned to the hotel feeling positive and strengthened. Her father had called as he said he would, their meeting to take place the next morning at ten. But now, the old restlessness and uncertainty nudged at her confidence. Absently, she watched a father play with his two little girls in the hotel pool.

One of the little girls called out, "Throw me the ball, Daddy."

And then the other child, "Swing me, Daddy, swing me."

Amidst the children's voices, the father laughed and shushed them. The two girls—one a cute little towhead, the other sporting a long brown braid—seemed to vie for their father's attention.

Maegan scanned the outdoor setting. Azure blue water in an L-shaped pool. The tall trunks of palm trees reaching for the sky.

Hotel guests lounging on beach-towel-covered chaises. Soft music from outdoor speakers and waiters serving margaritas. The stuff of happy vacation magic. With her growing uneasiness, the scene depressed her.

What would a family vacation have been like, to have had a father who played with her, protected her, made her squeal with laughter?

People in her life seemed like stones skipping and skimming over water, then sinking. Audrey, a mother who didn't want her. Roger, a father she never knew. Dixson, a stepfather she wished she'd never known. Neville, a stepbrother who hated her. Pearl and Winston, the only solid place to land.

She watched the father help his little girls from the water and wrap them in towels. They walked together toward the hotel, leaving wet footprints on the cement, the father urging his daughters to "come along." What would it have been like to have that experience, that family memory?

Were marriage and a family in her future? Despite her childhood, she wanted both. She'd make sure the children were loved by a mother and a father. They'd take family trips, go to soccer games, and graduations. Her gaze lingered on the trio as the man opened the hotel door and they disappeared inside.

She left her chaise, wishing she'd taken time to change to her bathing suit, and sat on the edge of the pool, her feet on a step in the shallow end. The water between her toes and circling her ankles refreshed her. Guests walked by, probably on the way to their rooms to shower and change before going to dinner and exploring the desert's night life.

Except for Pearl, she hadn't seen her "family" since she'd moved to Los Angeles five years ago. She dangled her hand in the pool, swishing the water away as if pushing that part of her family away. If only she *could* push them away.

"Find the good thoughts," she murmured.

Her youngest stepbrother, Winston. A musician, played electric guitar. How she loved to hear him play, sometimes soulful, sometimes jamming the rafters off the house. He'd been her friend, watching out for her, when he was around. Sometimes Neville and his father tried to pull him into their schemes. Pearl had written that the police sometimes came by looking for a Dupre—Neville or Dixson.

Let those thoughts be, she chided herself. Think about tomorrow. What would her father be like? Maybe a reserved man. Maybe a man glued to his work. Perhaps he was sour on life. Maybe he worked the gray areas of the law. He might be troubled and worried by people in his life, ones he acknowledged, which didn't include her.

Images and ideas faded to a muddle.

Whatever he was, whatever he did, she wondered if he'd want her, if he'd want to know her. If he didn't, she wasn't sure what she'd do. But on the other hand, what if she didn't want him? The last act of a play would soon unfold.

An early evening breeze, ever so slight, carried the water's faint chlorine scent on its breath. She brushed her auburn hair behind her ears, gathered her bag and hat, slid on her sandals, and left the pool area. The Palm Springs Art Museum lay just behind the hotel, beyond which rose a trail up the side of the mountain. She could see a white gazebo a short hike up the path. The view of Palm Springs from there might be interesting.

As she entered the parking lot beside the museum, she heard snatches of conversation. "So glad the museum has evening hours."

"I'm looking forward to seeing a real Van Gogh." Several women, a gray-haired man, a family with three children, and a group of tourists from a gleaming blue bus made their way from the lot toward the front entrance. A group of senior citizens emerged from a van, Heritage Manor on its side.

As she continued through the parking area on the way to the trail, Maegan neared a kiosk painted desert purple, sage, and deep gold. A poster advertised a special museum event. Six paintings by old masters hung on exhibit, among them a Monet, a Van Gogh and a Picasso. To her left, she noticed a stairway descending to double doors and a small sign, "Museum Side Entrance." A walk through the museum would be more relaxing than a hike to a gazebo. And cooler. She walked down the stairs, now in shadow, hoping the side entrance would be open and save a walk around to the front of the building.

A man wearing flip-flops, slapping on the concrete steps, began his way down the stairs behind her. Maegan completed her descent and stood in front of glass-paneled doors. As she peered into an empty museum hallway on the other side, she gripped the large brass entry handle and jostled the door. Locked. She noticed a sign: "After 5 pm Use Front Entrance."

Maegan turned as the man neared the bottom of the stairway. "We have to use the front entrance," she said and started up the stairs, passing him. He extended his arm, blocking her progress. "Hey!" she responded.

Dark round sunglasses covered his eyes. A brown crocheted hat slanted on his long, unkempt blond hair that partially hid his face.

"Please get out of my way," she asked as she maneuvered to his other side.

"Hey, hey," he said and laughed as he withdrew his other hand from the pocket of his khaki cutoffs to block her again.

The fight-or-flight instinct flowed through Maegan's body. Should she scream? The man had a runner's body, sinewy and taut in his faded green T-shirt. *Run!*

Maegan darted to the side. Almost past him, she felt him grab her arm. His grip tightened. She screamed, kicking at his shins, and striking at him with her free arm. Her purse and its contents clattered onto the concrete.

"Don't scream. Don't scream," he said as he pulled her toward him. "Jesus, Maegan, it's me—Winston."

She stared at him for a moment, at the guitar tattooed on his forearm, the miniature guitar shaped earring dangling from his earlobe, the pierced nostril. His voice had a velvety rasp.

"What are you trying to do?" Breathless, she shook herself from his grip. "Take off those damn glasses."

Winston did so, dropping them in his pants pocket. "I had to be sure it was you."

"Did it ever occur to you to just ask?" Maegan peered at him, anger and fear mixed in her eyes. "What's with the blond hair and the pierced nostril?"

"Part of my new image." Winston tapped his one earring with his index finger, making it swing.

Maegan rolled her eyes. "How did you recognize me?"

Winston shrugged. "Pictures from Pearl. We stay in touch."

"How did you find me?"

"I'd just finished rehearsal with my group at The Blue Coyote next to the hotel. Win Spence and the Blasts."

"Spence isn't your last name."

"I'm sure not going to use Dupre," Winston said, frowning. "Anyway, I have a gig there in the evenings. Almost done for the season. After the earthquake this morning, I ran outside toward the hotel. A chick I like works there. Wanted to see if she was okay. I thought I saw you out on the sidewalk. I was sure once I got a better look at you in the lobby."

Maegan put her hands on her hips. "So, what's going on, that you need to scare the shit out of me? Why not just say 'Hi' to me in the hotel like normal people?"

"I was excited to see you, but I'm never sure about where Neville is. He pops up out of nowhere and keeps an eye on me. He's in and outta Palm Springs all the time. Got people all over town. Runners, dopers, wannabes. Regular human internet. People who know people. 'Don't you ever make no peep to the police, little brother, or I'll break your fingers,' he says. When I saw you, I wanted to tell you to stay the hell out of his way if you ever spot him. And hope he doesn't spot you first. He's really gone down the path. Mean SOB. I'm telling you now."

"Worse than when we were kids?"

"Much. He's got it in for me because I got my music, and I won't get involved in his operations. Like he's tryin' to build a dynasty. Like he can't stand people with dreams and ambitions." Winston paused. "And he still rants about you, Maegan, havin' that special bank account and us as kids—him and me— havin' to scratch. He'll make trouble for you just out of meanness. And he'd really like to get his hands on that money." Winston sat down on the steps. "I'm pluggin' away with my group. We're gonna cut a CD with a small recording company next month. What are you doin' here?"

"I'm going to meet my father tomorrow."

"What?" Winston's forehead wrinkled. His eyebrows arched. "The guy who left Audrey before you were born?"

"Yes."

"How'd you find him, or did he find you?"

"How I wish." She sat next to her half-brother and told him how she'd made it happen.

"I know that's something you've wanted all your life. Happy for you, little sis."

At least Winston seemed the same, inside. She put her head on his shoulder. "I'm glad you didn't get separated from your music."

"Neville and Pop keep trying, but I don't want that life. I just keep my mouth shut. Go along to get along."

"Don't let them take away your dreams." It sounded good—better than she felt.

Chapter Sixteen

Winston Dupre

May 2008—Cathedral City, California

"Welcome to the 'Bu na Vista' apartments," Winston murmured to himself, as he locked the door to the black Ford Escape that he'd bought from his drummer's brother. The "E" from *Buena* had been pried loose from the sign in front of his apartment complex two months ago. Just another notch on The Bu na Vista manager's list of things gone to hell and not tended to.

He walked from the covered parking strip toward the iron gate leading to the apartment courtyard and pool area. After closing the gate quietly, he continued to the row of apartments on the left of the complex toward number 5. Lighting in the overhang above the weathered Spanish-style doors gave a dull glow. A cat, tufts of hair missing from its body, ran by, casting a furtive glance in Winston's direction. The faint aroma of doughnuts emanating from the Swiss Doughnut Shop across the street hung in the air, the day's supply of early morning cholesterol underway. He glanced at his watch. 3:30 a.m.

Thoughts—the life-changing kind—had been running through his head on the drive back from his gig in Palm Springs to Cathedral City.

He walked slowly toward number 5, pausing by the pool, by a metal-framed chair, the strips of webbing faded and sagging. The night air had finally cooled enough to be comfortable. He sighed and sat down in the chair, the legs of the metal frame scratching backward on the concrete as he lowered his weight onto it.

After being with his half-sister earlier at the museum and then playing at The Blue Coyote, he felt inspired. He didn't realize how much he'd missed her and their talks. Maegan had faith in him, even offered to help him. He wanted to be a good guitarist. Hell, he wanted to be a *great* guitarist. But Neville always tried to pull him off track. "Store this stuff in your apartment," he'd say. "Deliver this." Neville could be quite persuasive. Winston regretted taking money from him when things had gotten tough.

Maegan had succeeded after all the shit that had happened to her. Why couldn't he? She'd told him something important: She was about to *meet* her father for the *first* time. He admired her and her spirit. It made him resolve to *leave* his father—and brother—for the *final* time. He'd had enough of the drugs, the shady deals, always looking over his shoulder. He gritted his teeth as he hauled himself from the chair and walked the few steps to his door. The bulb above number 5 flickered and went out.

Winston started to slip his key into the lock only to find something strange. The door was unlocked. Winston tensed. Had neighborhood punks broken in and made off with some of his sound equipment? *Goddammit.* He entered slowly and groped for the switch by the door. At the same time, a lamp clicked on, and Winston heard a man's voice.

"Where the hell you been, little bro?" the voice said.

Winston jumped. Neville sprawled on the couch, his head propped up on pillows against the sofa arm, a bottle of beer dangling from his hand.

"Jesus, man," Winston stammered. "When did you get into town?"

"Tonight," Neville said, smirking.

"How'd you get in?"

"Piece o'cake lock, little bro. Easy to pick."

Neville Dupre's red-eyed stare bored into Winston as he placed the bottle on the beige carpet. Pulling up his sweat-stained tank top, he used it to wiped his face, revealing the well-defined abs of his short, powerful body.

"So, where ya been?" Neville asked.

Winston swallowed. "You know. Still at the Blue Coyote." He couldn't tell his brother about running into Maegan; that guy would do anything to get at her. He had to let his stepsister know Neville was in town.

Neville raised himself up on one elbow, his bicep sleek. "Yeah? Where's your guitar?"

"Locked it up at the Coyote." He walked toward the kitchen alcove for a glass of water.

His brother sat up, swung his feet onto the floor, thighs powerful, his body panther-like, ready to spring.

Winston ran water in the glass, took several swallows. "Make any money tonight?"

"Yeah, little bro," Neville said. "But I guess not as much as you."

"What are you talkin' about?" Winston held onto the glass, tightening his grip. "You make way more money than me."

"My man Carlos saw you earlier tonight."

Winston put the glass on the counter. He turned, watching his brother.

"Yeah, you were comin' outta the Hyatt on the way to the Blue Coyote." Neville stood, stretched his arms and turned his upper body from side to side. "Takes money to hang at the Hyatt."

After meeting Maegan, he'd walked her from the museum back to the hotel and then cut through the hotel out to North Palm Canyon Drive. Where had Carlos been lurking? Had Carlos seen him with Maegan?

Neville grabbed the beer bottle, took a couple of pulls from it, looked Winston up and down. "You scorin' or sellin' on the sly at the hotel?"

"Just tryin' to book a gig in the hotel lounge." Winston edged from the sink, nearer toward the door.

"Lookin' like that?" Neville snorted. "They wouldn't let your scruffy, long-haired ass in the pisser, let alone the lounge." Neville closed the space between them, looked him up and down again, extra slow. "By the way, asshole, they don't have no live music there. What are you up to?"

"Okay. Listen." Winston thought fast. He had to protect Maegan. Neville would go after her if he knew she was in town. "I might be on to a big score. Found out about it from a guy at the Blue Coyote. Guy works at the hotel. South American stuff. I was gonna tell you about it."

"You ain't never set up any drug buys."

"Always a first time." Winston shrugged as he watched his brother glower at him.

"Yeah? Carlos scouts that side of town for me. Ain't no action 'round south Palm Springs unless I make it." Neville grabbed his arm, tightening his hold. "What're you up to?"

Winston winced as his brother's grip dug into his flesh. "Hey, let go."

"I've told you before. You're lucky I don't break those long, fancy fingers of yours, Mr. Guitar Man." Neville glared at him. "I repeat, what are you up to?"

Winston felt his adrenalin surge. Neville was mean enough to do it.

"Dammit, Neville, I got or had a girlfriend who worked there."

"Really." Neville laughed, loosening his grip. "Do tell me more."

"She dumped me." Winston pushed on. "I wanted to talk to her."

"How'd that go, lover boy?"

Winston shook his head. "She'd quit and no one would tell me where she went."

Neville grinned, flashing his palms like two flags. "Well, now *that* I believe. At least *somebody* around here's got good sense."

Winston watched his brother, every muscle tense. Neville leered at him, sauntered toward the door, pulled it open, then paused. He shook his finger at Winston, a leer on his face, and left.

Chapter Seventeen

Neville Dupre

September 1982—Beaumont Valley, California

Neville slouched in a tire swing hanging by a rope from a branch of a large oak. His thick mop of black hair made his face sweat. He looked down at his calves, enjoying the sight of hair on his legs. He hoped for some on his chest, too. His firm, squat body had no fat. At twelve years old, people said he was maturing early and built like a fire plug.

He looked around Pearl's scruffy front yard, the rundown house. Car exhaust smell from the freeway sometimes blew their way. His old man, Dixson, was supposed to help fix the place up while they lived with Pearl till they found a spot of their own. But old Dixson never did nothin'. He was always "busy."

Pearl wanted the place painted, the shutters hung straight, and the porch made safe. Secretly, Neville hoped Pearl'd fall down the porch steps with a load of pies, what with the broken railing and crumbling cement stair and all. The old broad was always on his case.

He scuffed his feet in the dry dirt, chewing on a toothpick as the sun slipped lower in the sky. Late afternoon but still hotter than shit.

He wiped away the sweat above his upper lip where he could feel hair growin' like a someday moustache. It was the third time in two weeks he'd had to watch his little stepsister, Maegan. He didn't want to be no babysitter for no five-year-old brat. If his friends found out, they'd rag on him good. He yanked the toothpick from his mouth and threw it on the ground.

His stepmother, Audrey, and her mother, Pearl—he was supposed to call her "Gramma Pearl"— were doin' somethin' for their dumb church. A bazaar. Had one every damn month, seemed like.

He watched Maegan wheel a doll buggy through the dust. She stopped to pull a small blanket over a Chatty Cathy doll inside. An old red purse of Audrey's hung on her arm. On her head, one of Pearl's straw hats.

"Hey, Maegan. What ya doin'? Tryin' to smother your baby? It's hotter than hades. Why the hell d'you think I'm sittin' under the tree?"

Maegan's eyes grew big. "You're not 'posed to swear. I'll tell Mama."

Damn kid. Always gettin' him in trouble. Like when he came home late, skipped school, or got in a fight. She'd hear him and his little brother, Winston, talking, then she'd run and tell Audrey or Pearl. A royal pain in the ass. Why'd his father go and get married again? To that Audrey? They'd been doin' fine. He could do what he wanted—back then.

Maegan passed by, looking at him, all innocence, shaking her finger at him. Neville shoved his foot out in her path. She fell forward, hitting her head on the buggy handle. She flopped in the dirt, letting out a howl as the buggy tipped on its side. The doll, blanket, small pillow, and buggy mattress fell out. He jumped from the tire, looked around, pulled her up and dusted off her dress. He picked up her hat, checked her head. No mark. He threw the stuff in the buggy, plopped the hat on her head, and gave her the old purse.

She stood there, wailing.

"You ain't hurt!" he insisted.

"I'll tell Mama!" she cried.

Little shit. His eyes narrowed. "Hey, Maegan," he asked, "want a cookie?"

She sniffled and turned away. "Can't have any till after supper."

"No one'll miss one or two. Wait a minute. I'll get some. Make ya feel better."

He ran up the porch steps into the kitchen. The aroma of fresh-baked somethin' hit his nose. A plate of cookies sat on the table. Pearl had made Maegan's favorite, sugar cookies with faces on 'em. She never made his favorite. He liked chocolate brownies.

He grabbed two. About to leave, he noticed a crock with a chipped lid sitting on the table that had the word "Bazaar" painted on it. Never there before. Must have forgotten to take it to church with 'em. Probably more cookies. Neville looked inside. *Whoa!* It was full of money—lots of coins and small bills. He looked around. Maegan was still outside. He cocked his head, a hint of a smile curling the sides of his mouth. He put each of the cookies on napkins from a holder on the table.

"Hey, Maegan," he yelled. "Come 'ere. Have your cookies inside."

He heard Maegan clump up the steps. Soon she appeared in the kitchen doorway, still sniffling, carrying her purse, the hat sideways on her head.

"Come 'ere. Sit down. Have a cookie. You want some milk?"

She sat at the table, shaking her head, nibbling on a sugar cookie, watching Neville.

"Hey, take a look in here." He removed the lid from the crock. "Gramma Pearl left us a real surprise. She said you and me could both have some."

Maegan stood on the chair, leaned her hands on the table, and peered inside the crock. Neville curled his lip. There was always money for the little shit. Her real daddy sent a check every month. He and Winston "sucked hind tit," as their old man said. Dixson Dupre didn't like the arrangement and tried to get at Maegan's money, but Pearl watched that account real close. She'd tell Dixson to go out and make his own money. The old woman always said that Dixson "worked at not workin'."

"Did Gramma Pearl say we could have some?" Maegan looked at Neville. He nodded. She reached into the crock and fished out a shiny quarter.

"You takin' any?" She looked at Neville.

"Not this time. I want you to have the fun."

He watched Maegan pull out two more shiny coins. He was just itchin' to take some. But he had another idea to fix the little fucker *real* good. He watched her take out a big handful of coins. She liked the newer pennies. Dumb kid liked the shine.

Maegan sorted her coins and stacked them. "Now I can get some more clothes for my dolly."

Neville jiggled the table. The stacks fell. Her lower lip began to waggle.

"Don't go all crybaby on me," Neville barked at her.

"I'm not a crybaby!"

"Here, take some paper, too." He reached in the crock, pulled out a five-dollar bill and smooth-pressed it on the table for her. Then he pulled out more fives. And some tens. "Here. Put all that stuff in your purse."

She put the money in her purse, reached into the crock for two more coins and dropped them in, one by one.

Neville watched, adding, "You can get those doll bunkbeds you've been wantin'."

Maegan's face lit up.

He glanced at the clock hanging by the door. Audrey and Pearl could get back from church real soon.

"Come on. Let's go outside again. You need to finish walkin' yer doll." Maegan looked at him and nodded. Once outside, his stepsister trundled off, pushing the buggy through the dusty dirt. She stopped to straighten her hat, putting her purse, now heavier, inside the buggy beside the doll. Then she continued around the corner of the house.

Neville scurried back into the kitchen. Quickly, he made sure everything was neat and in place. He ran back out to the tire swing, pulled a new toothpick out of his pocket, and hung it from the corner of his mouth. He swung back and forth, smirking.

After about fifteen minutes, his stepmother and Pearl came home. *Wait'll Pearl misses that money,* he thought, *and they find it in Missie Maegan's purse.* Time for little sis to get her little ass in real trouble.

Chapter Eighteen

Pearl Spence

January 2010—Beaumont Valley, California

That time I thought I lost the bake sale money from the church bazaar—*oh, my stars!* It was back in 1982. The bake sale had taken in $429.55. That's a lot of money to lose. Sure did make me sweat. Reminded me of the time I was little and lied about breakin' a bottle of milk. Money was tight and my dad found work wherever he could— The Big Depression and all. My mother made real sure I learned a lesson about the value of a dollar, about being wasteful and careless. With that bake sale money maybe lost, I could feel my mother shakin' her finger at me from the grave.

How did I come to think I lost it? Well, late in the afternoon, the day I was supposed to turn the bake sale money in at the church, Neville watched Maegan while Audrey and me took care of business. I'd put a barrel painted bright yellow in the pie shop for donations of old clothes. Got some nice stuff for needy folks. Every few days I'd bring the clothes home, wash 'em and put 'em into plastic bags. The day the money and all the clothes was due at the church, we hauled six big plastic bags to the Honda. The last thing I told Audrey was, "Bring the crock. It's on the table." I'd taken it from its hidin' place in my closet.

How could I be so damned careless? Dead tired on my feet, that's how. Runnin' the pie shop. Keepin' Audrey and her husband Dixson and those two sons of his. Bein' overweight— stress eatin', I think they call it now. I was fifty-five and my knees was payin' the price. My heart would later.

Well, when we got to the church, Edna Smythe took the clothes and then asked for the money. I told Audrey to give it to her.

My daughter said to me, "I thought you brought it."

"I told you to pick up the crock," I said.

"I sure didn't hear that," my Audrey answered right quick.

Edna turned kinda peevish when I said I guessed we'd forgotten it. I said I'd bring it over later the next day. By then I really wasn't sure where the money was. I knew if Dixson found it, he'd take the money—crock and all.

When we got home, I was glad to see that crock sittin' on the table where we'd left it, and Neville and Maegan gettin' along. Him in the swing my husband put up when Audrey was little, and Maegan playin' with her doll buggy and Chatty Cathy.

Never knew what was goin' to happen with that boy Neville. Times I thought he was a weasel like his father, Dixson. Other times he'd be okay. I kept hopin'.

I looked in the crock and heaved a big sigh of relief. I hid the crock back in the closet. Next day I took it to the church like I promised and turned it over to Edna. She was tallyin' the books. We was all workin' hard, raisin' money to build a new church.

"How much you got, Pearl?" Edna asked.

Feeling kinda proud, I said, "Total of 429 dollars and 55 cents."

"Wonderful. Would you help me roll the change and double check your final tally? Shouldn't take too long. I know you're busy."

So she dumped the money out of the crock onto the table and we started rollin' quarters and such, stackin' bills. When we counted it all up, there was only $351.05; I was $78.50 short. Edna was lookin' at me, her eyebrows curved like the tops of question marks. I got real warm and red-faced.

"I don't know what happened. Audrey and me counted it twice."

"Well, Pearl, if you've found it necessary to *borrow* a little, just bring it to me by Saturday."

"I didn't 'borrow' no money from the bazaar bake sale," I said, glowerin' at her. The creases between my eyes got deep like the look I was burrowin' into her face.

"Now, I didn't mean to blame . . ."

"Oh, you blamed just fine, Edna." I reached inside my purse and pulled out six wrinkled ten-dollar bills, three fives, some singles and a handful of change. I dug around in the bottom and found two quarters. From my house money; that was money I worked hard to make. I slammed it on the table. Now I *would* be short. I never touched Maegan's special money for runnin' the house.

"Pearl, I didn't mean anything," Edna back-pedaled. "We all get short on occasion."

"Well, I'm *not* short." I stared hard into her eyes. "Are we done here?"

Edna nodded and cleared her throat. "Sorry for any misunderstanding."

"Uh-huh." I pushed my chair from the table and left the church.

I drove up the lane toward my house like a railroad engine runnin' late. I could feel the steam and smoke comin' out of my ears. I pushed down hard on the brakes, making a cloud of dust when I parked. I stomped up the steps and into the living room. My daughter was home.

Audrey looked at the scowl on my face. "My goodness, what is it, Mama?"

I planted my hands on my hips. "Did you take any money from that crock?"

Her eyes got big. "Of course not."

"How about Dixson?" I waited with my eyes locked on hers.

Audrey looked down. "No. He didn't come home last night."

Not again, I thought. But I couldn't deal with two problems at once. Not today. Before Audrey could say anything else, through the window I saw Neville ridin' his bike into the yard. I stomped out of the house, back down the steps. He was just leanin' the bike against the front porch, comin' right home after school for a change. When he saw me, the look on my face, he pulled the bike out, ready to hop back on. For a heavyset person, I can move real fast. I grabbed those handlebars and yanked on 'em, pullin' the bike toward me.

"Hold it, Mr. Neville," I told him. "I want to talk to you. You take somethin' wasn't yours yesterday? Know anything about some money missin' from my bazaar crock?"

"Nope." He jerked the bike back, full of attitude.

"I think you do." The little varmint. I lost my grip on the handlebars.

"Well, I don't." He backed away with his bike right fast, hopped on, and called over his shoulder with a laugh, "Maybe Maegan does."

I stomped back up the porch stairs, small pieces of crumblin' cement flying out from beneath my feet.

"Maegan!" I yelled. Then I saw her playin' at the dining room table with her doll.

She looked up. "Yes, Gramma?"

"Did you take money from the crock that was on the kitchen table?"

She nodded. "Now I can buy more dolly clothes."

What? I pulled out a dinin' room chair and sat beside her. "What made you think that money was yours to take?"

She looked at the ceilin', swingin' her feet. "I don't know."

I crossed my arms in front of me. Gave her a good scowl. She knew that look.

"Neville said you said it was okay." She looked down at her hands.

I felt my blood heat to the boilin' point. "Where is the money?"

"In my big red purse."

"Go get your purse, child."

Maegan trundled down the hall to her room and returned with the purse. I opened it and dumped the money out on the table.

"You took this?"

"Yes, Gramma." Her lower lip quivered. She could tell from my voice somethin' was very wrong.

"Honey, you don't take money that ain't yours." I gathered the bills and coins into my pocket. Sure glad I'd got my house money back.

That night I had a "sit-down" with Audrey and Dixson. Said I wasn't goin' to tolerate any thievin' games or anyone teachin' Maegan bad behavior under my roof. It was the pure principle of the whole thing rubbin' me raw. I told them they had to get a place of their own.

I knew that Dixson was a no-good. I just didn't know how no-good a man Dixson would turn out to be. And that Neville seemed to be comin' into his birthright.

Chapter Nineteen

Audrey Spence

August 1984—Beaumont Valley, California

Audrey paused as she peeled a Granny Smith apple for Pearl's pies. She relaxed her white-knuckled grip on the paring knife and placed the apple, skin still clinging to it, on the table. Pearl always said that apple pies put her diner on the map. But Audrey hated the place with its endless supply of apples and the sweltering heat from the shop's two oversized ovens. It was already hot enough outside without heating up the inside. A black metal fan sitting on top of a used commercial refrigerator provided just enough breeze to blow a strand of hair across her forehead. She used the back of her hand to brush it out of the way.

From where she stood in the diner kitchen at the wooden table her father had made, its surface heavily scarred from years of pie making, she could see her mother and two regular customers through the order and pickup window. Del Reams and Joe Ingram stopped every day for pie, coffee, and "the news." They always sat on the same two stools at the counter. She felt her life, like theirs, had fallen into the same rut. Coffee, pies, and—for her—"the blues."

She finished peeling the apple, peeled more, and sliced them in a dull rhythm, as usual—*klunk, klunk, klunk.* The white apron covering her jeans and T-shirt, once morning-clean, now had bursts of blueberries, apples, and coffee spattered down its front. Her mind kept wandering to her husband, Dixson, who seemed so restless and dissatisfied. "Moody" was a better description. She never knew what might set him off. He was touchy about everything. They couldn't seem to talk much anymore.

His baseball career had ended when he wrecked his knee playing for the Rancho Cucamonga Quakes. The local doctor said he'd have to quit. It was a bitter disappointment. And no longer able to climb utility poles, the electric company let him go. He seemed to adjust, at first, and got a job down the street at the Bowden Family Hardware Store. Mr. Bowden seemed to like him and his former baseball skills just fine; even made him manager. But then, with no baseball and a bad knee, Dixson changed. He shrugged at knee surgery since he still would be unable to do sports.

Over time, tight money became a raw bone they chewed on every month. Especially after Neville tricked Maegan into stealing from Pearl and they had to get their own place. Audrey despised the rundown 1950's house near Interstate 10. The rent was cheap, but the traffic noise made a quiet moment almost impossible. Surrounded by a rusty cyclone fence with a dirt patch for a yard, the place resembled a prison more and more each day.

She regretted telling Dixson about Maegan's special bank account. The money couldn't be touched by anyone but Pearl until the girl reached thirty, and then Maegan herself would take control of it. Until then, money came every month for Maegan's support. Dixson said it should be used for him and his boys, too; after all, they were Maegan's family. The thing that flamed his anger most was that Pearl had been put in charge of the money, not Audrey, Maegan's mother—and *his wife*.

Audrey just couldn't seem to do anything to please her husband. He was mad she'd gained weight. But he made her so nervous, she ate. His words cut deeper than any knife. *You're gonna be fat like your mother. I didn't marry that.*

And then about two years ago . . . a lump rose in her throat.

She looked out into the diner. To her surprise, she saw Dixson through the café's front window. He crossed the street toward the shop, his limp more noticeable than earlier in the morning at the house. Or at least more noticeable for her benefit or anyone else watching him. He was supposed to be working. She dropped her knife on the table and grabbed a glass from the sink ledge. From the refrigerator, she took a pitcher and, holding the glass, felt the cold water fill it as she poured. She took several swallows of water, like a gunfighter gulps whiskey for courage. She pressed the glass against her forehead seeking its coolness.

Behind the café counter, Pearl joked with Del and Joe. Lunch time at Pearl's Place had been busy, noisy. Audrey was glad the rush had ended. It would be several more hours before Maegan came by on her way home from school. Not Neville. After school—*if* he went to school—Neville wandered off with his friends. And he often tried to influence Winston to do the same.

Del Reams nudged Joe, sitting at the counter next to him. "Hey, Pearl, sure you don' wanna sell this apple pie recipe? Make ya a rich woman."

"What're you gonna buy it with, your good looks?" Pearl laughed, clanging her spoon on the inside of her coffee cup as she stirred in a teaspoon of sugar. She leaned her hip against the green Formica lunch counter.

"Pearl, how about another slice to go with the rest of my coffee?" Joe Ingram pushed his plate toward her. She pushed it back.

"Your wife'll kill me if I let you have another one." Pearl swiped her spoon at him. Joe ducked, slapping his hand on the counter, laughing.

Audrey had to smile at the way her mother handled her loyal and well-fed customers.

She glanced out the window again. Dixson could see in. He stood, beckoning for her to come out. Audrey slipped her apron off, put it on the table, and walked from the kitchen into the dining area.

"Mama, I think Dixson needs to talk to me a sec."

Pearl scowled in his direction. "I see him, signalin' like a baseball coach. Doesn't he work today? Honey, don't be too long. We need those fresh pies. Supper crowd'll soon be along."

Audrey grabbed a paper napkin from a metal dispenser on a table on her way out and wiped her face. She opened the shop door and stepped onto the sidewalk. Her jeans and tee shirt clung to her. With his lopsided walk, her husband moseyed nearer the curb under a struggling oak tree.

"What's up?" Audrey asked. "Any special reason you're not working?"

"Don't give me any crap," he growled, glancing through the window in Pearl's direction.

Audrey looked over her shoulder. Pearl watched them. "What's the matter?" she asked.

"My damn knee. Bowden gave me the afternoon off. Gotta go to the doc for a cortisone shot." His voice hardened. "I need some money."

"I don't have any money with me." Her voice sunk low in her throat, the resolve to stand up to him about money matters shrinking, like her backbone, like always. The money wasn't for any doctor. He'd drink it or gamble it away.

"Where the hell's some cash? Couldn't find any at the house." Dixson cocked his head toward the diner. "Go slip some from the till."

"I can't do that."

He wouldn't dare hit her, not with Pearl watching. And Del and Joe. Pearl held part of her pay back so there'd be money for rent and food, and Dixson didn't like it. He also knew that Audrey usually had a few dollars on her for running the house.

"Can you wait until I'm done at work?"

"I'm not hangin' around here," he said with a snarl. "I need it now."

Audrey glanced again in Pearl's direction. Her back was to them. Dixson followed her gaze. He grunted and grabbed Audrey's upper arm. "Where the hell you got some stashed?"

She felt his fingers dig into her flesh. They would leave bruises. She didn't want Pearl to know. Long sleeves, long dresses, sunglasses. Lots of ways to hide the marks. And he wasn't like this all the time. Sometimes . . . he treated her so nice. "I've got a little with me."

"That's more like it." He released his grip.

She reached into the V-neck of her T-shirt. His gaze followed her hand, eyeing her breasts. She pulled out twenty dollars.

"This ain't all you got," he said, knowing she'd hang on to what she could. "Come on, fork it over."

Audrey sighed and pulled out another twenty. He grabbed the bills. With his free hand, he jerked her arm downward, hard. It hurt her shoulder and threw her off balance. She stumbled against the tree. She righted herself as he crossed the street, walking back in the same direction he'd come from, his limp less noticeable. She couldn't cry, not now, not here. She rubbed her arm and shoulder, watching him walk away. She turned toward the shop.

Pearl was watching. Sweat increased under Audrey's arms, making her feel hotter, fatter, and emptier.

She walked back into the shop, saying nothing. Del seemed very interested in a newspaper. Joe poured sugar into a spoon and watched the white granules slide off into his coffee. Pearl looked at her with questions on her face but said nothing. The air hung heavy with a knowing and a curiosity from lives lived longer than hers. Audrey rushed back into the kitchen. She slipped on her dirty apron, picked up the knife and grabbed a Granny Smith apple.

Whole apples. Pealed. Whole apples. Sliced. *Klunk, klunk, klunk* . . . sliced to pieces, like her, like her life.

She wondered what would happen when she got home. If he gambled and won. . . if he lost . . . if he was drunk . . . and she worried about Maegan and Winston. So far, he hadn't touched them.

Chapter Twenty

Dixxon Dupre

August 1992—Beaumont Valley, California

Dixson Dupre leaned his elbow on the bar and finished a long, cold swallow from a glass of Bud draft. He plopped the empty glass down, slid the back of his hand across his mouth. *Shit.* That damn smell on his fingers. He wanted to hawk a spit on the floor but didn't. The stink of turpentine clung to his hands like skunk spray.

"Hey, Palani, gimme another," he ordered as he let go a belch.

The bartender nodded. "Here ya go, man."

Dixson glanced around the small, narrow tavern stuck between Harry's Tack & Feed Store and Morton's Pharmacy. It had a worn, comfortable feel. A magenta-and-green neon sign hanging in the front window announced "The Aloha Oasis." Another neon below it advertised his favorite beer in bright-red letters: "Budweiser on Tap." On the door dangled an 8" x 11" cardboard sign attached to a piece of twine that announced "We're Open" in big block letters. He smiled to himself, having closed the place more than a few times, drunker than a cross-eyed roadrunner.

"How's things goin' over at Bowden Hardware?" Palani asked, his yellowed smile contrasting against his dark, Hawaiian skin. He swiped a cloth across the glossy bar surface in front of Dixson.

"Lousy," Dixson replied. "Same damn thing every day. Put on a white shirt, Bowden's Hardware stitched on the back. Wear a 'Service with a Smile' pin on the front pocket. Feels like a bowling shirt. Old man Bowden thinks it's real class-assy. Then I poke around helpin' people find light bulbs, ant spray, furnace filters. Write up some orders. Make a few keys. Mix paint. Goddamn oil-base paint spilled today. Bitch to clean up. Turp smell is still on my hands."

"Least you're workin'," Palani responded as he waved at a man entering the bar.

Dixson grimaced. "I hate turpentine. Makes my eyes water like that damn chili powder my ever-lovin' mother-in-law uses in her cookin'."

Palani nodded. "Gotta admit, Pearl's chili is sure good."

"Yeah, yeah." Dixson scowled, smelled his hands. "Damn turp fumes hang in the back of my mouth. Can even taste it." He ran his tongue across his teeth and lips.

Bowden's Hardware was a lousy place to work, but it wasn't far from his house. Only a ten-minute drive. He belched again. Friday night. Pay day. The guys would be comin' in. He took his pay envelope from his pants pocket, pulled out a twenty and laid it on the bar. "Run me a tab."

Palani eyed the small brown envelope. "How 'bout it, man? Wanna bet on the Laker game playin' tomorrow in Los Angeles?"

"Sure, what the hell." Dixson followed basketball, so he pulled out fifty bucks. "The Lakers, by two."

"Okay, man." Palani jotted the transaction in a small, tattered notebook and slipped it along with the bet money in his back pocket.

"It's about time I win somethin'," Dixson whined. "I'm tired o' bein' piss poor."

Before he'd married Audrey, she told him that money came every month for her little girl. Dixson couldn't believe his good luck. Child support money could help him and his boys, too. But after they married, he learned it wasn't the usual child support set-up, and Audrey had no control over it. It was money from a mysterious special account. He could never get his hands on anything. The funds went directly to the account and that old bitch of a mother-in-law controlled it. The money was only for Maegan.

When he'd gone to the bank in Beaumont Valley to try to withdraw a few dollars from the account, the teller told him he'd have to see the manager. "I'm sorry, Mr. Dupre," the manager said, "but the terms of the account are very clear." The manager looked at him over the rims of his glasses. "Only Pearl Spence is authorized."

Dixson had even confronted Pearl. "I'm Maegan's stepfather. Audrey is her mother. *We* should have control of that money."

Pearl laughed from deep within her frame. "Dixson Dupre, that's not for me to say. And I wouldn't trust you with squat."

Maegan had whatever she needed. Him and his sons and Audrey were always scratchin' to get by.

Old Pearl was cagey. Several times he'd slipped over to her place while she was at church. He'd rifled through all the hidin' places he could find. Copped a few bucks here and there, but no sign of major money or bank paperwork.

"I'll have another Bud." Dixson held up his empty glass.

"You're on a roll, Dix." Palani put a tall glass in front of him, foam dripping down the sides, removed the empty one. "How's the wife?"

Dixson shook his head. "Gettin' fat on chili and pie."

Audrey used to be a looker—good enough for him to marry and give Neville and Winston a mother. The boys' own mother took off with another baseball player from the farm team they both had played on, The Cucamonga Quakes. Never could find her. Good riddance. He'd have had a baseball career with the LA Dodgers if he hadn't blown his damn knee. He swallowed the last of his beer.

"Thanks, Palani, see ya Monday." He edged off the bar stool. "Think I'll head home early tonight. Got a few things to do."

Dixson walked outside, hopped into his used pick-up and drove down the street toward home. At the convenience mart, he stopped and bought a six-pack of Bud, a pint of gin, and a pack of smokes. *If this is as good as it gets, I might as well enjoy myself.*

Audrey used to turn him on when she had a hot body. Now she only looked good after a few beers and a couple shots of the hard stuff. His sons were lucky, probably out cattin' around. "Get it while you can, boys," he said under his breath. He slid the bag onto the bench seat and heaved himself into the truck.

He should have taken Alice Monroe's unspoken proposition. The gal always came into the hardware store on Fridays, looking for nails . . . or oven spray . . . or somethin' or other . . . and flirted with him somethin' fierce. Good for a quick Friday night lay. Her old man was a trucker and stayed gone until later in the night. But Dixson only bedded Alice once. A guy could get shot messing with another man's wife this close to home. Come to think of it, that was her damn paint he'd been mixing when it spilled all over. Had to admit, she did get him hot and bothered.

He felt restless as he drove into the driveway of his house, past the open cyclone fence gate. Nothing ever seemed to go right. *Some palace*, he thought. The landlord appeared like a bad dream on the first of the month and got real testy if the rent was short or gonna be late.

Lucky, a large, long-haired mutt, barked and wagged his bent tail. He clumped down the porch steps toward him.

"Sure would be nice if everybody was as happy to see me as you." Dixson patted Lucky on the head, then with a quick, hard move, he kneed the dog in the side, pushing him away. "Now leave me the hell alone."

No one else was on the porch to greet him. Usually someone was around. But not tonight. Audrey and Maegan had walked from the diner to church to help with some damn thing or other.

Every day he dropped Audrey off at work. Maegan took the bus to the high school, walked to the diner after school, and stayed until her mother was done. He picked them up. Every day. Suited him just fine. He had the truck to run around in, day or night. Dixson dropped down on the top step, snapped open a beer, and swigged. Lucky sidled in beside him and tried to push his head into Dixson's palm.

"Don't you get it? Get the hell away from me or I'll beat you good!" He slapped Lucky's muzzle with the back of his hand. The dog backed away, tail lowered, and lumbered down the porch steps, disappearing around the corner of the house.

Dixson's belly rolled over a worn leather belt, giving his once-athletic build the look of a cheap, sagging mattress. He cracked open the smokes and reached into his rumpled shirt pocket for a book of matches. *Damn.* Moisture sat on his upper lip. The unlit cigarette dangled from the corner of his mouth as he stared out into the street in front of the house, the cars parked at odd angles along the edge of the curbless road. In the distance behind him, traffic whirred by on Interstate 10. His thoughts roamed.

Neville was getting to be a handful, always over in Palm Springs messing around. Wouldn't be bad if he brought home some real money. Dixson might have to cuff that boy up. Old Pops could still throw a punch. The kid was twenty-two, tough and smart. Audrey called him a bully and didn't want him around. "He should have his own place by now," she grumbled.

Winston, the young one, Dixson couldn't quite figure. Always carried that guitar. Audrey called him the sensitive one. Dixson might have to shake him up, too. Put some starch in him. Dixson felt prickly, edgy. He wanted to beat the crap out of somebody. This was no life.

The phone rang. He hauled himself up and went inside. "Yeah," he answered.

"Don't forget we'll be at Pearl's after the Friday-night church supper. Pick us up there," Audrey said, her voice tired and whiney as usual. "Should be done in a couple of hours."

"Yeah, yeah. You already told me this morning. Why the hell can't Pearl bring you home?"

"You know she doesn't like to drive too far at night," Audrey reminded him.

All his wife did was wheedle and want somethin' all the time. "Okay, okay. I'll be there." He slammed down the receiver.

He'd already decided earlier that'd work just fine. He'd leave right away, now that he knew how long they'd be. Give him a chance to rummage for stray cash old Pearl might have around. *This night's lookin' up.* He grabbed the rest of the six-pack and headed for the truck.

Pearl's house was across town. When he arrived, he saw a light on inside the house. Through the window, he could see Maegan sitting at the kitchen table, writing in a notebook, a stack of books beside her. *Goddamn it. Why isn't that kid with her mother at church?* Nothin' was goin' right.

Heaving a sigh, he sat down on the steps, pulled out the pack of cigarettes.

"Hey, Maegan?" He called over his shoulder, his voice carrying into the kitchen through the screen door. "Bring me some matches." He leaned back on his elbows and waited.

He hollered again, "Hey, Maegan! You deaf?"

He heard the chair scrape on the floor, then footsteps. Maegan appeared beside him, holding a match book. "I didn't know you were here."

"Well, thank you, little Miss High and Mighty. What *you* doin' here?"

Maegan lowered her eyes. "My homework so I can go to the school football game tomorrow afternoon."

"Ain't that nice." He looked at his stepdaughter's bud breasts and long legs. She was on her way to being a looker.

Maegan turned to go back in. He grabbed her ankle. "Why not sit down with old Dad and have a beer?"

Maegan shook free and went back in the house

Dixson laughed and scratched his crotch. *Down, boy. Get it out of your head.* He snapped open another beer. "Here's to nothin'!" He raised the can in a grandiose toast and took a swallow, then chugged the rest of it. With a series of fumbles, he clamped a cigarette in his mouth and lit up.

Seemed to him some of Maegan's precious money could be used to rent a nice house, give him real pocket money, and maybe buy better booze. A private visit to Pearl might be necessary. He could be real persuasive when he had to be.

He grabbed the wobbly porch railing and pulled himself up. On his way into the house, he stubbed his toe on a potted geranium. Winston's little league baseball bat and a used guitar case leaned against the stucco wall by the front door. Winston got along with Pearl; stopped in to see her a lot. She kept the bat he'd once hit a home run with. Church game . . . big deal. Kid was no ball player. Lucky hit was all that was..

Once inside, he stood across the kitchen table from Maegan. She didn't look up.

"My, my, ain't we busy." He snatched the paper from under Maegan's hand. "Fancy arithmetic, huh?"

"Geometry."

He shoved the paper back at her and picked up a book. "This ain't even in English."

"It's French," she explained.

Dixson grunted and tossed the book down. *Stuck-up little bitch.* He walked around the table and stood behind her, rubbing his crotch. *So young, so pretty. Get away from her. Now.*

He grasped his hands together, feeling the sweat in his palms. *Get away from her.* His breathing grew agitated. *No.* He looked over his shoulder. *No! Don't do it!* But he couldn't stop himself. He cupped his hands over her breasts.

Maegan screamed. Moving fast, Dixson clamped his hand across the girl's mouth and pulled her from the chair. It thumped onto its side. She kicked, but he held her tight, backing across the floor into the dark living room, toward the couch.

He tightened his grip. "You scream again, and I'll hurt you real bad." He saw her eyes open wider. "And your mother and Pearl, too."

He dropped her on the couch and knelt over her, grabbing at her arms, kneeing her body down, giving a hard smack to her face. Fumbling, he ripped at her shorts and panties. He opened his fly, felt himself growing hard. He jammed his knees between her legs. Maegan squirmed back and forth.

"Damn it, hold still." He smacked her again.

Suddenly, he felt a searing blow across the base of his neck.

"Get off her!" the woman yelled.

He turned, gasping. A baseball bat struck him again, on the shoulder. The pain grew. His erection shrank. His mother-in-law came into focus.

Pearl screamed, *"Get off her!"*

Audrey pulled at him. *"Leave her alone!"* she yelled.

"Mama! Mama!" Maegan beat on his chest.

Pearl hit him again before he got his arm up. She kept swinging at him as he rose to his knees, flailing his arms to ward off the blows, moving to get to his feet. Maegan, sobbing, worked away from under him and into Audrey's arms. Audrey wrapped her in a throw from a nearby chair.

Pearl stepped back. "You animal!"

Dixson lunged toward Pearl and grabbed at the bat. She pulled something from her apron pocket and shook it in his face. Red powder. Suddenly, his eyes were on fire.

"You old bitch!" He clenched his eyes, tears streaming down his cheeks. He coughed and fell on his bad knee. Pain telegraphed up his thigh bone to his hip. He felt a whack on his head and fell forward, slamming his face into the worn carpet. He passed out.

When he opened his eyes, he saw Pearl standing guard in front of him with a tin of chili powder and a baseball bat.

"You stay right where you are, Mr. Dixson Dupre." Pearl glowered at him. "We called 911."

Next thing he knew, a heavy knocking on the front door filled the room and Audrey let in the police officers—one a man and the other a woman. Then came the questions. What happened? Who did what? Where? When? There was a lot of talkin', Pearl doin' most of it. Audrey piped up on occasion. Maegan did some noddin', answered a question or two.

The male officer pulled Dixson up and turned him around. Dixson felt his wrists handcuffed behind his back.

"Unlucky for you, we were close by," the officer told him. "I take you for a runner if you have the chance. Looks like the women will be pressin' charges at the station."

As Dixson slouched down the porch steps to the patrol car, he looked over his shoulder. Audrey called, "Oh, Dixson, what did you do? What were you thinkin'?"

Audrey had her arm around Maegan while the woman officer talked to the girl. Pearl stood with her tin of chili powder in one hand and the baseball bat in the other, watching him, a grim look on her face.

He felt a hand on the top of his head pushing him down into the back seat of the police car. *Son of a bitch.* When they arrived at the local police station with its small jail, the process began. Name, nature of the crime, mug shot. Possessions taken and put into a bag. Fingerprints, body search, check for previous warrants. Another officer walked him to a cell.

"I know my rights," Dixson said. "I get a phone call." He had to get to Audrey to tell her not to press charges. He had to stop her.

"Not tonight, buddy."

Dixson slumped onto a cot, fell into a beer sleep.

The next afternoon Audrey appeared outside his cell, alone this time. "Oh, Dixson, what did you do?" Her eyes were ringed with red, dark pouches.

"Aw, please, Audrey, honey," he pleaded. "I lost my head. I didn't get inside her. Please don't press charges. I had too much beer. It'll never happen again. You know I've never done anything like that before. It was a stupid mistake. I'll make things right with Maegan and you and Pearl. I promise."

"Dixson, it's already done." She looked at the floor. "You know I love you. I didn't want to, but Pearl and the officers . . ." Her voice trailed off.

He stepped back from the cell door. The realization flooded through him that he'd probably go to prison. Four years, five years, eight years? More? Maegan was a minor.

"I'm so sorry," she said. "I love you." She lowered her gaze.

He glowered at Audrey, who looked up and quickly looked down again.

You dumb bitch.

Chapter Twenty-One

Pearl Spence

August 1992—Beaumont Valley, California

I watched the police car drive off with that no-good Dixson, wonderin' how a man could do such a horrible thing. I turned to see Audrey holdin' Maegan in her arms, rockin' her back and forth, the child sobbin' and clingin' to her mama. The poor girl's cheek looked bruised. We straightened her clothes, wiped her face with a damp cloth, and brushed back her hair, all the time talkin' to her real quiet.

It took Maegan a while to calm down. Me, too. Audrey acted kinda dazed, what with her daughter in her arms and her husband occupyin' the back of a police car. We was lucky, though. Dixson would have succeeded with an unforgivable act if Audrey and me hadn't gotten home when we did. So I guessed we should be thankful. But that drunken, vile man had slapped and treated Maegan rough.

I fixed us all some hot chocolate and we just sat, me in my recliner, Audrey and Maegan on the couch. Maegan kept askin', "What made Dixson do that? Mama, I was so scared. He hit me and tried to hurt me."

We had trouble comin' up with answers. A child should be safe in her own house and her grandma's house.

But we talked, answerin' Maegan's questions, explainin' sometimes people can't control themselves. "Impulses," they're called. We told her Dixson would be gone from her life and from our lives and she was safe right there with us. Audrey had tears in her eyes.

Maegan finally fell asleep in Audrey's arms. My daughter gently moved away, settled Maegan on the couch and covered the girl with the throw. Audrey sat herself in a chair.

"What are we going to do?" Audrey said, talkin' to the floor.

"We're gonna take care of that girl," I answered. "She's had a terrible fright."

I could see the love in Audrey's eyes as she looked over at Maegan. She got up and stepped over to the couch. Gently, she adjusted the throw around her daughter and sat down again.

"And we're gonna press charges," I continued in a hushed tone. I saw a funny look on Audrey's face. She teared up again.

"Mother, Dixson had a bad night," Audrey murmured. "Too much beer. I'm sure he'll never touch Maegan again . . . not like that."

"Honey," I said, "some things a person does just plain cross-the-line. A man isn't supposed to covet his daughter or stepdaughter. Dixson's done it once. It could happen again."

"But he's my husband," Audrey whined. "He'll have a record."

"And she's your daughter." I looked hard at *my* daughter. "It's up to you to protect her."

"I'll be watchful. He won't do it again. I'm not going to press charges. He'd never forgive me," she answered, again looking at the floor.

"You don't have to, honey. I'll take care of pressin' the charges."

Audrey looked up. "Please don't," she whimpered.

"Get hold of yourself, girl," I said.

Maegan stirred on the couch and sat up, rubbing her eyes. "Gramma Pearl, can we stay here tonight? I don't want to go home."

I had my daughter and granddaughter safe under my roof. But each of our minds was in a different place—Audrey sayin' don't press charges, me sayin' press charges, Maegan feelin' confused, afraid and hurt. Seemed like poor Audrey could see her family fallin' apart.

The next mornin', I went to the Beaumont Valley Police Station where Dixson was bein' held for forty-eight hours. Audrey stayed with Maegan. I filed charges for attempted rape of a fifteen-year-old minor. Found out that's a felony. Dixson would be arraigned and a court date set. We could tell how we caught him in the act unless he just goes ahead and pleads guilty. Old Dixson would go to prison for at least seven years, pay a fine, and he'd have to register as a sex offender. He brought it on himself.

When I got home and told Audrey, she burst into tears, sayin' her life was ruined. I asked her about her daughter's life. Audrey mummed up, which was a good thing 'cause Maegan came into the living room in her bathrobe. Don't know how much she'd heard.

But I wasn't done yet. Late in the day, after Audrey got back from seein' Dixson at the jail, she and Maegan went to Walmart for somethin' nice for Maegan. Maybe a cute blouse and jeans to make her feel better. My granddaughter acted kinda skittish and nervous. After they'd left, I called a number the lady officer had given me.

The Beaumont Valley Women's Center was in an old store front near the doctor's office. I'd seen the sign but never knew what it was for until the policewoman told me the people who worked there helped women who'd been raped or abused.

I wanted someone to talk to my granddaughter. I knew Audrey and me had a big difference of opinion. I hate to say anything against my daughter, but I wanted Maegan to not be like her mother when it came to men. You don't let men slap you and try to rape you.

At first Maegan said she didn't want to talk to anyone but me or her mama. But I kept pushin' that it might be a good idea and make her feel better. I'd offered to take her to our pastor, but Maegan finally said if she was gonna talk to anyone besides her mama or me, she wanted it to be a lady. I told her about the Beaumont Valley Women's Center. I told her I'd go with her and be nearby. She lowered her head. I thought she was gonna say no, but she whispered, "Okay."

I was also thinkin' maybe my daughter should talk to someone there, too.

Chapter Twenty-Two

Pearl Spence

August 1992—Beaumont Valley, California

I got kinda mad at myself for not realizin' what was goin' on. I'd noticed how Dixson liked to look at Maegan—sly, out of the corners of those shifty eyes of his. He'd sneak a quick look like a child ready to steal jellybeans. Sometimes his look wasn't quick enough. I'd catch him leering at her. Fifteen years old Maegan was, and real pretty. He knew I watched him—knew I didn't like him, ever since I caught him rummaging in my house for money. Claimed he was lookin' for matches. Maybe he'd been a good man once, good at baseball. But not anymore. He'd gone flabby, dishonest, and sloppy.

Even before his attempting to rape Maegan, I'd tried to talk to Audrey, seen bruises on her. "Oh, Mother, sometimes I just do things that make him mad," she said. I told her my worries about Maegan, told her to be watchful. "Oh, Mother, what a terrible thing to think," she protested. "He's been her father since she was two."

Audrey felt she needed Dixson. He loved her, she said. Said he just got a little tired and stressed from work was all. *Tired? Stressed?* From that job? I think Mr. Bowden kept him on only because we was friends. The girl was kiddin' herself. She wasn't happy. A mother knows these things. I saw her sad face tryin' to hide behind fake smiles, her droopin' shoulders tryin' to carry burdens too heavy.

I stayed with her and Maegan for a few weeks after Dixson got hauled away. Women comfort each other; learned that from my mama. I heard Audrey sob at night. Why did she have such bad luck with men? First Maegan's run-away father and then the child's no-good stepfather. Tried to talk to her. She claimed she was confused and sad.

"I know he did a terrible thing," she told me. "I hate what he did." Audrey's voice grew soft. "But I love him. I miss him."

"Oh, child, how can you say that?" I said right quick.

"I know, I know," she said. "But he's not a bad man. Something terrible made him do what he did. It's all my fault. I'm always so tired and I've let myself go. Please don't tell Maegan."

"Your fault? How do you figure that? And I don't carry tales," I said. "But hear me. I don't want to see that man again, and, if you're smart, you'll move on, put him out of your thoughts. Remember, secrets and whispers build a house on sand."

I worried about Maegan. She hung near her mama and me and stayed away from her friends. She cried, didn't want to go to school. I kept takin' her to the Women's Center to talk to a counselor. I finally brought Audrey and the child to live with me. Dixson's boys moved in with friends. Winston told Maegan he was sorry about what happened. Neville, his surly self, said nothin'.

It was a happy day when the judge sentenced Dixson to eight years over at Chino Men's State Prison. It was also a happy day when Audrey started goin' to the show with a girlfriend on Sunday afternoons. It took me a while to figure out she wasn't goin' to the show but drivin' over to the prison to visit that man. She also told me she was goin' for a walk on her break to lose weight. But she was takin' Dixson's phone calls down at Josie's Hollywood Hair Salon, a few doors from the diner. Her sneakin' around like that made me real angry and hurt. Did she think I wouldn't find out? People talk. I couldn't convince her to stop that foolishness. Then things really backfired.

One day Maegan was walkin' to the diner after school. As she passed Josie's hair place, she saw her mother inside at the receptionist's desk, her back to the front window. Guess the salon was real busy. Maegan went in, unnoticed, and headed toward her mother. Just then the phone rang as usual for appointments. Josie, the shop owner, answered it and said, kinda loud, "Hey, Audrey. It's Dixson." Josie told me all this the next day.

Maegan ran from the shop. She came into the diner, breathless, cryin', "Gramma, Gramma!" Soon Audrey came runnin' in the door. I had to close up; explained to the customers I had a family emergency. We had a terrible scene. I knew things would never be the same between Maegan and Audrey.

"Gramma, why doesn't she choose me first? I'm her daughter. I was here before Dixson. I hate him." The words tumbled out. "And I hate her!"

I could see Maegan felt betrayed. And she was.

Chapter Twenty-Three

Maegan Spence

August 1992—Beaumont Valley, California

Maegan sat on the couch with one leg crossed over the other, kicking her free foot back and forth, absently picking at her nails and pushing at the cuticles. She hated Dixson for what he'd done, but it was all so confusing. He'd been her stepdad since she was two, and she'd loved him like a real dad. She was sorry he'd hurt his leg and couldn't play baseball anymore. She sort of understood that the loss might make him sad, make him want to drink. But then, when he *did* drink, he'd be so mean to Audrey and Gramma Pearl and her that she'd grown afraid of him. Not just afraid. He'd begun to make her feel strange at times, looking at her with a funny smirk on his face, more like a horny boy in high school than a dad. Then he'd always look away real quick.

She also remembered thinking it was her imagination because she was noticing the boys more. Or she'd flip-flop, thinking maybe she was wearing something or doing something to make Dixson look at her funny. She wore jeans, tees and shorts just like the other kids. She helped her mom and grandma, went to school, did homework, and sometimes saw her friends. Normal stuff. Except she noticed his hand stayed on her shoulder or hung around her waist longer than usual. His hug lasted longer. It felt weird. Then she'd say to herself, what terrible ideas to have about your father. Except he did turn out to be terrible.

Gramma Pearl's voice barged into her thoughts. "Time for us to leave, Maegan. Audrey, you comin' with us?"

Audrey shook her head. "I told you before. I don't want to go to the Women's Center."

Gramma Pearl just scowled at her, shaking her head back and forth, and strode out the front door. Maegan followed at a slower pace.

Maegan rode in silence as Gramma Pearl drove them to the center, a whirlpool of dread circling inside her. She was going to talk to a stranger. Dread slid into embarrassment and then into fear. She just wanted to stay home, sit in her room.

When they arrived at the center, Gramma Pearl spoke to a receptionist behind a desk who confirmed their appointment. Maegan stayed near her grandma, looking at the floor most of the time. The receptionist pressed a button on her desktop.

Soon another woman came out from behind a closed door. Maegan peeked at her. Dressed in black slacks and a frilly pink blouse, she was heavyset and looked soft like a pillow. Brown hair reached to below her ears and she parted it to the side. The frames of her glasses, striped in pink, green and brown, caught Maegan's attention.

"Hello, Mrs. Spence," said the woman. "Hello Maegan. I'm Mrs. Harris."

The lady shook hands with Gramma Pearl. Maegan felt a nudge. She fumbled and shook the woman's hand, too.

"Welcome. Please, let's step into my office," said Mrs. Harris, who then walked to the doorway.

They followed her into the room. Maegan looked up quickly and back down, in time to see a desk in the corner. In the middle of the room was a circle of three upholstered chairs which Mrs. Harris gestured toward, her palm up. "Please, sit down," she said quietly.

Mrs. Harris spoke with kindness in her voice. But, for all that, the woman was a stranger in a strange room. Maegan wanted to leave, but they all sat. Maegan sank into the chair and deeper into herself, cocooned inside her head.

"Maegan," said Mrs. Harris, leaning slightly toward the girl, "I'm very pleased you and your grandmother are here. I'm so sorry for what you have been through."

Maegan welled-up and a sobby-gasp escaped her lips. Gramma Pearl reached over and patted her hand as Mrs. Harris put a box of Kleenex on a small table beside her.

"Maegan, whatever you're feeling, if you're thinking you did something that made Dixson do what he did, put those ideas out of your head. The man did what he did because of problems of his own. The fault is his."

"Just what I told you, honey," Pearl said, nodding.

"You obviously have a good grandma who loves you," Mrs. Harris continued. "People who do what Dixson did have impulses they won't or can't control. But we're not here to talk about him."

Maegan pulled a Kleenex from the box and wiped at her eyes and nose.

"I hear you're very smart and do well in school. What classes do you like?" Mrs. Harris pushed her glasses up on her nose.

Maegan took another Kleenex. Talking to her lap in a soft voice, she said, "History. And English."

Pearl interjected. "Speak up, honey."

Maegan looked up, in time to see Mrs. Harris shake her head at Pearl who put her hand over her mouth and nodded.

"Do you have a favorite teacher?" the counselor asked.

Maegan responded slowly and again in a low voice. "Yes. Mr. Patti, my English teacher."

Mrs. Harris smiled, her eyes warm and friendly. "How about a best friend?"

Maegan nodded. "Michelle," she whispered.

"That's wonderful. And what do you like to do after school?"

Maegan thought a minute. "Sometimes I go to the French Club meeting. Sometimes I talk with my friends until their moms pick them up."

Pearl patted Maegan's hand. Mrs. Harris shook her head at Pearl again, who again put her hand over her mouth and nodded.

"What do you do after your friends leave?" Mrs. Harris asked.

"I walk to my grandma's pie shop and do my homework or help until my mother is done work and then we go home." Maegan seemed to run out of breath.

Mrs. Harris nodded and said, "You're a busy young lady. I can also see you are a very strong young lady." Maegan broke out in tears and grabbed at the Kleenex box. "It's all right, Maegan. Let those tears out. That strong girl inside is just taking care of loose ends, getting ready to come out and help you get on with your life."

Maegan saw Mrs. Harris once a week for ten weeks. At first Maegan continued to just sit there, either not talking or only answering questions, hugging herself. One day, after a few visits, she started talking, first a little and then more. She began to realize that she looked forward to the sessions. Mrs. Harris really listened to her, and Maegan could tell her things, like the way she could still smell Dixson's awful breath or feel his hands on her skin. That her mother talked about missing Dixson. How could she miss that terrible man? That her brother Neville scared her.

She could talk about not being able to sleep because when she closed her eyes she saw Dixson, felt him on her, and saw herself trying to get away from him. Or when she did fall asleep, she'd wake up all sweaty and scared. If she'd had a terrible dream, Mrs. Harris would listen. Mrs. Harris also told her that if a boy or a man was making her uncomfortable, she should tell someone and avoid them.

Pearl didn't talk about Mrs. Harris, except that she seemed like a fine woman who was giving Maegan recipes for "the confidences" that she'd need and use all her life.

Chapter Twenty-Four

Winston Dupre

October 1992—Beaumont Valley, California

Winston ran down the steps from Pearl's house, clutching his stepsister's note. He stopped, read it again.

> Gramma Pearl,
> I can't stand it here. My mother still talks to that terrible man, still goes to see him. I hate her. I just have to leave Beaumont Valley. I love you.
> Maegan

He shoved the note in his pocket and grabbed Audrey's old bicycle that was leaning against the porch. The chain banged on its rusty guard as he pedaled down the drive to the road. Dust billowed, making him cough. His eyes watered. The only way Maegan could get out of town was if a friend with a car helped her or if she caught a bus.

Maegan had been doing pretty good since Dixson's rape attempt, but recently she'd become gloomy and didn't want to go to school. She was bound for college; not like him, dropping out of high school. He had to find her.

He'd come to Pearl's for his old guitar and found the note on the kitchen table, propped against an apple pie covered with Saran wrap. He shouldn't have read it, but he got nosy. Too much had been going on. Audrey had made him and his brother move out of the house they'd all shared before Dixson went nuts. Winston had moved in with a friend. No one knew where Neville holed up. Shortly after that, Audrey and Maegan had moved in with Pearl.

How he wished Dixson wasn't his father. He despised the man. A bolt of anger with shame right on its heels rushed through his body. The only family he'd ever known had been torn apart. He loved Maegan, his stepmom, Audrey, and Gramma Pearl. Did he love his brother and his old man? Maybe. Once upon a time.

A bus could take Maegan to Palm Springs. Or Los Angeles. Or Phoenix. Winston bet on Palm Springs, maybe Uncle Seb's place. He sometimes hung out in Palm Springs on weekends and sometimes Maegan had asked to go with him, but he'd said no, mainly because he'd be with his brother. Neville liked to roam around among the tourists, boosting purses, picking pockets, selling stuff on the sly. Not Winston. He played his guitar in Hardy Park, checked out the music scene in the local clubs. That's what he liked to do. He'd never be like his brother—or his father.

Winston pumped the pedals, gritted his teeth. His brother often went to Uncle Seb's. Uncle Seb was okay, but the man ran a little drug business with Neville on the side, and old Neville couldn't stand Maegan. If Neville found her, where he could get at her, with no one else around? Winston shuddered at the thought.

He glanced at his watch, its plastic band tight on his wrist. A bus left Beaumont Valley for Palm Springs in about fifteen minutes, at

2:00. He'd caught it many times. She might try to take that one. He couldn't let Maegan run away. She was fifteen and so pretty. He just knew somethin' bad would happen. Uncle Seb was too lazy to keep an eye on her and Neville'd love to get *his* eyes on her.

He pedaled harder. A barking dog with a blind white eye charged out of a yard, nipped at his ankle. He zigzagged, pedaled harder. The animal dropped back, still barking. Winston turned onto the main road, wiping sweat from his forehead with the back of his hand. Something glistened on the roadside. Glass. He swerved into the car lane to avoid it. He swerved back to the honk of a horn.

"Hey, kid, watch yer ass." The driver of a VW minivan veered around him. Winston flipped him off.

He pedaled, making good time, pushing to go faster. All at once, pedaling became difficult. He looked down. The front tire bulged, flat on the bottom. "Aw, hell." He hopped off and pushed the bicycle toward a roadside fruit stand. Sagging wooden bins bulged with fresh-picked produce.

"Hey, mister. Leave my bike here, just for a bit?" Winston asked the vendor. "Flat tire. Don't want nobody to steal it."

The man behind the counter looked him up and down, saw the tire. "Okay, kid, but not for long. I'm busy, and I'm no bike sitter."

"I'll be right back," Winston shouted, taking off fast.

Winston couldn't let her run away. She always wanted him to play his guitar; he liked that. They talked about personal stuff all the time. She'd even talked about going to the Women's Center. He liked being her big brother. Winston ran beside the busy road, the soles of his old sneakers grinding on the gravel shoulder. Soon he could see the blue and silver Greyhound bus waiting in the terminal parking lot. He prayed to find Maegan in the crowd.

"Goin' ta Palm Springs! Leavin' for Palm Springs!" The driver yelled and walked around beside the bus, gesturing to riders to board. "Next bus not 'til 9:00 p.m." People and children milled about. Some held cardboard boxes tied with twine. Others carried large shopping bags or suitcases.

"Maegan!" he called.

Then he saw her, standing near a man with a blue parrot perched on his arm, watching them. The bird stopped mid-chatter and cocked his head toward Winston, one black eye riveted on him. The man coaxed the parrot to sing to a small group of people drifting around them. A coin clanged in a shoe box. On a sign propped against it, "Every little bit helps. Thanks."

Winston ran to her, calling her name.

Maegan turned, saw him, and started to walk away.

"Pretty girl," the parrot squawked, dancing on the man's shoulder. "Pretty girl."

Winston grabbed her arm. The man looked from Maegan to Winston. "You know him?" the man asked.

Nodding, she shook her arm free from his grip.

"It's okay, man," Winston said. "I'm her brother. We gotta talk a minute." He pulled her aside.

"What are you doing here?" Maegan hugged a striped tote bag.

"You can't run off. You'll break Gramma's heart."

She glared at him. "You read my note!"

The driver edged by, tapped his watch. "You gettin' on or not?"

"No, she's not goin'." Winston tried to grab her hand.

Maegan slapped it away. "Oh, yes, I am! I'm not going back to that house. My mother still talks about Dixson . . ."

"Oh, Maegan. I'm sorry." Winston slipped his arm around her shoulders.

Maegan twisted like a corkscrew, stepped back, out of reach. Her body stiffened. "Don't touch me. You don't know what it was like. It didn't happen to you."

"Everything'll be okay. You'll see. I'm sorry." He lowered his arm to his side. "You're having one of those down times like Mrs. Harris said would happen once in a while, and she told you things you could do."

"Yes, one was leaving the house," Maegan snapped.

Winston thought a minute. "I think she meant like goin' for a walk or goin' to see a friend. Something like that. Not *leave* permanently."

"Why not? When will everything ever be okay?" Tears glistened at the edges of her eyes.

The two of them stood, neither moving nor yielding to the other.

"Won't you come back with me? Please?" Winston pleaded with the girl.

She took a deep breath and stared at the people boarding the bus.

"There's nothing but more problems in Palm Springs," Winston said. "Besides, where you gonna stay? Costs money to stay in a hotel."

"I'll stay with Uncle Seb."

"He know you're coming?"

"No."

Winston shook his head. "Might not be the best place to go. Sometimes Neville stays with him."

The mention of Neville's name registered on her face. Again, he reached for her hand. This time she didn't pull away.

"Win, what should I do?" she begged.

"Come back to Gramma Pearl's. You don't wanna be alone in Palm Springs." He held her hand.

Maegan looked down, nodded, and they started walking. She stopped and asked, "What if Dixson comes back?"

"He's not coming back. He'll be in jail for a long time. Besides, I'll be around."

Winston carried Maegan's tote as the two walked along the road. At the produce stand, he called, "Gotta take my sister home. Pick up the bike later."

"Haul your sorry self back here soon," the man shouted, "or I'll give the damn thing to the junk man."

Chapter Twenty-Five

Neville Dupre

May 2002—Beaumont Valley, California

A beacon of moonlight poked through the night's black shawl, draping a glow around the warm evening. It threatened to betray Neville as he slinked toward Pearl's house. Glancing over his shoulder, he stayed close to the large bougainvillea bushes edging the yard, out of sight from neighbors. Thursday nights a lady friend picked up the old woman and they went to church, singing and praying until late. He knew from Winston's gabbing that her royal highness Maegan was still over in La Verne at the university and Audrey wasn't around anymore. No better time to search for cash and maybe find the source of Maegan's mysterious money.

Back a few years, Pearl had left a check on the kitchen table, supposedly from Maegan's special account from her real father. When she'd realized he'd seen it, she'd snatched it away and shoved it in her apron pocket That was back when he was kind of welcome in her home, before his old man tried to rape Maegan. Dixson couldn't even do that right.

That money had always been spent on stuff for his stepsister.

Green-eyed anger heated his gut even now, made his footsteps more determined. Life had dealt him a short deck, but thanks to his smarts, he had a couple of business ventures—drugs, peddling stolen stuff. Even had a few guys working for him.

Tonight, he was after money that should have been shared with him, too, when he was growing up with Maegan. *Share and share alike, kiddo.* They were all kids under the same roof. But back then, when he'd asked Pearl for cash, she'd say it was Dixson's job to provide for Audrey, Winston, and him. Except Dixson couldn't find his way out of a bag of beer nuts.

He crept along the side of the small house, knocking off tags of stucco. The porch railing wobbled as he swung himself over and landed cat-like on the porch. A splinter pierced his left palm. Cursing to himself, he tried to pull it out, but it broke off. *Shit.* He resettled his black Nascar cap on his head and grinned. A savvy, street-smart surge sped through him, pushing a mere splinter off his radar.

A rustle over in the bushes. He froze, looking for a dogwalker who might be out nosing around. Seeing no one, he stepped to the door, hoping the locks hadn't been changed and his old key still worked. He held his breath. The deadbolt turned. The lock clicked. He slipped inside. Kitchen smells met his nose. Apple pie—almost made him miss the old woman.

The red crock should be on the counter to the right of the old sink. The money pot. He made his way in the semi-darkness. After he took whatever bills she'd stashed in it, he'd slip down the hall and search her bedroom. She had to have special hiding places in there for the real money—maybe even money from her Social Security check.

He set the crock on the table, took off the lid. He put it beside the crock. Before he could dig into the contents of the container, the sudden glow of headlights bobbing up the lane, bathing the kitchen in gentle light, snapped him to attention. What the hell? Who was coming? Was Pearl's friend bringing her back from church so soon? The lights neared. But it wasn't the car of Pearl's friend. It was Pearl's old Honda. *Pearl's car?* He thought Pearl didn't drive anymore. The car stopped and the driver's door opened. Moonlight silhouetted the figure of a woman. *Maegan.* What the hell was she doing home? She got out, hugging a large rectangular box to her body.

Where to hide? He didn't want any run-ins with the cops. Maegan, the mighty, almost lawyer, would press charges for breaking and entering. Or stalking. Or whatever the lousy bastards could drum up after they'd checked his record. No time. He rushed past the table, knocked against a kitchen chair, tripped, and stumbled. As he hustled into the living room, his cap jostled on his head. When he dove toward the couch, the cap flew off. He jammed his sore hand. *Shit!* He ended up well hidden—without his cap.

Trapped behind the sofa, he heard Maegan at the front door. He hoped to God she didn't notice his cap or recognize it if she did. Soon as she went down the hall to her room or to the bathroom, he'd grab the hat and get out of there. To silence his heavy breathing, he bit his lower lip. The door opened, followed by the click of a switch. Light filled the room. He heard the box drop on the kitchen table.

"Gramma Pearl? Are you here? You really should lock that door." The scuffing sound of a chair being straightened.

"Why is the crock on the table, Gramma?"

Neville tensed his muscular frame.

"Why is the lid off?"

Silence. Neville couldn't tell what was going on. Time hung stone heavy. Then quick steps. Rummaging sounds. The bang of a cupboard door.

"I don't know where you are, Neville, but if you're still here, you'd better come out. I almost didn't see your stupid Nascar race cap on the floor by the coffee table."

Why did she have to come home? He crawled from behind the couch, grinning.

"Now don't do anything silly, little sister."

"What do you want? As if I didn't know. That crock is always left on the cupboard. You must be hard up." Maegan glared at him, holding a broom, the kitchen table between them. "I'd recognize that greasy cap anywhere."

He picked up the hat, running his fingertips around the edge of the bill. "Just thought I'd take a little of what's due me."

"What do you mean, 'what's due you'?" Maegan gripped the broom like a baseball bat.

"You still don't get it, little sister." Neville shifted his gaze. "What's in the box?"

"If you must know, my cap and gown. I graduate from law school in two days." She shook her head. "You'd really steal from Gramma Pearl?"

"Actually, not stealing; jus' takin' a share of the extra money that comes in every month. Some of that should have been mine all while we were growing up."

"Get out before I scream or call the police or both," Maegan said, a hard edge to her voice.

Neville eyed the broom. "Maegan, I could pull that away from you real easy and knock you silly. Just remember this: I'm gonna get that money of yours, and I don't mean the piddly-assed stuff in the crock. You got money comin' to you every month, probably for the rest of your days. Your so-called old man's got enough money guilts to last a lifetime, after leavin' Audrey with a bun in the oven the way he did."

Maegan tightened her grip on the broom. "Money arrangements are none of your business."

"Remember my promise." Neville took a step toward Maegan. He heard her take a deep breath.

"You stay away from Gramma Pearl and me." Maegan raised the broom as if to strike.

He laughed and moved toward the door. "Watch your back."

"Get out!"

Chapter Twenty-Six

Maegan Spence

May 2002—Beaumont Valley, California

Heart pounding, her grip on the broom tight, Maegan rushed to lock the front door as Neville's footsteps clumped down the porch steps. Not sure he'd leave the property, she ran to the back of the house, flipping on every wall switch or lamp along the way. She checked the back door, closed the bedroom windows, and returned to the kitchen. It was then she noticed her shaky hands. She sat down at the table, placed the lid back on the crock.

Neville liked to lurk around, squinty-eyed, seeing what he could find out, always coveting the money she received each month. The money that paid for her school and bought food. He'd turn up in town, suddenly standing in front of her, coming up beside her, waving at her from across a busy street. He gave her the creeps.

In a few weeks, she'd leave Beaumont Valley for Los Angeles. She couldn't wait. The pressure and tension caused by Neville, the lingering judgment of neighbors who knew Audrey and the circumstances of Maegan's birth, and the attempted rape by Dixson always lurked in the background. How could she forgive Audrey's loyalty to Dixson? The feelings about her mother would never heal.

She'd start with a clean slate, like a newborn; only, this time, better equipped for what might come her way. As the innocent, illegitimate child of foolish young lovers, she had grown up amid taunts from stepbrother Neville, abuse from a drunken stepfather, and a mother buried in regret and self-pity. But Gramma Pearl's love and solace never failed her. Nor did Winston's. He kept her safe when he could.

Maegan put the crock back on the counter where Pearl kept it all these years. She sat again at the kitchen table, facing the window and the front door, the broom in front of her on the red-checked tablecloth. Fatigue, nerves, and anger clawed at her back muscles. The tightness in her neck and shoulders made turning her head uncomfortable.

Tears gathered in her eyes. This should be a happy time. She'd graduate in two days after so many years of classes and hard work. *Damn Neville to hell.*

A sound from outside startled her. Heavy treads on the porch steps. Maegan reached slowly for the broom. A key turned in the lock. The door opened.

"Good Lord, Maegan," Pearl said, "every light in the house is on and it's hotter than the devil's hell in here! How come everything's shut tight? And what's that broom doin' on the table?"

Maegan ran to Pearl, hugging her tightly.

"Goodness, honey, I've only been to church," Pearl said. "And what's in that box?"

"Oh, Gramma . . ." Maegan wanted to tell her about Neville, but the words stuck to her tongue. She wasn't going to let him ruin this moment, not like he'd ruined so many others. She'd tell her later, warn her to be watchful.

She ran her palms down the sides of her jeans and opened the box on the table. "Look, Gramma, my cap and gown."

She held the black gown in front of her, plopped the mortar board on her head.

"Well, aren't you somethin'! We've gotta get that robe ironed. Looks like a wrinkly old prune." Pearl glanced at her arm and laughed. "Or my wrinkly old arm."

Maegan watched Gramma Pearl take the broom from the table, put it back in the cupboard. "The broom," Pearl said over her shoulder, "Did you see a critter skitter across the floor?"

"Sort of."

"I'll have to set some more traps," Pearl said.

Chapter Twenty-Seven

Audrey Spence

May 1979—Beaumont Valley, California

A collection of grumbles filled Audrey's head. She'd wanted to go shopping or to the movies, but her girlfriend Shirley was the one driving, picking her up. Why had she let Shirley talk her into going to this old baseball game? She didn't get out that often, what with little Maegan at home. But Pearl had said, "You go and have fun." Thank goodness her mother was there to babysit. But now it seemed like a waste.

All at once, the baseball crowd cheered, and fans jumped to their feet. Shirley poked her in the arm with her elbow. Audrey's popcorn spilled from its box. "A home run, a home run!" Shirley shouted.

Audrey, now on her feet, watched a batter rounding the bases. A player on the other team had fumbled the ball; the fans were frantic. Shirley's team, the Cucamonga Quakes, won the game.

Shirley grabbed her arm. "Come on! I know one of the players."

The next thing Audrey knew, they were clumping down the outdoor stadium's wooden steps to the dugout area where the players were grabbing their equipment and congratulating each other.

"Jimmy, Jimmy!" Shirley called. "Great game!"

A tall wiry player came toward them, his spikes scuffing along the dugout's dirt floor. "Hey, great to see you, Shirl!"

Players exiting the dugout elbowed past them. Jimmy grabbed one of them by the arm, pulled him aside.

"Ladies, I want you to meet Dixson Dupre. He hit the homerun that saved our asses."

After an exchange of high fives between the two men, Shirley introduced Audrey. The next thing Audrey knew, Dixson was saying, "See you there," and moved on. The three of them walked to Jimmy's car.

"What about your car?" Audrey whispered.

"Oh, we'll come back and pick it up," Shirley replied.

They drove to an after-game celebration at the home of one of the players. In the player's backyard, a string of bulbs stretched from one corner of the patio cover over to a large oak tree and back to the other corner of the cover, forming a triangle. The glow lit up the night. Players, girlfriends, and friends bustled around a keg of beer and a long table with chips and snacks. Others sat on folding chairs, benches, and a pony wall defining the patio. She heard "Y.M.C.A." by the Village People playing in the background.

As Dixson waved and walked over to join them, Shirley winked at Audrey. The four laughed and joked until Jimmy took Shirley's hand and said, "I want you to meet the coach and some of the guys."

Audrey smoothed her tee, thinking, *Here I am, left standing with a guy I don't even know.* Dixson's voice caused her to look up.

"I'm glad you came to the game tonight," he said. And he took her by the elbow in the direction of the beer and food. Dixson laughed and nodded his way past some of the players and their congratulatory remarks. He was a hero for saving the game and wore the mantle well.

Soon they were sitting together on folding chairs at a card table where they talked for much of the evening. Where they lived, where they went to high school, how Dixson was being scouted by a major team and worked for a power company, how they both had small children at home. Dixson was divorced with two little boys; she had a little girl. She didn't say she'd been abandoned, just that she was raising her little girl with the help of her mother.

Audrey glanced at her watch, at the lateness of the hour, knowing she'd better find Shirley. Except she couldn't see Shirley or Jimmy. The crowd in the backyard had thinned.

"I need to be going, but I don't see my friend," Audrey said.

"Shirley and Jimmy left," Dixson said, "but I'll take you home."

Audrey knew she'd give Shirley an earful as soon as she saw her again. She didn't know Dixson, a guy she'd just met, and now he was going to take her home. She'd kill Shirley. But Dixson proved to be a straight-up guy. Sure, they made out a little, but he didn't push the matter.

Audrey became a regular at the Cucamonga games through the summer. Dixson became a regular in Audrey's life.

Even Pearl liked him. "He seems to be a good person. Has a decent job with the utility company. Maybe a baseball career. How do you feel about him having two little boys? Sure he's not just lookin' for a mother for those kids?"

Audrey didn't respond. After all, it would be nice for little Maegan to have a father. And even brothers. Not be an only child. Dixson was steady and regular, unlike Roger who'd run off or the other flakey guys she'd met. Plus, he was fun and a star player on a local farm team. She was in love. The only thing he did that she didn't like? If he thought he'd played badly or the team lost, he'd go all moody on her until he "pushed out his anger."

Dixson proved to be good with Maegan, playing with her, reading to her. Winston, Dixson's youngest son, took to Audrey and she to him, but the older boy, Neville, was more stand-offish. Dixson just said, "Give him time. He'll come around."

They were married at the home of her mother's friend in November. Thelma had a nice backyard with a little, white, wooden arch in it and rose bushes on each side. The team came, as did customers from Pearl's coffee shop and miscellaneous friends. Neville, nine, and Winston, four, stood with their father along with best man Jimmy White. Audrey chose Shirley, long forgiven, as her maid-of-honor. Two-year-old Maegan was flower girl, Shirley holding tight to her little hand.

Audrey couldn't remember ever being so happy.

Chapter Twenty-Eight

Audrey Dupre

May 2002—Beaumont Valley, California

Audrey stood in the doorway of her daughter's bedroom, watching the girl pack a large brown suitcase lying on the bed. Sun light gleaming against the yellow-painted walls failed to brighten her heavy heart. Maegan was leaving. Audrey's stomach tightened as she searched for words, followed her daughter's every move. She fidgeted with the smooth plastic button of her blouse.

"I wish you weren't going," Audrey said.

"Well, I am," Maegan snapped. "Are you blind?"

Audrey bit her lip, stopped herself from lashing back. "I wish you'd go to work at Abel Brookings's law office over in Riverside. You could still live here or nearby."

"No way! Too many memories. I'm leaving this place for good." Maegan glanced at her mother, her eyes lingering in a hard look.

"But why?" Audrey heard the whine in her voice, took a deep breath. "You said Brookings liked you."

Maegan carefully wrapped her two framed degrees in a towel— one from the University of Redlands and the other from La Verne

University College of Law—and slid them in among her folded clothes. She zipped her suitcase. "Mother, if you ever listened to me—we've been all through this." She pulled the heavy travel bag to the edge of the bed.

"Let me help you with that." Audrey stepped into the room. Maegan's hand shot out, a police officer stopping traffic at an accident scene.

"I can move it." Maegan grasped the handle and slid the heavy suitcase onto the floor. She reached for a small, rectangular make-up case still on the bed, assorted cosmetics and toiletries scattered around it.

Audrey bent down, straightened a blue throw rug with an upturned corner before someone tripped on it. Maegan ignored her and continued to pack.

Audrey knew she should have listened to Maegan more. She'd tried to. But there was always so much to do. And when they moved in with Pearl after Dixson . . . did anyone listen to *her*? Did anyone realize it was possible to love her daughter and a troubled man at the same time? Did anyone remember how handsome Dixson had been? How good their marriage was at first? No one knew of his promises on the phone or in person when she visited him in jail. How sorry he was. How things would be different when he was paroled. A person can change. A person can still be good, even with a bad mistake. He deserved another chance. Did anyone ever try to understand?

"I'm listening now, honey," Audrey said quietly.

"For the last time." Maegan's voice grew emphatic. "I'm going to Los Angeles. I've got a job at Higgins, Sharp and Whitelaw. One of my professors helped me get it." She slipped her toothbrush in a plastic holder, grabbed a tube of toothpaste, and put them both in the small case. "I'm not changing my mind." A pause. "And don't call me 'honey.'"

"Shhh. Don't be so loud. Pearl's just out in the kitchen." Audrey didn't need *her own* mother butting into the conversation. That had always been part of the problem—Maegan relying on Pearl more than on Audrey. She felt a flash of jealousy. Who wouldn't?

Maegan put her hands on her hips. "Don't shush me. Can't you wish me well? I have a chance to get away from here."

"I didn't say I wasn't happy for you. It's just . . ." Audrey stopped, tried to think of another way to say it, but couldn't. "I don't want you to go. Besides, you could also help here with money. Lighten the load on Pearl." She paused. "And me," she added softly.

Maegan stepped closer to her mother. "I've stayed here this long *because* of Gramma Pearl, and I've always helped her and always will, wherever I am."

"What about me? I did the best I could." Audrey's face flushed, tired of being ignored and blamed.

"Please! Did you ever try to protect me from Dixson and Neville?" Maegan turned her back, threw a comb, brush, and shampoo into the case. "You've always come up short." She shoved in the last of her cosmetics, banging containers together, rearranging them. The case snapped shut. "You've always been so"—she faced her mother, her mouth twisting for words—"self-absorbed."

Audrey took a deep breath as Maegan pushed by her to pick up a leather belt coiled on a wicker chair by the door. Anger and regret absorbed the air between them. Audrey thought about how *she'd* been hurt, too. Abandoned by Roger. Wed to Dixson who'd changed before her eyes into somebody else. How could she have known he'd attempt rape? If only she'd been a better wife and lover, maybe that wouldn't have happened. And now, she had a daughter who hated her. God, she'd undo all of it if she could.

Audrey turned to Maegan. "I've always loved you."

"Oh, get out of my way," Maegan said.

Audrey felt her daughter's elbow as she pushed by to return to her packing.

"You're weak, *Mother*. Clinging to Dixson, betraying me."

The words slapped Audrey in the face. Maegan's cold stare cut through her. She murmured, "I'm sorry—for everything." She reached for Maegan's hand, her heart ready to burst. "Please, don't keep shutting me out."

Maegan pulled away just as Pearl entered the room.

"And how you doin' in here?" Pearl smiled at Maegan. "All packed, honey?"

Maegan nodded. "I am."

Pearl patted Maegan's hand. "We'll have coffee and pie when Winston gets here to see his little sister off."

Audrey slipped by Pearl into the hall. "I'll make the coffee," she mumbled, her eyes stinging.

Chapter Twenty-Nine

Caleb Marley

May 2008—Palm Springs, California

The morning sun baked the chrome handle of the plate glass door. By mid-afternoon the hardware would be searing to the touch. Caleb glanced at the bold black letters on the door: "Caleb Marley, Private Investigator." He used to rent the office. Now he owned the building. That thought always gave him a good feeling. He walked into the reception area, nodded at Clarissa, his receptionist, and continued to his private office.

On his desk to one side sat a closed laptop and a Fantasy Springs Casino cup filled with pencils and pens. He unclipped his cell phone from his belt, took off the earpiece, and placed them by the landline, absently rubbing the nicked and scratched surface of the oak desk, with him since he opened his office some thirty years before. When he remodeled the office to 1950s retro, he'd kept the desk. Sentimental value.

Clarissa had readied two files for him as he'd requested. On one file, the name "R. Hemmings." On the other, "J. Bevins." Each connected by a single name: Maegan Spence. He eased himself into a tan leather desk chair and removed his wire-framed sunglasses, rubbing the pink indentations on either side of his nose.

A ceiling fan, which he'd also kept when he'd remodeled, rotated on low, cooling his pale, high forehead with its receding gray hair, wispy thin on top. He leaned back in his chair, his fifty-five-year-old body still semi-firm thanks to the treadmill in the office corner. He observed the slow turn of the fan's white blades against the cool, gray ceiling, their movement reflected in the glass of a large, framed picture of a World War II Corsair hanging on the office wall.

His gaze followed the fan's circling white blades, their soft whir unobtrusive. Strange, he thought, how life circled and turned, cycling people into events, changing their lives, cycling them out. What forces directed a person's life? Dice tossed randomly? A plan by an all-seeing power? People used words like "Chance" or "God" or "Fate" or "Destiny." Bad luck. Good luck. Karma. Perhaps it was pure witch-craft—ancestors manipulating their progeny. As good an explanation as any. With years of handling other people's problems, he still had no answers.

He looked away from his "thinking fan"—installed almost thirty years ago. It was the same day he had asked Emma to marry him, the same day he first heard from a young man named Roger Hemmings, Jr. The call had been a prayer answered. Caleb had just hung up his license and needed business.

At that time, Hemmings had given Caleb a phone number, information about an Audrey Spence, and an Uncle Seb who owned a Palm Springs shop called The Desert Tee. Hemmings didn't know the man's last name. Pearl Spence was the mother of Audrey. Several weeks later, Caleb had returned the young man's call.

"Mr. Hemmings, based on what you've told me, I believe I've found her. Audrey Spence lives in the small village of Beaumont Valley with a Pearl Spence, her mother. The young woman, apparently a nice girl, got herself pregnant. Local gossip has it that she got tangled up in Palm Springs with a college boy on spring break. Has a little girl named Maegan. Neighbors say Audrey, the mother, has trouble warming up to her baby."

Roger Hemmings did not reply.

"Mr. Hemmings, sir, anything else I can do for you?"

Hemmings' voice, strained, asked, "What last name does the child use?"

"Spence."

"What kind of person is Pearl Spence?"

"Seems to be well respected," Caleb replied. "Hard working. Runs a cafe called Pearl's Place. Famous for apple pies. Attends church. Law abiding."

Hemmings cleared his throat. "I want you to get the name of a local bank president in Beaumont Valley. I'll deal with him directly. I want the address of Pearl Spence. Also, I want a report twice a year on the little girl, Maegan, with pictures and videos. This is all confidential. You will be well paid."

"I'd like to ask a few questions," Caleb said.

"You have all the information you need," Hemmings responded.

They worked out a satisfactory financial arrangement.

Caleb made sure his reports on Maegan Spence arrived on time. Never spoke to the man but that once.

Now he swiveled the chair gently from side to side, steepled his fingers beneath his chin. Over the years, the man had sent a check every month. Some months, that check kept the doors open. He sat upright, closed the file.

Diligence to Hemmings's case and others had paid off. He'd built his private investigator's business into the best in the Palm Springs area. Had calls from all over the country. People seemed to find themselves in trouble on their visits and vacations in Palm Springs. *Must be the sun,* he smiled to himself.

He opened a file labeled "Jennifer Bevins," a lawyer at Higgins, Sharp and Whitelaw—a large law firm in L.A.—who recently had seen fit to engage his services. Her instructions? Keep an eye on her friend and co-worker, Maegan Spence, who would be in Palm Springs and might be in danger. She gave him the dates and hotel information.

Interesting. Two people wanted him to watch the same person, Maegan Spence. Were Hemmings and Bevins linked? What danger was the Spence girl in? And from whom? Roger Hemmings?

He returned to the first file. Hemmings had called early yesterday, much to his surprise, for the second time in thirty years.

"Mr. Marley," Hemmings had said, "I'm flying to Palm Springs, Bermuda Dunes Regional Airport, to meet Maegan Spence, the girl you've been reporting on all these years. I'll be there tomorrow and will need last-minute information on her. She's staying at the Hyatt in Palm Springs. As you know, she's an attorney with the firm of Higgins, Sharp and Whitelaw in Los Angeles."

Caleb had worked fast, made some quick phone calls. He'd put a tail on Maegan Spence that very day, then returned Hemmings's call early the next morning.

"Mr. Hemmings, she's arrived at the hotel. She went to Beaumont Valley yesterday. Visited a local church."

"Please meet me at the airport," Hemmings said and gave his arrival time.

Two calls from Roger Hemmings. Separated by thirty years. A call from an attorney named Jennifer Bevins. Three women named Spence. Pearl, Audrey, and Maegan. How were these people all connected? Who had been hurt? Loved? Angered? Betrayed? He needed answers. In his business, accurate information kept you alive, possibly literally.

He leaned back, focused again on the fan, letting his thoughts turn with it. This was "think time" before he had to leave for Bermuda Dunes. He'd already figured out some of the connection between these people.

Chapter Thirty

Roger Hemmings

May 2008—Palm Springs, California

"We'll be landing at Bermuda Dunes Airport in about twenty minutes, sir."

"Thank you, Hector." Roger Hemmings nodded at his longtime assistant and looked through the window of his firm's private plane. Below him spread the Coachella Valley with its agricultural fields and bustling towns, defined by Mounts San Jacinto and San Gorgonio on the west, and Chiricao Summit to the east. He last saw the Coachella Valley thirty years ago, flying home from spring break. He chewed lightly on the inside edge of his lower lip. The sound of the Learjet 45 hummed in his ears.

Golf courses splashed swaths of green on the arid soil, with developers' sprawl crawling onto crop land and date gardens. Swimming pools glistened in the clear sunlit morning. Resorts, hotels and casinos dotted the landscape. He sighed, wishing, for a moment, his flight to Palm Springs was for pleasure.

Hector stood beside him. "Here, sir, let me make sure you are secure."

Roger placed his hands on the arms of the seat, raised himself, and wriggled back on the cushion. Hector carefully strapped his legs in place and checked the seat belts across his lap and chest.

"Please give me the girl's file." Roger pointed to a briefcase wedged in the rack of a small table by his assistant's seat. Hector opened the case, gave him the file, and then strapped himself in. Sam Alton, another employee sitting beside Hector, did the same.

Gauze-like clouds, indistinct in appearance, stretched across the sky, unlike the distinct threats the young woman had made to expose Roger and reveal his secret if he didn't meet her. He wondered what a meeting would accomplish. He'd survived, and so that he *could* survive, he'd learned to push regret and guilt into an inner void where feeling no longer existed. But today's trip made the remorse resurface, as strong as when he was twenty, when the anger, the disappointment, and the self-pity almost consumed him. His mouth felt dry, but he didn't want to drink. His catheter bag was quite full and would soon need to be emptied.

Roger turned his attention to the burgeoning file he held in his lap. Inside, a picture of a young woman: Audrey Spence, the girl he'd met on spring break in Palm Springs his junior year at ASU. A matchbook from Zelda's Disco. A napkin from The Palms Bar. Another napkin from Sandy's Coffee Shop. Pictures of Audrey taken at later dates with a telephoto lens. Pictures of their daughter, Maegan. That's all he had. That and the memories of Audrey's and his stolen time together. Slowly, he closed the file and clutched it in his hands, gazing through the window, wondering what might have been—something he had stopped doing years ago.

A jabbing pain traveled from his neck, disappearing somewhere down his spine. He needed Valium. *No*, he thought, *I want to be clear headed.* "Hector," he asked, "has Caleb Marley arranged for transport to the Hyatt?"

"Yes, sir. He promised to have a vehicle waiting."

Roger nodded, then replied, "He knows we need an oversized SUV, right?"

"Of course, sir."

Roger's thoughts returned to that week, three decades ago. He'd run from the tennis club, breathless, to the hotel to clean up. Then hurried to meet Audrey, the girl he'd met in the T-shirt shop. He'd almost missed her. Running, running. For a moment, he studied his knees and lowered his head. *Being able to run.*

He grasped the file of memories in his lap. Other memories he'd dropped into different files. Mental files. The kind he couldn't lay aside. His life fell into a collection of them. He shook his head at the irony of events.

He had arrived back in Phoenix from Palm Springs before noon. After telling his father about the attack in Hardy Park—"What the hell were you doing in a park?"—and after being taken to the doctor to check on injuries from the mugging, he'd escaped his parents and stopped at a convenience mart for beer on the way to a friend's. He was so high on life and Audrey, he thought he'd never come down.

He'd rushed into the store, grabbed two six-packs of cold beer from the refrigerated section along the back wall and hurried down the aisle toward the cash register. Another man, wearing jeans and a black hoodie, the hood masking his face, stood at the counter. The man glanced over his shoulder at Roger. He turned back, shouting at the clerk, gesturing with his arms. That was when Roger saw the gun. *Pop!* The clerk clutched his shoulder and dropped behind the counter. Roger backed away, turned, and ran back up the aisle for cover. *Pop!* He gripped the pain in his left leg. The beer he carried dropped on the floor. *Pop!* Another shot hit him in the back. He fell and then blacked out. The shooter had been captured soon after; in his pocket, the money he'd stolen. Seventy-four dollars.

Roger ground his teeth, remembering the pain, the realization of what had happened and what was to come. He'd closed the first mental file chronicling his existence and labeled it *Former Life*. He dropped in verbs he'd never use again—"run," "swim," "stand," "walk." He dropped in nouns—"hope," "dreams," "love." He dropped in a name—"Audrey Spence."

The next mental file he called "The Crip." He found words that a once tall, healthy college kid had to learn. "Paraplegic," "physical therapy," "rehabilitation," "psychological counseling," "catheter." He packed in new feelings—"depression," "anger," "tears." And always Audrey.

He murmured her name.

Hector's voice. "Sir?"

"Nothing," replied Roger.

The third mental file was the largest, the hardest to name. Over time he'd settled on "My New Life"—in a wheelchair, in a specially-fitted van he could drive. He learned that challenging himself blotted out memories and feelings of hopelessness. Law studies, success in his father's Phoenix firm. Basketball on Wheels.

The plane quivered slightly as the landing gear lowered, bringing him back to the present. Moments later, touchdown. As the pilot taxied the Learjet to the terminal, Roger wondered what he could possibly say or do to make up for years of silence. He didn't know how he felt about meeting his daughter. Curious? Happy? Embarrassed? Remorseful? Did he love her? He had agreed to come, but he didn't like being forced. He thought he'd closed the "Former Life" file forever.

His aide unfastened the seat belts and helped him transfer to a lightweight traveling chair, strapping him in. "Hang on, sir," Hector said and pushed him toward the exit. Sam opened the door, lowered the stairs.

Despite Hector's care descending the steps to the tarmac, Roger bounced in the uncomfortable chair causing him to white knuckle the armrests. He could see a man, probably Caleb Marley, the private detective he'd hired so many years ago whom he'd never met, waiting by the closest hangar, a large, black GMC Savanna SUV nearby.

"Mr. Hemmings?" the man asked, a flash of concern lighting his face for just a moment. Roger was used to this when someone met him for the first time. He nodded.

The three men waited as Sam brought a sleek, motorized wheelchair from the plane's baggage area toward the black SUV Caleb Marley had rented.

"Thank you, Sam," Roger said.

Sam placed the heavy chair into the rear of the rental and waited for the lightweight aisle chair to be vacated. Roger placed his arms around Hector's neck, felt himself eased into the passenger seat of the SUV. Sam would return the aisle chair to the plane and remain at the airport with the pilot. His assistants were used to the routine.

"Are you comfortable, sir?" Hector asked.

Roger nodded as Hector strapped him in before sliding himself into a rear seat. Marley pulled away from the air terminal and drove toward a freeway on-ramp. Soon they sped along Interstate 10 toward downtown Palm Springs. Except for a few exchanges about the flight, they rode in silence.

Roger watched the unfolding desert landscape of billboards and commercial warehouses lining the freeway. If only his past life could be put in a warehouse, stowed away, out of sight and mind. If only nothing else had happened. Facing life in a wheelchair, he'd found the prospect of seeing rejection in Audrey's eyes too daunting. How could he have visited her or brought her to Phoenix? She would have quickly discerned what their life together would be. He'd simply made a pre-emptive strike. He'd rejected her first—never making contact.

He turned to Marley as the man drove toward the hotel. "The girl, Maegan, chose this place. Something about not wanting family members to know or interfere. What's that all about?"

"Some members of her family are, shall we say, unsavory and envious of her special bank account. I have the information in a file for you," Caleb explained. "She checked into the hotel yesterday."

Roger struggled with uncomfortable thoughts but could not stop them. *What should I say to her? Will she recoil at the sight of me? What will she look like?*

Marley eased the SUV under a portico at the hotel's front entrance. Hector removed the battery-powered chair from the back of the vehicle and helped Roger into it. Only then did Roger feel in control. He set his jaw as they entered the lobby.

A gentle hand touched his shoulder. He looked up. Marley pointed to a young woman sitting by herself on a black leather couch, her back partially toward them.

Roger waved the two men away. He moved slowly toward her; the low whir of the power chair announcing him. She turned toward him.

"I'm Roger Hemmings," he said and waited.

Chapter Thirty-One

Maegan Spence

May 2008—Palm Springs, California

Maegan couldn't find the bullets in her arsenal, words that had been loaded on the tip of her tongue, words she'd planned to fire upon meeting her father. Surprise flashed on her face before she could control it. Accusations and the demand for explanations receded in her mind as she stared at the man in the wheelchair. She wet her lips, her mouth dry, her words disarmed.

"I'm Maegan Spence," she said, rising to her feet.

Under other conditions, the momentary position of power she had as she looked down on this man might have been satisfying. But not now. The man being in a wheelchair startled her. She regained control of her facial expression. Legal training, like muscle memory, kicked in, telling her to keep cool even though faced with a "surprise." Road bumps in law were common. She knew how to handle them, made herself do the same now. She stifled her desire to scream or vent her rage—or cry, although all surged close to the surface.

"Is this a new malady or an old excuse?" She gestured toward his chair, her voice a knife honed with sarcasm. Put the adversary off balance. Her own venom surprised her. Usually, she could mask her feelings more.

A dark scowl flashed across his face. A pause. The beginnings of a smile pushed aside the frown. "I like your mettle," he responded. "But before this gets messy, I think we should move to a place more private."

Maegan stood where she was. The man gazed at her face, his cerulean blue eyes scanning her hair, then her eyes, nose, and mouth. "You look like your mother."

She wanted to look away, but didn't, returning the scrutiny in kind, an adversarial technique. Study your opponent.

"Excuse me a moment," he said. Hemmings moved the small switch on his chair with his index finger and thumb. The chair turned, the distance closing between himself and two men near the concierge's desk. She recognized one—Caleb Marley, the detective, who nodded in her direction. He shook Hemmings' hand and strode toward the lobby exit.

Mr. Marley, your job is done, Maegan thought.

The two remaining men went to the hotel desk. Maegan noted her father's still apparent good looks, despite whatever had happened to him. Was it illness? An accident? She understood how her mother would have formed an immediate crush on him and allowed herself to fall in love.

A full head of white hair, thick like a Kennedy's, framed his fair complexion. Had he once been a redhead like her? His upper body was strong, with muscled arms and wide shoulders filling his golf shirt. But his back curved, like a concave lens. His stomach formed a pouch from being confined to the wheelchair. Casual khaki slacks covered his withered legs. Tasseled Italian loafers housed his now-useless feet.

The other man walked in her direction. Thirtyish, dark haired, muscled like a bodybuilder.

"Miss Spence, I'm Hector Aguilar, Mr. Hemmings's assistant. Please, let us go to Mr. Hemmings's suite."

Maegan glanced from Hector to Roger Hemmings. For a moment, she just wanted to dump her crate of hurt feelings into Hemmings's lap, experience the satisfaction and leave. But she'd waited a long time for this meeting. To know "the why."

They joined her father at the reception desk and the three moved toward the elevator. No one made polite small talk, and she chose not to speak in the elevator. She wanted answers. She wanted to stay calm, not become a raging witch.

Once in the top floor suite, she was left alone in the living room while her father and his aide went into the bedroom. The door clicked shut. She stood, facing the floor to ceiling windows which filled three walls. Downtown Palm Springs, and the Coachella Valley with mountains in the distance spread before her. Tightness in her stomach traveled up her spine and across her shoulders, her body a violin string stretched to breaking, the pitch rising higher and higher. As she took several deep breaths, she heard the bedroom door open and the whir of the wheelchair. She turned. Hector discreetly left the suite. They were alone.

"My apologies, Maegan, but some things must be tended to on schedule or . . ." He stopped. "Will you sit? I think we both have had some time to give complicated feelings a chance to settle. In addition to being father and daughter, we are both attorneys, open to reasonable discourse."

She felt her cheeks flush. *To hell with pretense. To hell with reasonable discourse.* "Why did you abandon my mother, never acknowledge me, and think money could replace human contact?"

"Maegan, I loved your mother, but as my life changed, I felt it best to sever all ties."

"Best for whom? My mother would have liked a word, an explanation. I've felt abandoned all my life. Why did I have to blackmail you into a meeting?"

Roger shook his head. "She never would have wanted me."

"Did anyone ever ask her?" Maegan felt her voice grow louder. "She's never stopped wanting or loving you. Did you get cold feet? What possibly could have changed her mind about you?"

"This." He tapped the arm of his chair.

"What happened? And when?" Maegan demanded.

Her father explained the circumstances of the shooting at the convenience mart when he returned to Phoenix, his transition into bitterness and self-pity. "I won't ask you to understand my mental state during all this. I interacted with very few people. My family, physical therapists, psychologists . . . "

"A simple phone call to my mother would have been the thing to do," Maegan interrupted. "You or a member of your family could have given her some peace of mind, given her something to explain to me. We could have done letters, phone calls." Maegan stopped. "Wait. How did you know she'd had a child?"

Roger Hemmings rubbed his lifeless knees. "As time went on, I wanted to call her. My father, a powerful man then and now, wanted me to have no communication with Audrey. He wanted no negative publicity, no scandal. He forbade any calls. I was shattered by his decision. We fought until my depression and rage interfered with my progress. Finally, he gave me a bit of an olive branch and hired a private investigator in Palm Springs, Caleb Marley, to find information about Audrey."

Maegan nodded. "I've met him."

"Marley located her and was able to obtain pictures. By then her pregnancy showed." Roger paused, a sigh escaping between his lips. "I felt the baby had to be mine. Your mother was a virgin before we made love."

Maegan gave herself a moment. "What did your father think?"

"He wanted me to drop the whole affair."

"And so, you did. How easy for you." Maegan turned away.

"Whatever you may think of me, I wanted to do the right thing. To me, the right thing was not to burden Audrey more by letting her know her baby's father was wheelchair-bound for life. The relationship that blossomed in Palm Springs could never be. We all make choices."

Maegan whirled around. "I beg to differ. You didn't give my mother a choice. Or me." She brushed her hair back. "How did the bank account come about?"

He gazed out the window. "I told my father I would stop all therapy and stop trying to make something of my life; that I would not study law nor join him in the firm. And I wouldn't keep my mouth shut about the whole situation . . . unless we provided for Audrey and the baby. You see, Maegan, you come by blackmail naturally." He smiled at her.

Maegan remained stoic. She wasn't prepared for all of this.

Her father continued. "My father had a dream that I'd become one of the firm's partners. My circumstances almost destroyed him. That's how we arrived at the idea of a special bank account, the monthly check."

"Easier to buy your way out?" She couldn't stop herself, the cutting remarks. "Did you ever marry?"

"No, I didn't. But the scandal of an illegitimate child would be harmful to the firm, then and now."

"Oh, yes, the firm. God forbid you harm the firm. Do you really think a baby born out of wedlock would make any difference in today's world?"

"Maegan, we employ many people and represent many people, conservative people. It wasn't just about me."

"No, much easier to abandon a young woman, destroy her self-worth. Forget about your child. Let us manage however we could."

"No one's life has been easy," Roger protested.

"I wasn't asking for easy. I was asking for a father."

Silence filled the room. She saw fatigue on his face, felt her own weariness work its way through her body.

Hemmings glanced at the bar. "May I offer you a drink?"

Maegan strode toward the door. "I've had enough for today."

"Please, let's continue our talk tomorrow," Roger requested. "Call me and we'll set a time to be together. As difficult as this has been, as much as I fought this happening, we've made progress today."

She put her hand on the door handle, paused. How easy it would be to make him wait for her call—the same way her mother had waited for his. Maegan had her answers. But turning, she nodded, and let herself out. Alone in the elevator, she could no longer keep control. She leaned against the side wall and wept. After several moments, she pushed the "down" button.

Chapter Thirty-Two

Maegan Spence

May 2008—Palm Springs, California

Maegan hurried from the elevator toward her room. As she rifled in her purse for the key card, a woman, wearing white shorts and a pink T-shirt with "Palm Springs" printed on it, emerged from the room next door. She carried a camera and a bottle of water. Maegan put her head down, shoved the card in the slot, hoping for the green light to flash—fast. She heard the woman ask, "Pardon me, but do you know if the art museum is nearby?"

The green light blinked. Maegan did not reply, but turned the handle, shoved the door open and stepped in.

"Thanks for being so friendly." The woman's scornful tone followed Maegan as she pushed the door closed and turned the deadbolt.

Oh, screw you.

She threw her handbag in the nearest chair and fell face down onto the bed. Tears came again, wetting the bed covering. The way he looked in the wheelchair. His eyes searching her face, seeming to take her in as fast as he could. Her heart jumping in her chest, trying to listen, trying to speak, trying to think. She could still see his long slender fingers on the arms of the chair, the brushing of his cheek with his fingertips. Answers from her father tumbled in her mind, word rocks plummeting down a mountainside. He'd had no choice in what happened to him. True. But Audrey hadn't been given a choice either, post-accident. Not a phone call or letter or email or text to inform her of what had happened. Maegan doubted Audrey would have chosen to break all contact.

She lay there, wallowing in her feelings, head on her arm, replaying his words. Her hand gripped the pillow. A combination of information overload and emotional exhaustion drained her.

She rolled over, stared at the ceiling, and began to sort through what she'd learned. He'd loved her mother. He intended to call or come back or send for her—this she believed. Then the shooting occurred. Roger's father probably would have been a problem no matter what happened. Whether a marriage between two young kids would have lasted, or if they even would have married, no one could ever know. But his intent seemed clear. He'd planned to return, to be there with Audrey and, by extension, with his daughter. An important point.

His story didn't sound like convenient invention, said to appease her. In his way, the only way his perception and reality would allow, he had been there for her with financial support that helped when she was young and, as she grew, provided her with an education. That had never been an issue. But he'd never been there physically or emotion-ally. For all the milestones of her life. For the terrible years with Dixson.

Maegan rubbed her face. Maybe there was no answer, no one to blame. And it wasn't his fault Audrey had married Dixson Dupre. She sighed.

Careful, she thought. No rationalization could take away the resentment she'd carried all her years for the abuse she and her mother had experienced. If her father had been there . . . well, life would have been better. *Or would it?* she wondered. *Christ, I'm wearing myself out. I can't ever know what might have been.*

She got up from the bed, wanting a drink. Her head ached. She opened the minibar, reached for a split of Kendall Jackson Chardonnay, changed her mind, and decided on a Diet Coke instead, along with a small blue can of Planter's Mixed Nuts. She sat at the round glass-topped table and popped the tabs on both containers. After a sip of Coke and several cashews, her thoughts continued to roam.

Trained to observe and evaluate, she was annoyed at her self-absorption during the meeting. She wished she could have slowed her mind, her actions, and her questions, studied him more. The man was in a wheelchair. She admitted to herself that, at first, his condition confused and shocked her. But now she found herself experiencing bits of understanding and empathetic concern.

Roger Hemmings was not a weak man. He had overcome two life-altering events. At only twenty he'd lost the use of his lower body *and* a true, innocent love. Would she have had the strength to overcome such odds?

But did she want him in her life? Or another question, perhaps, would *he* want to be in *hers*? She would call him tomorrow, more ready this time to listen than to judge. What had happened to him and to her mother was like a Shakespearean tale—two lovers in a tragedy, star-crossed.

She sipped her Coke. It was then she noticed the blinking light on the bedside phone. She picked up the receiver, pressed the number eight to access voice messaging. The call was from Winston. "Maegan, call me as soon as you get this." He left a number, his voice urgent.

He must have had a breakthrough with his music. That was the only thing that really excited him. The read-out on the digital clock told her it was 2:00 p.m. She didn't feel like talking to anyone, but his tone prompted her to pick up the receiver. She pressed nine for an outside line, then she dialed the familiar number.

"Hello?" Winston's voice, groggy.

"Hi, it's Maegan. Are you sleeping?"

"Yeah. I work tonight. How'd it go with your father?"

Maegan paused. "Is that why you called?"

"No. Meet me down in the hotel bar after my gig. Around 12:30 tonight. And don't leave the hotel. Neville's in town."

"What?"

"Just meet me." He hung up.

Maegan replaced the receiver. What could Neville do that he hadn't already done? He'd always played the bully, making no secret about wanting her money. That had been going on all her life. If she had to, she'd call the police. But Winston's voice had an urgency she found unsettling.

Anger rose again toward her father; toward the life she'd experienced by his non-existence in it. The only steady hand had been Pearl. Her mother, Audrey, so emotionally disabled, had found a handsome baseball player who, when sidelined by a knee injury, disintegrated into an abusive drunk. She cursed her stepfather, Dixson. She cursed his son Neville, who'd grown into a worse version of his father, even more vengeful toward her because of the money.

A rush of self-pity grabbed at her stomach. She brushed her hair back and shook her head. *Don't go there.* At least Winston seemed to escape the family mold. She had him on her side. She had her best friend, Jennifer. She had Pearl. She'd had Jack but he'd sensed her pre-occupation, her obsession, seeming to know she had to work it out, solo.

No one had enjoyed a picnic in this "family." Everyone had sur-vived in their own way, each life molded directly or indirectly by Roger Hemmings. She wanted to rid herself of the anger that kept surfacing. Anger at her father, her mother, her stepfather. Herself. Just when she felt the anger might be spent, some new thought would make it re-surface.

And now Neville again. Was she in danger or was Winston just worked up over nothing? She hated the continuing progression of her inner confusion, followed by anger, then hints of understanding, and then confusion all over again. She wanted direction and orderliness in her thoughts, especially now.

She glanced down at her hands, fingers interlocked, twisting in her lap. *Stop doing this to yourself.*

She decided to shower and take two Tylenol PM tablets. Later she'd call room service for a light meal. The most important thing to her now was the meeting with her father the next day. That's all she wanted to think about. Winston's call was an unwanted interruption.

Chapter Thirty-Three

Maegan Spence

May 2008—Palm Springs, California

The numbers on the digital clock shone into her dimly lit room. A little after midnight. *Gaslight* with Charles Boyer and Ingrid Bergman played on Channel 70, light from the TV screen spreading its grayness around her. Maegan loved this old movie, but it had taken on a new dimension. She identified with Bergman's character and the evil swirling around her. And now Winston wanted to meet in the hotel bar after he finished playing with his group. She really didn't want to roam around in the hotel in the middle of the night.

A part of her resented her brother's intrusion into this important moment in her life. She'd waited a long time to meet her father. Another part of her liked the renewed contact with Winston, even if the reason for the meeting concerned Neville. It had been too long since she and Winston had confided in each other.

She turned on a lamp by the bed, pulled on white cropped pants along with a blue tee, and shoved her feet into yellow flip-flops. A quick fix ponytail solved the hair. After checking herself in the mirror, she turned off the TV but decided to leave the lamp on. At the last minute, she also left a light on in the bathroom.

She closed the door to the room quietly, stepped into the deserted hall, and walked along the rust, orange and beige checked carpet toward the elevator. Even at this hour she could hear muffled sounds from behind closed hotel room doors. The drone of a TV. A woman's laugh. A loud sneeze. She pressed the "Down" button and waited, studying her toes. She needed a pedicure.

When the brushed bronze metal doors slid open, two men in suits, shirt collars open, and ties undone, emerged. They had an Abbott and Costello look about them.

"Little too much to drink," the taller one said.

The shorter, heavier man winked at Maegan and fell against the hallway wall. His companion righted him and the two tottered down the corridor, laughing. She stepped into the empty elevator, laughter far from her mind. Since the earthquake, an elevator ride filled her with fear, making her afraid she might be trapped. After the short ride down, she was glad to step into the lobby. It was nearing 12:30 a.m.

The night housekeeping crew worked discreetly. A vacuum whirred somewhere down a wide hall near the banquet rooms. A woman in a grey uniform and white apron brushed a feather duster across a coffee table in a seating area near the shuttered coffee kiosk. Maegan walked into the bar, into sand and sunset colors accented with deep purples, the lighting low, furnishings retro and minimalist.

"Sorry, you missed last call,'" the blonde bartender said, her smile surrounded by bright pink lipstick.

Before Maegan could reply, she saw Winston seated in a booth shrouded in shadow, waving at her.

"Not a problem," she said and walked toward her brother, who was halfway through a pilsener of beer. A glass of chardonnay sat on the table.

"For you." He pushed the glass toward her as she sat down across from him. "Man, did I have a shocker last night. Got home from seeing you and had the crap scared out of me."

"What happened?"

Winston continued. "Neville was waiting for me in my apartment. Picked the damn lock."

"What did he want?" Maegan didn't like the sound of this.

"One of his men had seen me here at the Hyatt. Neville wanted to know what I was up to. I told him I was working on trying to get a job in the lounge."

Maegan cocked her head, looked around for a stage. "Do they have music here?"

Winston continued. "Hell, no, and he knew it. Then I told him I was on to a big drug score, ready to surprise him." He cracked a wry smile. "Neville didn't like that answer either. Accused me of trying to get some drug action on the side. Finally, I told him the real "reason," confession-like. I had a girlfriend at the hotel."

"Oh, Winston," Maegan said, shaking her head. "I hope you aren't in danger from that creep."

"He's leaned on me before, trailing me, threatening me. I'm used to his tricks." Winston leaned toward Maegan. "It's you I'm worried about. No telling how long he'll be in town."

"Well, I'm only here for another day. Then I must get back to L.A." She realized she had a tight grip on the wine glass.

Winston gulped a mouthful of beer. "I don't like that he's got the Hyatt on his radar. He usually doesn't operate in a venue like this place. Likes the casinos, nightclubs, and bars. He could start dropping in to see if anything is going on."

Maegan nodded. "I have one more meeting later today with my father."

Winston nodded. "How's it going so far?"

"He's in a wheelchair."

"What? He's not *that* old, is he?"

Maegan shook her head. "A shooting in a convenience store. Paralyzed him from the waist down. It happened right after he got back from spring break and meeting my mother."

"Jesus. So that's what happened. What luck. What's he like?"

What's he like? Maegan thought for a moment. "As much as I hate to say it, I think he's a good person who got a bad deal. Still nice looking. Mellow. Polite and reasonable. The first time I talked to him on the phone a few months ago, he was cold and harsh, probably trying to discourage me. When I threatened to expose his secret—an illegitimate child—he agreed to meet. He sounded very angry. His proper life had hit a major pothole. But between then and now, something happened. He was open to me."

There, she thought, I've recognized he's not the monster I'd imagined.

Winston shrugged. "Maybe he did some soul searching and came to terms with everything. Do you like him?"

"I don't know. I don't dislike him."

"Do you think he'll be in your life from now on?

"We haven't gotten that far."

Winston took her hand. "Be careful on two counts. First, with your father; you're fragile. This meeting is huge. Second, be careful about Neville. He's a loose cannon and the last thing you need, now or ever."

They finished their drinks. Winston grabbed the tab, reached in his pocket, and put a twenty on the table. "I need to get back. We're jammin' tonight. Just be careful."

"You, too."

Instead of going back to her room, Maegan decided to go out by the pool. Winston had been right about the next big step. Would she and her father be in each other's lives after their meeting today? She didn't know what to think.

I really don't know him. Do I even need him?

Chapter Thirty-Four

Roger Hemmings

May 2008—Palm Springs, California

After the door had closed behind Maegan, Roger reflected on their meeting. He'd done what Maegan had asked. He'd met with her. She seemed to say what she wanted to say. So be it. Now she could go back to Los Angeles, knowing the facts, and he could return to Phoenix to get back to his life. They were strangers, and they'd remain that way. Nothing more could be done. But he was glad he'd met her. And as for Audrey, she had a life and a husband.

What might have been? What should have been? Hell, who knew why things happened the way they did? Fate? Bad luck? He'd paid his dues with therapy, prayer, psychiatrists, support groups. Fights with his father. His mother's tears. Self-pity and loneliness. His own tears.

Self-pity had been hard to deal with, making his rehab difficult. And the isolation added to his plight as he slowly accepted . . . not having a normal life. Not feeling connected.

Loneliness wafted through him, like a cold draft on a winter's night. He sat quietly playing with the links of his Rolex, rubbing the crystal on the case. Time settled around him—not in minutes, but in years. Unable to be retrieved. Thirty years. His daughter had found him. It finally was over. The thought rang through him, the last gong of a giant clock.

Except . . . was it over? Did he want it to be over? *Roger, you fool. There's still time.*

A swallow caught in his throat. His daughter may have been invisible to him, but he now acknowledged something he'd tried to bury. The first sight of her had slipped into feelings of delight and wonder. A connection . . . of strangers.

He wanted to see her again and he'd said it.

The room's stillness made the noise in his head louder. He should have been part of his child's life, of Audrey's life. How hard had he really fought with his father? The decision for him "to disappear" could have been reversed any time by picking up a phone or sending a letter. He ran his palms back and forth on the arms of the wheelchair. Maegan's illegitimacy had been a rationalization, something to hide behind.

You've made the connection. A connection, you stupid son-of-a-bitch. But Maegan may want nothing to do with me.

He moved his chair to a well-stocked bar of burnished chrome and glass, a bottle of Ketel One within easy reach. He retrieved and poured the vodka into a Riedel tumbler. He swirled the drink absently. *She may not want me.* What would he do? Continue with the status quo, hiding behind a special account and a private investigator? He took a long swallow, the thought and the drink mingling into a burning sensation. No, he couldn't do that.

What about Audrey? His first and only love. He needed to see her. To let her know he'd meant every vow and promise. Another swallow. Vodka burn. *Christ.*

Maegan looked like Audrey but favored his red hair and fair complexion. Freckled. Brown eyes. She had moved with purpose, feisty and determined. Her eyes met his, never backing down. The meeting had been more positive than negative. If he had been aggressive or pompous, he would have had a good battle on his hands. He sensed she was prepared to fight, to make sure she was heard.

How much he had missed. No one could be blamed but himself. Both Audrey and Maegan should have had the choice to be in his life—or not. His thoughts circled the mounting remorse until interrupted by a sharp click at the door. Then it opened. He turned his head. "Hector?" he asked.

"Yes, sir."

"Glad you're back. Do you have the new information Caleb mentioned?"

"I'll get everything," Hector said.

Roger maneuvered his chair toward a walnut computer desk, a free-standing piece in the corner of the executive suite, placed to overlook the city. Fatigue pulled at his upper-back muscles. He turned his head, rolling it from side to side to release tension in his neck.

Hector emerged from the master bedroom with a thick, well-used file and a new manila envelope, slender in size. He handed them to Roger and pushed the hotel's black leather desk chair aside. Roger thanked him and eased his wheelchair up to the desk, placing the materials on the polished walnut surface.

"Is there anything else, sir?" Hector inquired.

"No, I'm fine for a while."

"I'll be in the other bedroom."

Roger nodded and opened the large file. A stack of papers and photos, some discolored, many dog-eared. Caleb Marley had done a good job with his reports. Through the years, he or one of his employees had managed to take pictures with a powerful telephoto lens.

Photographs told the story he had chosen to miss. Audrey and toddler Maegan in a Beaumont Valley park. Another at a church bazaar with Pearl. Two young boys standing under a tree with a rope swing. Maegan beside a new two-wheeler, a huge bow on the handlebars. Looking at the pictures became painful. He stopped with a photo of her university graduation. Enough. He flipped through the written reports, knowing their contents well. Now that he'd met his daughter, these memorabilia had become more precious . . . and more painful.

He'd missed his daughter's life, by choice, to become a voyeur. A sigh escaped between his lips. He closed the file, his eyes roaming the view, his thoughts roaming the photographed memories and written words.

He placed the old, thick file aside and opened the new manila envelope. He removed the first picture. Audrey and her husband Dixson Dupre sitting in folding metal chairs outside a doublewide. Caleb had written the names and address in the bottom right-hand corner. Sunshine Mobile Park, #54 Evans Way, San Bernardino, California. Audrey appeared heavier. Not the slender, pretty girl with a ready smile he'd known. He wondered if she hated him. Her unsmiling face was turned toward her husband Dixson who looked straight ahead. A soft belly overhung his belt.

Roger tapped his index finger on Dixson's image. He'd read all about the man's aborted baseball career, checkered employment record, encounters with the law. Petty theft. Drug charges. The rape attempt on Maegan. Time in Chino Men's Facility. Caleb had kept him well-informed. He'd almost broken his silence, but his father stopped him with the same old arguments. Roger put his elbow on the arm of the chair, chin resting on his thumb, fingers across his pursed lips. He closed his eyes for a few seconds and took a deep breath, a breath of shame for his own actions. No, he realized it was a breath of shame for his own *inaction*.

Next was Pearl Spence standing outside her pie shop and cafe. She held the family together, gave Maegan guidance, a consistent home. The investigator described Pearl as tough and "honest as the day is long."

A flyer advertising Win Spence and The Blasts. The group played at The Blue Coyote, a bar in downtown Palm Springs. Caleb had noted Winston's interest in becoming a legitimate musician. *Interesting,* Roger thought. *The boy uses the name Spence.*

Finally, a picture of Neville Dupre getting into a black BMW M6. Tank top, shorts, flip flops. Sunglasses. Dark hair, short and spiked. Bulldog build. Next, a booking shot from an arrest, with "traffics in drugs and stolen property" written beneath it.

He placed the material back in the envelope and returned to the bar to pour another vodka. Guilt smacked him hard, in his thoughts and in his heart. He no longer wanted to hide behind a Beaumont Valley bank and a private investigator named Caleb Marley. What could he do now?

Chapter Thirty-Five

Maegan Spence

May 2008—Palm Springs, California

The night temperature lingered somewhere between warm and cool, feeling like a soft, terrycloth robe after a swim. Maegan, wrapped in the evening air, wandered by the hotel pool, the underwater lights glowing through the slow undulation of its water, flickering shades of aquamarine, turquoise, and bluish gray. She crouched beside the edge and paddled her hand back and forth in the heated water. A swim or a soak in the sunken spa would feel good, but both were closed until morning.

Near the spa, a wicker couch and two oversized armchairs clustered around a low, glass-topped table. She settled into the orange, striped cushions on one of the chairs and put her head back. She closed her eyes. So much on her mind. Her father. Winston. Neville. *I've got to relax. Just relax. Breathe. Just breathe.*

She sensed a rustling movement near her. As she sat up, a hand clamped over her mouth. Another hand grasped her forearm. A male voice hissed in her ear, his sour cigarette breath wafting onto her face. "Don't make a sound, bitch, or Grannie has an accident."

Her bones turned jelly-like. A would-be scream stifled in her throat. His words, at first a jumble in her head, sorted with a jolt.

Gramma! Gramma Pearl.

"You understand?" The man pulled her head back.

She nodded, looking into the leering face, the narrowed, glinting eyes. A sly smile curled his lip. She'd seen the face, the eyes, the nasty smirk many times, but not recently. *Neville.*

"You hear me?" he growled.

She nodded again. Neville removed his hand.

"What do you want?" she said, hearing the quiver in her own voice.

"It's time we have a little talk. Or Gram . . ."

"Don't you dare touch Pearl." Her voice steadied.

"Well, now that I have your attention . . ." he said with a self-satisfied tone.

He smiled smugly and relaxed his grip, pulling the other chair close to her, his powerful, squat body the opposite of Winston's lankiness. He sat.

How could two brothers be so different?

"This is what's gonna happen," Neville said, leaning in close to her, his eyes flickering across the pool area and back to her face. "You're gonna go to your bank. You're gonna set-up an automatic monthly transfer of that money you get and have it sent to Winston's account."

"Winston's account?"

"Oh, yeah, his account. My bank is none of your business." Neville looked her up and down slowly. "Old Win really sucked you in, didn't he?"

"What do you mean?" Maegan couldn't believe the vile man's words. *Is Winston a part of this?*

"Think about it. Old Win runnin' into you, tellin' you to look out for me, keepin' you on the old scope ever since you got to Palm Springs. Think we're stupid, Maegan?"

"I don't believe you. He *never* treated me like you did."

Neville sniggered. "Ever hear of a leopard changin' its spots?"

Maegan stared at the short, muscular man, his frame perched on the edge of the chair. A vulture picking at his prey. She felt stunned. *Another betrayal? By Winston?*

Neville thrust a small piece of folded paper at her. "Here's all the information you need. Do it within three days. Call the number on the paper when it's done. And don't cross me or go to the police. If you do, Pearl pays the price."

"I don't even use that money. It's being saved for Gramma Pearl."

"Well, Maegan," Neville replied, "you're just gonna have to work a little harder for Grannie Pearl now that we're all gonna get our share." He reached over and pinched her cheek.

She slapped his hand away. "You make all sorts of money with your so-called enterprises. My monthly payment isn't that much."

"How much is it?"

She wanted to lie. Fear stopped her. "Thirty-five hundred dollars."

"'Not that much'? Wish I'd had that all *my* life. Actually, I don't even care if it's ten bucks. Was a time I had nothin' and you got everything you wanted. Now it's time for you and that old broad who threw me out to feel what we felt. I'm gonna enjoy takin' it away from you."

Maegan started to respond, but Neville stood up.

"We're done here. I better get a call in three days sayin' the money transfer is all set up."

He leaned down and patted her knee, the second-hand cigarette breath once more in her face, and sauntered toward the hotel. He disappeared through the lobby doors. Maegan stared after him, trying to comprehend what had just happened. Neville was always a bastard. But now, Winston, too?

She did depend on that money, not just for herself. She was still making her way as an attorney, putting in sixty-plus hours a week. At some point she hoped to find her grandmother a nice little house, or retirement home, using that money toward the payments. The dear woman deserved it.

Each year, a small cost of living increase had been added to the allotment. Her grandmother would bake a special cake when they got "a raise." She'd watched Pearl budget the money and save each month, saying, "These easy dollars could stop anytime." The money was never meant to be their total support. Everyone—Pearl, Audrey, herself—worked. Gramma Pearl would squeeze Maegan's cheek and say, "That money helps provide for a sweet little girl." She'd also overheard Pearl mutter, "That money's nothin' but that no-good lout's guilty conscience talkin'."

She couldn't let anything happen to Gramma Pearl. Neville's threat frightened her, made contacting the police not an option. Let him have the money. She'd figure something out. She'd work harder. As for Winston, she had his number now. What he'd done hurt. It would feel good to tell him off.

And Roger Hemmings. What about him? She had one more meeting. He'd already answered most of her questions. Her instinct told her he was probably a decent man with bad luck. But why continue to pursue a connection? She'd managed for thirty years without him and didn't need more complications. The conscience money, absent father, weak mother, no-good stepfather, no-good brother—correction, no-good *brothers*. She was sick of the betrayals. Today would end everything. She wanted nothing more to do with any of them.

Chapter Thirty-Six

Winston Dupre

May 2008—Palm Springs, California

Winston twisted under the sheet, tossing on his double bed. His brain wouldn't turn off. After meeting Maegan, he'd gone back to The Blue Coyote for a late jam session. Chet Manconi, a well-known guitarist from Los Angeles, dropped in unannounced and played a few sets with the group. Manconi liked him. This could be Winston's chance at the big music scene. Images floated behind his closed eyes. "Win Spence and The Blasts" on a Sunset Boulevard billboard. Star treatment at Hollywood's famous House of Blues.

A ringing cell phone prodded him back into reality. He opened one eye as the phone kept haranguing and glanced at the clock on the nightstand. "8:30 a.m." He'd just fallen into bed at five o'clock. His friends knew better than to call before two in the afternoon.

He fumbled for the phone. "Yeah?"

"You two-faced bastard."

He propped himself up on his elbow. "Who the hell is this?"

"You and Neville are two of a kind," the woman said.

"What?" He shook his head. "Maegan? Is that you? What are you talking about?"

"Neville paid me a visit last night. My special money will be transferred to your account every month. I hope you two have miserable lives."

"What did you say?" He kicked away the sheet and swung his body into a sitting position, his long fingers scratching his neck, toes digging into the brown shag rug.

"You heard me."

"I don't understand." The phone went dead in his ear.

He tried to think. Neville? Bank account? What the hell was Maegan talking about? He reached for his wallet lying beside the clock and pulled out a Hyatt Hotel business card with Maegan's room number jotted on the back. Quickly he tapped in the number, asked for her room. Five rings. No answer. Then the robot voice. "If you would like to leave a message . . ."

"Maegan, I don't know what Neville said or did. Will you pick up the phone? Come on, pick up the phone if you're still there."

About to hang up, he heard her say, "How clear do I have to be? You really hurt me."

Winston swallowed. "Will you tell me what happened?"

"As if you don't know."

"I don't know," he protested. "Tell me. Please."

Maegan's breathing brushed softly into his ear, as if she was deciding what to do.

"After you left, I went out to sit by the pool . . ." As Maegan's story unfolded about Neville's visit, Winston felt the hairs on the back of his neck and forearms bristle.

"And that, Winston dear, is why I never want to see you again," she said finally.

"Whoa, listen to me. What he said about me isn't true." He gripped the phone. "I told you he's a mean SOB. I don't know how he knew where you were or how he got my bank account number. Maegan, I've never wanted your money. Don't you know that? Why are you selling me short so fast?"

She didn't answer. She didn't hang up either. He waited.

Then Maegan's voice, softer. "I don't want to believe him."

"Well, believe *me* because it's not true." Winston ran his hand across his bare chest. "He dropped in at the lounge last night before I saw you. Wants me to meet him later this afternoon at his place. Didn't really give a reason. From what you've told me, I imagine he's gonna let me know 'the deal' with your money; how it's gonna move from you to me and then to him."

"I use some of that monthly payment for Pearl."

Winston felt like he'd been stabbed. Because of Neville, he could lose his sister and his grandmother, the only decent people in his life.

"I'll talk him out of it," Winston promised.

"I don't think that's possible. I just want to be done with him." She paused. "I want to go with you this afternoon."

"What? No." Winston flipped a strand of his long hair from his forehead. "Not a good idea."

"I'm arranging for the transfer today before I see my father. I think I have the right to tell Neville in person that it's taken care of, since he's stealing from me. I'm going with you."

Winston shook his head from side to side. "Go to the police. Don't let him have the money without a fight."

"He's threatened to harm Pearl if I don't cooperate."

Winston gritted his teeth.

She repeated. "I want to come with you."

"He won't like it."

"Good." Maegan paused. "I'll have one last chance to annoy him. He won't hurt me. He has to protect the source of the money."

Winston heard the determination in Maegan's voice. *Better she goes with me than confronting Neville somewhere else, alone.*

"Neville will go nuts if you tick him off," Winston warned. "If he gets weird, do what I tell you to."

"He can get as weird as he likes. He's getting what he wants," Maegan answered. "But okay."

Winston closed his eyes, picturing scenarios only Neville could devise. "I'll pick you up at the hotel at four this afternoon."

He hung up slowly. Goddamn his brother and his slick moves. Maybe Neville or one of his guys followed him when he met with Maegan. Maybe Neville copied down his account number during one of his so-called drop-ins to Winston's apartment. He stood, straightening the twisted waistband of his briefs, knowing one thing for sure. If he went along with the money transfer, he'd look like the one doing the stealing. *Shit.*

What was he going to do? He walked to the narrow galley kitchen, filled the glass pot of his coffeemaker with water and poured it into the machine. From a Folger's can on the counter, he loaded the brew basket with high-test caffeine and pushed the "On" button. The machine began to gurgle. He needed to think. Over the years, he'd managed to stay out of real trouble, despite Neville trying to suck him in.

How would Neville get his hands on the money? Make Winston withdraw it every month and give it to him. Neville didn't deal with banks. And if he didn't do what Neville wanted, the guy'd plant drugs in his apartment or SUV and have someone call in a tip to the police. Or worse, Gramma Pearl might get hurt. Or he might break Winston's fingers. Whatever happened, Winston knew he'd be the one who'd take the fall. Goodbye to dreams of a music career. He waited for the brew to finish draining into the pot.

He rinsed a green cup sitting in the sink and poured steaming coffee into it. A heavy flavorful aroma scented the kitchen, but he hardly noticed as he thought about his brother's jealousy, starting as kids. Maegan's money. Her education. Resenting Winston's love of music and his guitar playing. Now, Neville messed with his relationship with Maegan. Despite the screwed-up life they'd had, he and Maegan had always remained close. *Damn Neville.* She'd almost believed the lies. And Neville threatening to harm Pearl? *Jesus.*

Yet another threat from a few nights ago landed hard in his mind, words Neville had said when he accused him of having drug action on the side. Winston looked at his left hand holding the coffee, like holding the neck of his guitar, fingers clamped across the frets. He raised his right hand, splaying the fingers.

He padded toward the bathroom, carrying the steaming coffee, willing himself to get clear-headed. How was he going to handle Neville?

Chapter Thirty-Seven

Maegan Spence

May 2008—Palm Springs, California

Maegan stood by the sliding glass door of her hotel room. The bright day contrasted with her dark thoughts. Before taking Winston's call, she'd decided never to see her brothers or father again. She'd had enough of all of them. After learning Neville had lied, she felt sorry that she'd condemned Winston before hearing his side. How foolish. She was glad she'd decided not to run away, but to face Neville head on. Today would be her final contact with him.

She idly watched morning traffic as it headed south on Palm Canyon Drive. A delivery truck double-parked across the street at The Desert Vegan Restaurant caused traffic to swerve around it. Three pedestrians in a crosswalk brought the one-way traffic to a halt. Palm Springs was waking up, preparing for another day. She inhaled deeply as she prepared to face the rapidly changing events of her life. An emotion-driven mixture of anger, love, fear, and distrust had taken over her thinking—about her father, Neville and Winston—making her angry with herself. She knew how to think objectively, play hardball, be proactive, not reactive. *Damn, damn, damn.* "Work smart, not hard," was her favorite professor's motto. *Time to start thinking smart,* she admonished herself.

What had made her so ready to accept lies about Winston? After being ambushed by Neville, she'd allowed her anger to overflow onto Winston without thinking. A confidante and protector since they were kids, she'd turned on him in an instant. Her neck and cheeks flushed, a combination of shame and embarrassment.

She'd acquiesced quickly to Neville's demands to turn over the monthly money. She ordinarily wouldn't give in that easily on a case or in a courtroom, but his threat to harm Pearl had put her off balance. She narrowed her eyes. Threats had come her way before. It was a matter of who could outsmart whom.

She opened the slider and stepped onto the balcony. There had to be some way to handle this. *Think.* She idly watched a tan blonde in white capris, red halter top, and gold sling-back heels get out of a blue Porsche convertible. The woman stood for a moment, running her fingers through her long hair. Car horns honked as male drivers showed their appreciation. Maegan smiled to herself. The gal knew what she was doing. Sexy glitz attracted attention, like a peacock flaring its tail.

An idea pushed at her. *Glitz.* If the sparkle was taken away, the item would get little or no attention. Neville was attracted to the glitter of the special money, motivated by pure meanness. He just didn't want her to have it. What if the chance at easy money was taken away? How could that happen? *Think!*

She glanced at her watch, stepped back into the room, and closed the door. Ten o'clock. Time to call her father. She dialed his room. When he answered, she said, "This is Maegan. When can we talk?"

Roger Hemmings didn't hesitate. "Why don't you come up now? Have you had breakfast?"

"No. I've had other things on my mind," Maegan said. If her father only knew the trouble she'd endured because of his money.

"We can order room service, combine breakfast and lunch."

"All right."

Maegan hung up. She was hungry. Already dressed in black linen slacks and a white tunic, she grabbed her purse and left the room, grateful the elevator moved quickly to the sixth floor with no other passengers on board. Hector opened the door on the first knock and stepped aside.

She heard her father's voice: "Come in."

Her father beckoned her to join him at a table by the windows. In the center of the white tablecloth sat a clear, glass vase with stargazer lilies, their magenta color bright in the morning sunlight. "May I pour you a cup of coffee?"

Maegan nodded as she sat across from him, noticing Hector discreetly slipping into his bedroom.

Her father picked up a white ceramic pot from the table and poured coffee into a trendy black and white mug. He moved the vase that seemed a barrier between them to nearer the table's edge and put the mug in front of her, a menu already at her place. No one spoke. Roger sipped his coffee and looked out the window. She did the same. An uncertain silence, running with an undertow of unspoken thoughts, settled around them.

Then she heard his soft voice as he turned to her, "Have I answered all your questions?"

Maegan regarded the kindness in his tired eyes, lines at their outer edges sloping down, meeting those curving up from a slight smile. She said, "Actually you have. I think there's only one left, and I'm not sure of its answer or how I feel."

"And that is?"

"Now that I know the whole story, what do I want?"

Without hesitation, he said, "I know what I want. To be in your life."

Maegan didn't respond. Her heart beat harder in her chest as she brushed at an imaginary speck on the tablecloth with the back of her hand, suddenly feeling his honesty and vulnerability filling the white space between them. "I have people in my life I want to tell you about."

He nodded, interested in her story.

She told him about her mother, Audrey, and Dixson Dupre, and Audrey's betrayal. She told him about Neville. "They've caused me a great deal of unhappiness."

"I'm sorry," he said softly. "Please, go on."

She told him about Gramma Pearl, her best friend, Jennifer, and her stepbrother Winston. "These people fill my life with happiness."

"No boyfriends?" her father asked.

"No, not at the moment. Relationships have been hard." She paused. "His name is Jack. When he's around. I've often been too busy with work or the memory of Dixson's attack or Audrey's abusive marriage. They always rise to the forefront. However, I do have a life, friends. I know what and who fill my life. I have a career. I'm not sure—please forgive me—about adding an unknown quantity. Where do we go from here?"

"Yes, I am an unknown quantity. Please consider what I have said. I would like to be your father, to be able to tell people about my lovely daughter."

She swallowed, studying his eyes, unable to stop a sarcastic jibe. "What about the so-called stigma I bring as your illegitimate daughter?"

"I'm guilty, Maegan, of the attitudes of my times." He waved his hand. "I'll deal with that. Many things change in thirty years."

Maegan slowed her thoughts. She didn't want to be pulled along with the goodwill tide of the moment. Careful, she admonished herself. "I appreciate what you've said. But I need to think. I wanted to meet you, to hear your story. I wasn't so sure about what might follow, whether you'd want me or whether I'd want you."

"You know my feelings."

"Perhaps we take it a step at a time. Start with baby steps."

"Whatever you decide, I'll always be here for you—as will your trust fund." He picked up his menu. "Shall we order?"

Maegan thought about excusing herself after hearing her father's words. She felt a little breathless, but instead looked down at her menu. Thinking about food was nudged aside by a question. What would this man, as an experienced attorney, think about Neville's scheme?

"Before we order, there's one more thing I'd like to tell you. A change of subject, sort of. Something I feel you should know."

Roger cocked his head. "Yes?"

She told him about Neville's demand and threat. "I'm going with Winston today at four o'clock to see him and tell him the money is his."

"What?" Roger was stunned.

Maegan nodded. "I can't endanger my grandmother, and neither can you by stopping the money. Unless you have another idea."

Roger's face took on a look she'd seen on other attorneys' faces and knew well. A game face, ready for case or courtroom hard ball. He sat up, his eyes intense, like a plan was going on behind them. "Well, we've got quite a weasel on our hands. I think we can fix his ass quite easily."

"How? How can we make the money go away?"

"I told you that money will always be there for you. I know a good attorney in Los Angeles. We'll rearrange some paperwork and procedures."

"Who? How?"

"Lou Brinker of Johnson, Brinker, Stein, and Associates. On Wilshire Blvd. Have you heard of them?"

"Yes."

"Brinker will set up an account at a bank in L.A. which will receive the money. A bank that doesn't have any branches in Beaumont Valley or Palm Springs. You will be the authorized signatory. You'll need to sign some papers. This account will be exclusively for the monies, a trust account, paying out so much a month to a special separate account. Much more difficult to manipulate than a simple deposit to your regular checking account or for outside interference to occur. As far as anything Neville might be able to learn by nosing around at your current bank and its local branches, the money will have stopped. Continue any regular banking activity in your local account as usual. Just don't mix the two. Tell Neville our second meeting didn't go well, we don't like each other, and I cut you off. You won't be receiving any more special money."

Maegan shook her head. "He may not believe me."

"Are you a good actress?" Her father looked at her, eyebrows raised.

"What do you mean?"

"Tell him what a bastard I was, how insulting and indignant a prig, how much you hate me."

Maegan thought a moment. "Just one thing. His threat to Pearl."

Her father snapped his fingers and started to reply but she held up her hand. "I've got it. I'll call Gramma Pearl and tell her I found you as she encouraged me to do. I'm going to tell her I'm sending a car and driver to pick her up. That would be Hector, if that's all right. I want her brought to the hotel to be with me in case Neville decides to visit her in Beaumont Valley. I know she'll want to hear all about it, meet you, and size you up. Be ready, she's outspoken. She can stay with me in Los Angeles for as long as she wants after I'm through here in the desert."

"I knew you were bright and decisive," her father said with a smile. "I think we have a plan. Is it necessary for you to go see Neville? You might not be safe."

"I want the satisfaction of his thinking he got what he wanted and then drop the bad news. No more money. Winston will be with me."

"And you trust Winston?"

"Completely."

Her father smiled at her. "Well, I see you're tough, too. Can I talk you out of it?"

"No," she replied with a shake of her head.

They held each other's gaze, smiling. The smiles became soft laughter, just like it was a meeting in the conference room at her firm, plotting a case. They discussed the final arrangements. Maegan would call Gramma Pearl after she left her father and before she went with Winston. Hector would be apprised of his trip to pick up Gramma Pearl.

Roger returned to his menu. "Shall we order?"

"Yes," Maegan said. "I'm hungry."

Chapter Thirty-Eight

Pearl Spence

May 2008—Beaumont Valley, California

Maegan's phone call made me happy as an apple tree burstin' with blossoms. What a surprise, her bein' in Palm Springs. Best of all, we were goin' to see each other. Before I could recover from that good news, she'd told me about findin' her father.

Well, those words made me sit my tired bones down on a kitchen chair. When she'd said *he* was in Palm Springs, too, and she wanted me to meet him, I didn't know what to feel—happy or madder than a buckin' horse with a burr under its blanket. I knew one thing: I had a few words to say to that man.

"Gramma, one thing to know," she'd said, "so you won't be surprised."

"Surprised!" I replied. "I couldn't get more surprised. I think my favorite granddaughter is tryin' to give me a heart attack."

"Oh, Gramma."

"Well? What's to know?" I asked. "I bet he's got a floozy girlfriend with him and a wife in Phoenix."

"Now, Gramma. What I want you to know is . . . he's in a wheelchair."

"Well, well. A jealous husband go after him? Break his legs?"

"No, he was shot," she said quietly.

"Some client he'd cheated, no doubt. I knew it. Just a no-good . . ."

"No, Gramma, nothing like that. We'll talk later."

After her phone call, I was more curious than any cat ever thought of bein'!

Part of me was glad for her. Another part of me was sorry and sad for the life she'd lived because of him. My Audrey would've had a happier time, and there sure wouldn't have been no Dixson Dupre or that squirrelly son of his, Neville. But one thought pushed all that nasty stuff aside. I was proud my granddaughter had the spunk to find the man and the brains to know how to do it.

Whatever Roger Hemmings had done, without him, I wouldn't have my beautiful granddaughter. I wondered what she'd thought of him, what she'd said to him. What he'd said to her. Oh, to have been a bug on the baseboard—but I knew she'd tell me all about it.

Maegan said she was sending a black SUV to pick me up with a driver by the name of Hector. Kind of an old-fashioned name. Imagine, a car and driver to pick me up! She said to pack some clothes, that after a few days in Palm Springs, she'd take me back to Los Angeles with her. Stay at her place a couple of weeks, a little change for me.

Well, I sure did rush around the house, as fast as my bad hip would let me. Gathered up my new summer outfits from Walmart. Some tops and skirts. A couple dresses. Two sweaters. And as Maegan said, "Gramma, don't forget your toothbrush." At least she didn't have to say, "Don't forget your dentures." Praise God, I still got my own teeth.

I put on an orange, red, and pink print skirt and orange top, my support half-stockings and my taupe-colored oxfords with the Velcro straps I'd worn only twice. Even had a nice purse to match my shoes. Fixed my face with a little powder and then put on my good gray wig. My hair's so thin, doesn't hold a perm anymore.

That Hector man arrived right on time in the shiniest, big, black SUV I'd ever seen. Read the name on the back doors: "GMC Savanna." My, my . . . fancy. Real gentleman he was, muscles like a wrestler, but gentle in the way he talked and moved. He helped me into the passenger seat; even buckled the seatbelt for me. Then he loaded my suitcase and a Stater Brothers shopping bag stuffed with two pair of extra shoes and my slippers into the back of the SUV.

We drove into Palm Springs around five, about my dinner time. I had a couple packages of crackers in my purse from my last trip to Denny's for their homemade minestrone soup. I'd munched on 'em to tide me over. Next thing I knew I was in an elevator ridin' to the sixth floor of the Hyatt Hotel. This Hector man said he'd take my things to Maegan's room, and I'd be comfortable here. Next thing I knew, I was in The Executive Suite, meetin' a man in a wheelchair. Oh, glory be! I knew who it was.

And me alone. No Maegan in sight.

"I'm Roger Hemmings," he said, extending his hand.

I looked at his hand and nodded. Didn't offer mine. He rubbed his palms together and put his hand back on the arm of his chair. I stood there lookin' at him. Expensive clothes. Striped golf shirt with a fancy logo. Found out later it said, "Silverleaf Country Club." Beige slacks, his feet in brown, tasseled loafers. His legs boney thin, his chest and arms muscled. Thick hair like that actor Robert Wagner.

"Where's my granddaughter?" I asked.

The man raised his eyebrows. Did he think I was gonna make chit-chat?

"Maegan had some business to attend to and will join us shortly. Won't you sit down, Pearl?"

"That's *Mrs.* Spence," I said, making sure he knew what-was-what.

"Mrs. Spence," he nodded.

I looked around at the fancy furniture and sat in a leather chair, near the sofa, one I could get in and out of easy, 'count of my hip, and in case I wanted to leave in a hurry.

After I sat, anger bumped up my neck and landed on my face in a scowl. *Wait'll I see that granddaughter.* What was so important she couldn't be here with me for this meeting? Not that I couldn't handle it by myself, mind you.

"May I pour you a cold drink or get you a cup of coffee?"

"I don't drink, coffee keeps me up at night, and I have a few things to say to you, Mr. Roger Hemmings."

Chapter Thirty-Nine

Roger Hemmings

May 2008—Palm Springs, California

So, this is Gramma Pearl who handled the monies so diligently. The woman watched him, dark eyes glaring from beneath a deep frown. He powered his chair to be across from her and set the brake, but before he could speak, her voice cut into him.

"You threw my Audrey aside. Like a piece of trash. Such a pretty girl she was. A nice girl. And so innocent." She harrumphed and reset her purse firmly in her lap, her opening salvo an assault, a pommel of words.

"Mrs. Spence, if I may . . ."

"No, you may not, Mr. Fancy Lawyer." The woman's expression hardened. "You left Audrey with a little girl and a lot of heartache. No matter what I said or did, she wouldn't make anythin' of herself. Up and married the first man that looked at her." She caught her breath. "Shame, shame on you."

His face flushed. "Mrs. Spence, no one wishes things were different more than I do, believe me."

"You're hard to believe, leavin' a baby girl without a daddy. Did you think that special money would make everything okay?" Pearl harrumphed again. "It's nothin' but your guilts tryin' to smooth your conscience."

He wanted to speak, but knew he'd never be heard. Not yet. Maybe never.

"And just so you know," she continued, "we would have been fine without your money. Audrey and me, we supported ourselves. Wouldn't have been no fancy university for Maegan, but somehow, we'd have managed college for her. Scholarships or student loans or somethin'. I never went to college, and Audrey wouldn't go, but don't think we're not smart. I owned a pie shop for years. Everybody in town knew Pearl's Place. And I know things. I read. Talk to a lot of people." The woman twisted the pliable handles of her taupe purse with her fingers. "Meagan told me you was in a wheelchair. Said she didn't want me to be surprised." She paused. "So what happened?"

"A shooting during a robbery at a convenience store." Roger looked at the floor for a moment, then sought Pearl's gaze. "Right after I returned home. Right after I'd met Audrey. A bullet hit my spine."

She looked him up and down, shook her head. "Bad luck. That's pure bad luck. I'm a God-fearin' woman. Don't wish that on no one— no matter what they done."

"Thank you."

"Don't thank me, mister." Her look riveted into him. "If you was planning on bein' with Audrey—and I'm not sure you was anything more than a college kid with one thing on his mind—you mean you or a friend or someone in your family couldn't have called the girl? Tell her what happened?"

Roger opened his mouth to reply, but Pearl ignored him.

"No. Just let her think she's used goods. Worthless. Like it's all her fault. You ever hear of wantin' to feel good about yourself? Self-esteem? Oh, I read. You cheated my girl, cheated her out of . . ." Pearl stopped. Slowly, she removed a tissue from her purse, wiped her mouth, and looked out of the window.

Roger clasped his hands together, uneasy.

Pearl turned back to him, narrowing her eyes. "Ever think of what *you* missed, mister? First time your baby girl said "Mama," her first steps, her first time on a bicycle. You could have been part of that, no matter what had happened. There could have been pictures. Telephone calls. Videos. We'd have come to Phoenix to visit. So much to share even if you and Audrey never got together."

"Not all the choices a person makes are good ones, Mrs. Spence."

"You can say that again!" Pearl coughed several times. "You got any water?"

"Yes."

Roger rolled himself to the bar. From the mini refrigerator he took a bottle of Arrowhead water and opened it. He selected two glasses from the tray on the counter and poured, the water's sound loud in the tense quiet of the room. He placed one glass in his beverage holder and, returning, held the other out to Pearl, who accepted it with a nod.

She took a short swallow, followed by a longer one, then lowered the glass, placing it in the palm of her other hand. "Since Maegan didn't have time to tell me what happened, I'm listenin' now. Owe you that, even if it comes thirty years too late."

The woman before him sat upright, rigid. He cleared his throat, and then he began telling her about being mugged in the park, being called home by his father, and the shooting in the convenience store. "A fateful sequence of events, Mrs. Spence."

She pursed her lips. "Well, that's quite a tale . . ."

Roger cut in. "It's not a tale. You've heard the truth. I'm not happy with how the situation was handled."

"You shouldn't be."

Pearl grew quiet. Roger felt he'd said enough. A row with this woman would accomplish nothing. She seemed to be studying him. He grew more uncomfortable, his skin too tight.

Pearl narrowed her eyes and asked, "Did you love Audrey?"

"Yes. We planned a life together, as much as teenagers in love could plan. Yes, I loved her."

"Kind of hard to believe," she said.

"Believe what you will, but they say your first love is the truest. And mine was true. Will you excuse me a moment, Mrs. Spence?" The woman nodded.

He found the strain of the meeting drawing on his energy as he turned his chair toward his room. Suddenly, it became important that she believed him. He wanted this woman to understand, even if she'd never approve or accept him. He returned with a large, expandable file. "I want to show you some things. Will you join me at the table, there, by the windows?"

He waited while Pearl put her water glass on the side table, looped her purse on her arm. She placed her hands on the arms of the chair, pulled herself to the edge of the cushion, and pushed herself to a standing position. Taking several short steps, her hand on her hip, her gait slow, she walked to the table.

The two sat across from each other. Roger opened the file and placed items from it in front of her, like pieces of evidence.

"This is the flyer I picked up at her Uncle Seb's T-shirt shop the day I met Audrey. It's for Zelda's Disco where we went that first night. This is a napkin from Sandy's Coffee Shop. We met there several nights. She was afraid to let her uncle know. I could never bring myself to throw these mementos out."

"So, you're a saver." Pearl's look bored into him. "I save plastic bags."

"Mrs. Spence, I may never convince you, but I know what I have carried in my heart all these years and the memories I have. They've never faded. Here, there's more."

From the file he pulled four pictures taken by Caleb Marley. The woman looked at each one. Audrey walking with Maegan as a toddler. Maegan on her two-wheeler. Audrey leaving the pie shop. A teenage Maegan with two other girls eating ice cream cones.

"Where'd you get these?" Pearl pulled the picture of Maegan as a toddler closer to her.

"A private detective."

"What?" Pearl scowled at him. "You spied on us?"

"I wanted to know," Roger explained. "I cared. I still care, Mrs. Spence."

"Well, mister, if your love was so pure, why didn't you call my poor daughter? Her heart was broke."

"Look at me, Mrs. Spence." Roger spread his palms and looked down at himself.

"I see you, I see you—but a call, a letter—anything would have been better than nothing."

Roger shook his head. "I couldn't have handled her rejection. Or allowed my problems to become hers."

"You don't know what she'd have done." Pearl shook her finger at him. "You're the father of her little girl. And ever think of her problems? An illegitimate child, no education? What about your family. What'd they think?"

"They told me to cut all ties." Roger put his hands in his lap. "They said I had enough to deal with, being in a wheelchair. And, Mrs. Spence, I didn't deal with my situation well at first. At the time, I didn't have the stamina to fight them. Everything was too much. But I did insist on the special account."

"I see." Pearl rubbed her forearm upward from her wrist, smoothing the aging skin, rippling the same smoothness on the way back, studying each move.

Time lingered on the taut air between them. Pearl sighed, her body less rigid.

"Like you or not, you seem to be honest. Didn't try to say the child was someone else's, try to make me like you, or spin a tale. Didn't whine or want me to pity you." She smiled a small smile for the first time. "Reminds me of that TV show *Dragnet.* That actor Jack Webb used to say, 'Just the facts, ma'am.' One last thing I want to know."

"Yes?"

"What about you and Maegan?"

"I'll be her father, if she'll let me."

Pearl leaned forward. "And Audrey?"

"I'd like to see her and apologize, if she'll let me."

"And me? What am I supposed to do . . . with you?"

Roger inhaled, allowing the breath to slowly escape his lips. "I don't know," he said.

Pearl placed her palms on the table and pushed herself to her feet. "Mr. Hemmings, I'm tired. Goin' to my room to rest and wait for Maegan. I can see my way out."

Roger watched Pearl make her way toward the door, her purse on her arm. "Hector," he called. Hector emerged from behind a closed door near the entrance to the suite. "Please see Mrs. Spence to her room."

As the door closed behind them, he pulled his cell phone from his shirt pocket, opened his contacts, and scrolled to the number he wanted. He hit the dial button.

Chapter Forty

Caleb Marley

May 2008—Cathedral City, California

Caleb flipped the directional signal of his Ford Taurus and turned right from Date Palm Drive onto Ramon Road, a busy intersection in the late afternoon with drivers rushing in all directions. As he checked his watch, his cellphone, sitting in the beverage holder between the seats, began to ring.

He grabbed it with his right hand, pressed the green incoming call button, and hit the speaker icon. As he slipped the phone back into the beverage holder, he said, "Caleb Marley."

"Roger Hemmings, Caleb. My daughter Maegan's on her way to Neville Dupre's."

"*What?*" Caleb was stunned.

Hemmings continued, "Much has happened since we last spoke. Neville plans to harm Pearl if Maegan doesn't turn over her monthly deposit to him. Maegan's going to tell Neville our father/daughter meetings didn't go well, and I've stopped the money. She's with Winston."

Caleb shook his head. "Sir, that's not something you want to tell that guy."

"I couldn't stop her." Hemmings tone grew harder. "We're wasting time. Do you know where the bastard lives?"

"He keeps a place in North Palm Springs, off of Gene Autry Trail."

"I need the address."

"Hang on a minute," Caleb replied and made a quick turn into a Shell station and parked. He opened his contacts and scrolled through to the name Neville Dupre.

"Yes, I have it," Caleb continued. "644 Pinyon."

"Can you get over there?" Roger's voice became harried. "I don't know what Maegan and Winston may walk into or who else might be with Neville. I'm concerned for her safety."

"I can head over to Pinyon right now."

"Good, good," came Hemmings quick reply.

Caleb said he'd be in touch and hung up. Quickly, he scrolled through his contacts and hit the number he wanted. He chewed on his lower lip. *Come on, answer.*

"Palm Springs Police Department. Lt. Haster."

"Bud, Caleb Marley."

"I know one thing, Cal," Haster replied. "When you call, you're hot on something. Lucky I'm at my desk."

"Remember that slick little operator Neville Dupre?"

Haster laughed. "Yeah, still trying to nail that Teflon banger."

"This may be the moment." Caleb told him the situation.

"Don't know if we have probable cause based only on a father's intuition, but I can take a little drive over there." Haster paused. "How about you?"

"Yeah," Caleb replied, "I'm not too far from the place."

Caleb pressed the phone's disconnect button and pulled back onto Ramon, heading west, cursing the traffic, pushing the speed limit when he could. He turned right onto Gene Autry Trail and drove north toward Interstate 10. After several miles, the area became less populated. Scraggly vegetation sprouted along the road. A fine mesh of sand blew across the macadam. He spotted a street sign. It leaned toward the east, a victim of strong winds through the area. Pinyon Road.

He made a quick left turn into a potholed road dotted with scattered homes and vacant lots. In one driveway, a silver Honda sedan sat up on cinder blocks, its tires lying on their sides nearby. In another, two Harley motorcycles filled the driveway. In front of a 1950s stucco bungalow with a dangling gutter pipe lounged a brown pit bull on a thick chain, eyeing Caleb's car. He slowed the Taurus as he neared the 644 house. The house was as nondescript as the others except for two things: a shiny satellite dish projecting from the side of the house and a Black BMW parked in the carport. Closed shades covered the front windows of the small house.

Several months ago, he'd spotted Neville near Hardy Park and followed him home. He didn't realize the information would be useful so fast. He pulled up behind an SUV parked in front of Neville's place. A bumper sticker read, "Musicians Play Harder." Someone had tried to strip away the letter "P." Winston's vehicle?

Based on what Hemmings had told him, this little meeting was underway right now. He checked his watch. Six o'clock. It wouldn't have taken long for Maegan to say, "Sorry, Neville, no more special account, no more money." Caleb had an uneasy feeling as he turned off the ignition. Just then a dark blue Ford drove by. The driver nodded at Caleb, continued past an empty lot and parked. Lieutenant Haster.

The sun eased its way nearer the San Jacinto Mountains. Caleb wished it would hurry and set. He was tired of the glare. As he glanced around the neighborhood, an image of a black SUV appeared in the rearview mirror. It crawled down the street. As it drew nearer, Caleb recognized Hemmings' man Hector at the wheel. In the passenger seat, Roger Hemmings.

Hector continued down the street, turned around, and eased to a stop across from Neville's place. Just then a red Mazda pickup, the young driver wearing a yellow baseball cap, his tattooed arm resting on the open window, pulled into Neville's driveway. The truck had long-handled skimmers sticking out of the back. A magnetic sign on the side announced Scotty's Pool Cleaning.

Just as Caleb opened his car door, his phone rang. Hemmings.

"Caleb, have you seen her?"

"Nothing. No one in. No one out. Just this pool guy who's pulled up. I'll get rid of him."

Caleb approached the driver side of the red pick-up, at the same time watching the house for any activity. The driver lowered the pick-up's window.

"Hi." Caleb leaned down, looked through the open window. "Didn't you get the message that today's cleaning was cancelled?"

"Mr. Dupre didn't say nothin' to me about cancellin'." The driver looked toward the house and back at Caleb. "I don't do nothin' to piss him off."

"Someone must have forgotten to call you."

"You ain't shittin' me, are ya?" The driver squinted at Caleb.

"No." Caleb reached in his pocket and pulled out a money clip. "Here's fifty dollars for your trouble today. Sorry you made the trip. You'll get rescheduled."

"Well, okay." The driver slid the money into his T-shirt pocket. "I can call it quits. Ran late today."

Caleb handed him the bill. *Come on, fella, get out of here.*

Chapter Forty-One

Maegan Spence

May 2008—North Palm Springs, California

Maegan stood beside Winston in Neville's stuffy living room, an air conditioner rumbling in the background, cooling a little. Neville's scowl turned her palms sweaty.

"How come you're here?" Neville snapped, his eyes boring holes into her.

Maegan met his challenging look. "Because I have news about the money."

"The news better be good. What I said the other night still stands." He cast a sharp glance at Winston. "But first, little brother, some business talk. In there."

Neville cocked his head toward a hallway. A bedroom door stood open at the end of the hall. Maegan could see an unmade bed and clothing scattered on the floor. Winston spread his palms, shrugged, and followed his brother to the bedroom. At the doorway, Neville stepped aside. Winston went in first. Neville followed, slamming the door.

With nothing to do but wait, Maegan eyed her surroundings. Faded drapes covered the large, front window, which faced onto the street. Under the windows sat a couch. To her right, what appeared to be the bedrooms, the place where her stepbrothers talked. To her left lay the kitchen. Dirty dishes and to-go containers cluttered a tile countertop. A table and four chairs held a similar collection. Sliding glass doors, their drapes pulled aside, ran along the back wall of the living room and opened into the backyard. In someone else's hands, the house could have been comfortable, even cute.

Through the sliding doors, she observed a small backyard patio and beyond it a pool with cracked concrete decking. Leaves gathered in clumps on the pool's surface. Large bushes of bougainvillea and Mexican birds-of-paradise grew untended in the yard, their fuchsias, oranges, and yellows attracting hummingbirds and bees. Two chaises, draped with striped beach towels, sat at an angle. She wondered if Neville had a girlfriend. The thought of him as a lover made her shudder.

Everything about Neville made her ill at ease. The serpent tattoo wrapped around his arm and snaking upward toward his black tank top. His stained, khaki cargo shorts. His flip-flops padding on the soiled wall-to-wall carpeting. The man's heavy scent—a combination of Brut, sweat, and body odor. Mostly, his lust for the money coming into her special account.

She looked out beyond the pool. In a far corner of the yard sat a red sun-faded metal shed, its door hanging open, surrounded by rambling, untrimmed lantana bushes and vines. Mesquite trees cast peek-a-boo shade across the yard. Oleander bushes growing beside a cyclone fence edged the property. She hugged herself, rubbing her upper arms. *Great place for snakes.*

She wandered over to the tan vinyl couch and sat, its arms and cushions soiled by sweat and hair oil, the upholstered foam cushion beneath her saggy and hot. She felt clammy warm. Angled in the corner, near the sliding door, a large flat-screen TV aired a baseball game, the sound muted. She glanced at her watch. Her stepbrothers had been in the bedroom almost ten minutes.

The *National Enquirer,* dog-eared, lay by the couch. After scanning an article about another Hollywood marriage on the rocks, she dropped the tabloid back onto the floor. What was taking so long? Unless Winston had lied to her, he wasn't interested in any business deals with Neville. She hoped he wasn't really betraying her and siding with Neville about the money.

The bedroom door burst open. Winston hurried into the living room, Neville right behind him, saying through clenched teeth, "Listen, you little son-of-a-bitch, you'd better do it."

Winston motioned to her. "Come on, Maegan, we're outta here."

Neville rushed past them to the front door and blocked their exit. "You're not walkin' out on me, punk." His gaze darted to Maegan. "And we, sister dear, have unfinished business."

"Look," said Winston, "I'm not gonna sell any of your damn drugs, store 'em, or run 'em. I don't care how much money is in it." The words tumbled from Winston's mouth, his face reddening. "I don't care how sweet a deal it is, or who you *think* you know in the music business that could help me. Don't you ever get it, man?"

"Oh, little bro's tryin' to grow a pair, huh?"

With the front door blocked, Winston grabbed Maegan's hand and pulled her toward the glass slider opening to the back yard. In a moment they were on the patio, Neville right behind them.

"And you, sweet sister, what'd you have to tell me? Neville snarled. "It'd better be good news about my getting at that money."

Winston shook his head at Maegan; "Don't tell him now" written in his eyes as he side-glanced toward Neville, anger now flooding his face. But it was too late. Neville expected she had something to tell him. She'd stick with the plan made earlier and tell the lie.

"The meeting with my father didn't go well," she began. "Too much anger on both sides. I've been cut off. There won't be any more money."

Neville's bicep flexed, moving the serpent's head. "You know that's a piece of crap."

"It's true," she insisted.

"Yeah, and I'm Brad Pitt." Neville spat.

Winston walked across the patio toward the gate leading to the front yard. "Come on, Maegan. We're leaving."

"She's not leavin' until I have the truth about that money." Neville pushed her backward toward the pool. She stumbled against a chaise, tried to catch herself, twisted, and fell hard on the concrete decking. Neville loomed over her.

"For once in your life, leave her alone!" Winston rushed at Neville, shoving him away as Maegan slowly got to her feet.

Neville whirled, grabbed his brother by the arm and threw a punch. Winston staggered, righted himself, and lunged toward Neville. Maegan watched as the two men stumbled deeper into the yard, their years of pent-up anger toward each other erupting, their blows landing on each other's faces and torsos. They crashed into a bush, slammed against a tree trunk. She wondered if Winston could last against a street-tough like Neville.

She limped toward the patio door. *Phone. Police. Before someone's killed.* She looked over her shoulder as she neared the open slider. Winston, his face contorted, shoved Neville, who stumbled backward over lava rocks and dry brown lantanas by the storage shed. His body hit the outbuilding's metal side with a loud, urgent thump. The shed shook. Neville dropped to his hands and knees.

"Winston!" Maegan yelled. "Run!"

Winston hurried toward her as Neville shouted, "You're dead meat, you little bastard!"

Neville thrashed in the dirt, trying to right himself. Brittle branches scraped his bare arms and legs. He hauled himself to his feet, rubbing his forearm across his mouth. With Winston in his sights, he scrambled out of the lantana. Suddenly, he shook his head and brushed at his arms. His hands windmilled about his face as a black cloud erupted from the outbuilding.

"Winston!" Maegan cried. "Look!"

Winston turned, saw the cloud, and started running. "Maegan! Get in the house! Close the door. Call 911!"

A swarm of angry bees swooped down on Neville. He yanked his tank top up around his head and stumbled away from the shed.

Inside, Maegan grabbed her purse from the couch, dug out her cell, and tapped 9-1-1. She saw Winston flail his arms, run toward the house, grab a towel from the chaise, and throw it over his head like a desert nomad. He hurried toward the gate at the side of the house.

Neville swatted at the air. Bees swarmed onto his hands, black hair, tank top, shoulders, arms, body, and legs.

Maegan ran across the living room to the front door, opening it in time to see Winston running around the corner of the house and into the driveway.

"Here, Win, in here," she yelled. "Where's Neville?"

"The bees have him!"

A man in a Ford Taurus parked in front of the house swung open the driver's side door and got out.

"Stay in your car, man," Winston yelled. "Bees! Swarmin' like mad!" He ran into the house. The man slipped back inside his car.

As Maegan slammed the door, she realized the man was Caleb Marley. She held aside one of the drapes and peered out. Across the street, a GMC SUV. In it, Hector, and her father. What was going on? Why were they all here?

"Oh, Jesus," Winston stood at the rear patio door, his hands spread on the glass. "He's jumped in the pool. The deep end. *Christ!* He can barely swim!" He pounded his fist on the glass. "I can't stand here any longer."

His face wrapped in the beach towel, a slit for his eyes, Winston stepped into the yard. The swarm droned above the pool like a funnel cloud, growing blacker and heavier, descending on Neville each time he struggled to the surface. Winston grabbed an old hose coiled in the corner of the patio. As fast as his fingers could work, he attached the hose to the bib jutting from the stucco wall and turned the faucet on to full pressure, adjusting the nozzle to a hard spray. He pulled on the hose and ran with it toward the pool.

Maegan clasped her hands together, feeling helpless.

Winston aimed the hose at the swarm. The bees shifted away from the stream of water with almost ballet precision and maintained their attack. Each time Winston redirected the water, the swarm gracefully undulated out of its way, as if choreographed. Stunned, a few bees dropped into the water or onto the ground, but the spray wasn't strong enough to push the insects away.

The wail of sirens drew Maegan to the front window. A fire truck made its way down the street and stopped in front of Neville's house. Four firefighters emerged.

"In back," she shouted as she ran into the front yard and pointed to the gate. "Bees! My stepbrothers! One's jumped into the pool. Hurry!"

"Go back inside, miss!" a firefighter shouted.

Two of the men began dragging a pair of heavy hoses up the driveway to the side of the house and into the backyard. Another firefighter attached one of the hoses to a fireplug surrounded by weeds in front of the house next door and the other hose to a polished chrome valve on the side of their truck. A fourth donned a special suit and headgear. He opened an equipment door and grabbed a rescue hook with an extendable handle.

Caleb Marley and Hector ran up the walk, followed by another man in a rumpled suit. They followed Maegan into the house. Inside, Maegan glanced at the man with a questioning look on her face.

"Lieutenant Haster," the man said. "Palm Springs PD."

They watched through the back slider as Winston fled toward the side gate and passed a fireman entering the backyard, a firm grip on a large fire hose. All at once, water under high pressure arced into the air, falling onto the swarm like heavy raindrops. Bees began to drop on the deck and into the pool. The discarded garden hose, water still running, flopped back and forth on the ground. Suddenly, the high-pressure water stopped. Another fireman aimed fire-retardant foam at the disoriented bees from the other hose. More bees dropped into the water and onto the deck. Neville—by then secured in the rescue hook by the firefighter in protective gear—was drawn to the pool's edge.

Someone pounded on the front door. Maegan opened it to find paramedics, an emergency vehicle, an ambulance, and a police vehicle gathered in front of the house. Lt. Haster rushed past her out the door, followed by Caleb and Hector. Maegan followed and ran to Winston, who pulled the beach towel from his head as he entered the front yard, followed by a fireman carrying Neville.

"Everyone stand back," a policeman ordered.

Quickly, the fireman placed Neville on a gurney made ready by the paramedics who rolled it to their emergency vehicle. Neville's face, ears, neck, and arms swelled, turning red. Bee stings, angry and red, covered him. His gut appeared to be convulsing, jerking him from side to side.

"Stung by a swarm of bees," explained a paramedic into his emergency phone connecting him to the local hospital. "Anaphylactic shock. Swollen throat. Weak heartbeat. We suspect Africanized bees."

They administered oxygen, hooked Neville up to an IV, and gave him an injection of what Maegan assumed was Epinephrine. Moments passed. They maintained constant contact with the hospital.

"Not responding, not responding," repeated the paramedic.

After the passage of several intense minutes, working rapidly under pressure, they slowed their efforts, then stopped.

"He appears to have succumbed to severe anaphylactic shock," said one paramedic, shaking his head.

Maegan felt numb. "Oh, no." She took Winston's hand as he lowered his head.

Lieutenant Haster approached, speaking quietly. "I'm sorry, folks."

Maegan broke the stunned silence. "Thank you."

They watched as the gurney with Neville's body was rolled toward the ambulance, the driver waiting with the rear door open.

Maegan looked at Winston, at his pale face. Bees had left their marks on his neck and arms. The beach towel had protected his head. His Adam's apple moved as he swallowed.

Haster continued, "Neville will be taken to the hospital. A physician will certify the death and then the body will go to the morgue." Haster took a handkerchief from his pocket and wiped his forehead. "Law enforcement needs to talk to you both. When you're ready. At the hospital will be fine." Haster studied Winston. "Son, better let a paramedic look at you. These weren't ordinary bees."

It was decided Winston would go to the hospital in the paramedic's emergency vehicle. The stings appeared redder and more swollen than normal.

"Win, I'll drive your SUV to the hospital," Maegan said.

"Will you call Audrey and my father?" he asked. "I'm not feelin' too well."

She hesitated. "Yes."

He gave her his keys and Audrey's telephone number, then went to the waiting vehicle.

As everyone prepared to leave, Maegan ran up to Hector. "Why are you and my father here?"

Hector looked at the ground and then at Maegan. "Your father wanted to be certain you weren't harmed."

"Thank you," Maegan said. She looked out to the GMC SUV and nodded. Her father returned her nod. She understood now why Caleb Marley and Lt. Haster had also arrived.

She went inside the house for her purse. Neville's death left her feeling empty. As much as she hated him, she'd never wished him dead. And poor Winston, always in the middle. She looked around the room, wishing she'd never seen it, and stepped back outside, closing the door with a quiet click, realizing she'd just promised to call her estranged mother, Audrey Dupre, wife of Dixson Dupre, her attempted rapist, whose son was dead.

Chapter Forty-Two

Pearl Spence

May 2008—Palm Springs, California

My stars, by the time I got back to my hotel room, I felt like one of them big Walmart trucks had dropped on me. My feet throbbed. Back had a crick in it. My muscles was stove up. A headache drummed behind my eyes. Didn't realize how much of a strain it would be meeting Roger Hemmings, especially alone. Maegan was goin' to get a good talkin' to, leavin' me to fend for myself. For thirty years I'd hated that man for takin' advantage of my Audrey and abandonin' my granddaughter. And then, to meet him face to face—by myself?

I'd handled myself pretty good, I thought. Showed him I wasn't some old lady he could push around. And had to say, he wasn't the no-good, spoiled, rich kid turned holier-than-thou rich man I thought he'd be. Too bad he was in a wheelchair. Don't wish that on nobody. But I still didn't like him. The whole day made me weary. I wasn't sure what to feel.

I went into the bathroom and rummaged through the plastic cosmetic pouch Audrey had given me a few years back. When I'd unpacked, I'd put it by the sink. Had my toothbrush and Colgate in it. Never thought I'd use the foolish thing. Don't travel much or wear lipstick and all that fluff. Told Audrey she'd wasted her money. But something had told me to bring it and to drop in a new bottle of Advil while I was at it. Sure glad I did. The water running from the tap felt lukewarm on my fingers. Filled the hotel glass and downed two pills, prayin' they'd work fast.

Back in the bedroom, before I could lie down, I had to remove the hairpins and take off my Eva Gabor wig. Set it on the Styrofoam head I brought with me. Seems kind of a funny thing to travel with. Like having an extra head—which I sure could have used, my own achin' so. But it's what Lucille, the girl in the Glamor Tresses Wig Shop, told me to do. For perchin' my wig so it don't lose its shape. I set Miss Eva Gabor's head on the dresser in front of the big mirror and pulled the rubber band off my scraggly ponytailed hair.

Gettin' outta my good shoes was easy. Thank God, I could just whoosh open the Velcro closers. Set my new taupe purse on the nightstand where I could see it. Didn't even bother to turn down the bed. Just laid down and fell asleep.

Woke up with a start. Forgot where I was, then scared myself to death. The shadow of that damn Eva Gabor head lookin' at me seemed like someone was in the room. Took my breath away for a moment. Snapped on the bedside lamp. It was after eight.

I was a sight. My hair stuck out all over like I'd poked my finger in an electric plug outlet, all thin, gray, and wispy. Before I could get myself together, the phone rang.

"Hello?" I asked.

"Gramma, it's Maegan."

"Where you been and why weren't you here when I met Roger Hemmings? That wasn't anything I planned to do by myself." My voice had a sharp edge to it.

"Winston and I went to Neville's."

Oh, my stars! "You what?"

"I'm at the hospital."

Oh, dear God! "You alright?" I hauled myself to my feet.

"Gramma, Neville's dead."

"Oh, Lord." I almost knocked my purse from the nightstand. "I knew somethin' bad would happen one day. Neville was always the bully. Them two boys always fightin' like Cain and Abel. Never thought it would come to *murder!* Winston's gone and ruined his life."

"Gramma? Gramma . . ."

"Well," I sputtered, "what happened? Guns?"

"No one murdered anyone."

"Drugs?"

"Gramma, listen. It was bees. Killer bees."

"Bees?" I sat back down on the bed. "What do you mean, bees?" and I listened to Maegan's story. A terrible sadness, then a sense of relief fell over me as I thought about what could have happened to my granddaughter.

"I'll get back to the hotel as quick as I can. Winston needs some care, and he asked me to call Audrey. Love you, Gramma."

"Wait. What?" I stammered. All I heard was dial tone.

Call Audrey? Maegan had vowed she'd never talk to her mother again. Them two hadn't spoken in years. Audrey'd made a foolish decision when she decided to go back to that Dixson Dupre. The thought always riled me deep.

My heart and my head was in such a jumble. Too many things happenin' too fast, but I couldn't help but wonder what would happen next.

Chapter Forty-Three

Audrey Dupre

May 2008—San Bernardino, California

Audrey sat at the kitchen table in a 1980s Great Lakes doublewide, reading an article about England's Prince William. She studied the pictures in the April issue of *People* magazine and shook her head. William and his girlfriend had split up. She ran her fingers down the magazine spine to flatten the image and study the girl's picture, her flowing brown hair. She liked the girl's name—Kate Middleton. *Hang on to your prince, Kate.* She looked up from the article. *Then again, I hung on to mine*—she didn't finish her thought.

With the kitchen window open and a small table fan whirring, air moved around her upper body. The bangs of her permed hair tumbled about on her forehead, her hair frizzy in the heat. She glanced at the clock hanging on the wall by the washroom door. A shiny, plastic, black cat, its tail and eyes moving back and forth, a smirk on its face. Almost 9:00 p.m. She could hear the TV from the living room. Dixson watching the fights from Las Vegas.

Her thought flow continued. *And I lost my daughter.* Maegan hadn't spoken to her for over five years, and things weren't good before then. Audrey felt a tightening in her chest. Her only daughter would never forgive her for staying with Dixson. It hurt to know Pearl and Maegan had stayed close. Audrey felt a flash of jealousy. Seemed like her daughter had always liked her grandmother better.

The smell of ground beef, peppers, and onions she'd cooked for supper still lingered. How nice it would be to go to the supermarket and buy whatever she wanted. Prime rib roast. Thick steaks. Instead, she always had to shop on the cheap. Dixson had money. She often saw a roll in his back pocket. Where he got it and what he did when he went out at night, she didn't know. There never seemed to be much money to run the house.

She closed the magazine and put her elbows on the table, head in her hands. At least Maegan hadn't made the dumb mistakes she had. Pregnant in high school. Marrying a man like Dixson. He'd changed so from the handsome baseball player she'd first met. How different her life could have been. Sometimes she wondered why she bothered anymore. How nice it would be to just fall asleep and never wake up.

"Hey, Audrey, I need another beer!" Dixson's voice jarred her. She ran her hands through her hair. *Another beer.* The last thing he needed. Their life consisted of his lying around the house and working "deals" with Neville, and her going to work. She worried he'd be unable to get up in the morning and drop her off at Michael's Burgers for her early morning shift. She couldn't take their Honda and drive herself to work because he needed the car during the day. So he said.

"Where the hell's the beer?" Even louder.

She opened the refrigerator door and stood for a moment in the cold wash of air spilling onto her face, sweaty T-shirt and shorts, her bare feet. Slowly, she removed a can of Bud and took it into the living room.

"Took long enough." Dixson grabbed the can and popped it open, his eyes never leaving the TV. He swallowed with a gulp, burped, and sprawled back on the couch; sockless feet crossed on the coffee table. His open shirt exposed a bare belly bulging over his belt. "When are we gettin' someone to fix the damn air conditioner?" he grumbled.

"When you give me some money."

"There'll be some money comin' in a few days. Use one of the goddamn credit cards that's still good and get a repairman in here."

The phone rang.

"Get that." He winced at the TV screen. A boxer staggered backward while the referee held back his opponent. "If it's Neville, I'm here. Never know if he's gonna call on the land line or my cell. He was havin' a little meeting today with Winston. Otherwise, I'm not here."

"What meeting?"

"Never mind." Dixson flipped the back of his hand at her. "Answer the damn phone."

She bit her lower lip as she walked to the table by the couch and picked up the telephone receiver. "Hello?"

"Is this Audrey?"

"Yes."

"This is Maegan."

Audrey wasn't sure she'd heard right, unable to believe her prayers had been answered. She couldn't find words to reply.

"Is this Audrey?" her daughter repeated.

"Yes. I . . ." The rest of her reply caught in her throat.

"This isn't a pleasure call."

Audrey clutched the phone. Maegan's voice had its usual hard edge.

Dixson glanced at her. He waved a dismissive hand again and said, "Go in the other room. You're interruptin' my fight."

She turned away and pulled on the extension cord. She walked into the kitchen, the cord long enough to reach the kitchen table.

Before Audrey could gather her words, Maegan said, "I'm at Desert Regional Hospital. Winston asked me to call. He's been injured." She paused. "Neville's dead."

Audrey dropped down onto a kitchen chair as if her breath had been snatched from her. "My God. What happened?"

"A freakish thing," Maegan continued. "Winston and Neville were fighting in Neville's backyard. Neville banged into a shed. Next thing we knew—"

"You were there?"

"Yes. Next thing we knew, Africanized bees swarmed all over Neville. Winston ran. Neville jumped in the pool. Every time he came to the surface, he was attacked. The bees wouldn't stop. He died of anaphylactic shock."

Audrey's joy at hearing Maegan's voice withered. Neville's death would send Dixson into a frenzy. She picked up a pencil and small note pad kept on the table and wrote as her daughter gave her more information.

"Thank you for letting us know." *Do it now. Don't wait.* "Maegan, can we get together and talk? Please? It's been too long." Her voice cracked.

"By the way, I've met Roger Hemmings," Maegan said, as if not hearing her request.

"What?" Audrey dropped the pencil. It rolled across the table, onto the vinyl-covered floor. "How? When?"

"Gramma Pearl can fill you in. You may hear from him. Goodbye, Audrey." Maegan hung up.

Audrey sat with the receiver in her hand. The dial tone droned. How could all this come into her life in less than a few moments? A call from Maegan. Winston in the hospital. Neville dead. Maegan meeting Roger Hemmings. Pearl had never mentioned anything about Roger. She put her head down. *Too much. Too much.* Tears stung her eyes.

And now she had to tell Dixson his son was dead. She wondered why his sons had been fighting, although she felt she knew. Winston was always the good boy. Loved his music and Maegan. But Neville? His mean streak just got wider and wider. Nothing but drugs and gang friends. Always scheming. Like his father. She couldn't handle either one of them.

Dixson stood in the doorway. "Who the hell you been jawin' to?"

Audrey quickly wiped her eyes. "That was Maegan." She twisted her thin gold wedding band.

"Well, well. So, she finally decided to call." He scratched his chest on the way to the refrigerator. "What'd she want? Make more trouble? I've already done my time."

Chapter Forty-Four

Dixson Dupre

May 2008—San Bernardino, California

Dixson waited for Audrey to say something. He slammed the refrigerator door, holding a cold beer can in one hand, running the heel of his other hand around its top. "I asked you, what'd she want?"

Audrey looked out the kitchen window as she brushed the tabletop with her palm. "Maegan is at Desert Regional Hospital."

"So? She hurt?" With a snap of the aluminum tab, Dixson opened his beer and quickly drank before the spill dripped down the sides.

"No." Audrey slowly turned to look at him.

He waited some more, wondering if Audrey was going to open her mouth. "I ain't got all night. I'm hittin' the head."

He plopped the beer can onto the table and went into the washroom off the kitchen, leaving the door open. His knee ached. His back ached. His whole life ached due to a wrecked baseball career. And now Maegan. Again. He fumbled with his zipper. One damn crazy night at Pearl's, boozed up and drugged out, and he'd been payin' for it ever since. He felt his bile stir. Everyone made him the bad guy. What about a young girl runnin' around in shorts, actin' innocent, teasin'? And that damn bank account he could never get his hands on? Life was a real bitch. He zipped his pants, headed back out into the kitchen, and grabbed the beer, wondering when Neville would call.

"You got anything else to say?" He looked at Audrey, waited, then shrugged and went back into the living room. He again settled on the couch and focused on the TV. Then he noticed Audrey standing in the doorway.

"I have something to tell you," she said.

Dixson blew air between his lips and muttered from the side of his mouth, "Sweet Jesus. One damn interruption after the other. What the hell is it?"

Audrey ran her palms down her thighs.

"You just gonna stand there?" he hollered.

"Neville's dead."

"What?" He sat up, pressed the mute button on the remote. "What did you say?"

"That's what Maegan called to tell us. Neville's dead. I'm so sorry."

Dixson felt like he'd been punched in the gut. Audrey sat on the couch beside him, put her hand on his arm. He pushed it away. His windpipe grew taut. He had trouble breathing.

His voice, when he found it, sounded hollow, like it was someone else's, someone speaking in the distance. "What happened?" He stared at the soiled carpet, listening to each word, wondering how bees could kill a strong man like Neville.

"Winston's in the hospital." Audrey rubbed her fingertips across her forehead. "Maegan was there, saw it all."

Again, she laid her hand on his arm. This time he let it stay. They sat in silence. Slowly Dixson lifted his head. The boxers on TV continued to land blow after blow on each other until one staggered back and went down for the count. KO'd in the ninth. Dixson's hand went to his cheek and jaw, a reflex action. He felt the wetness on his cheeks, felt a knockout blow as if he'd been the one landing on the mat.

He shook his head and hauled to his feet. "Son of a bitch! Why Neville?"

His beer can sailed through the air, bounced off the fake walnut paneling by the kitchen door, and sent amber streams rushing down onto the rug. He lumbered into the kitchen and opened a small cupboard next to the refrigerator. Bottles clanged against each other as he grabbed a bottle of Jack Daniels. A bull-like rage grew in his chest. For a moment he remembered the black bull at Plaza Monumental in Tijuana. The powerful animal thundering around the ring. How it pawed the earth. Tossed its head. Powerful like his son. He and Neville had cheered the raw strength. Then the picadors struck. He groped for a glass in the cupboard, found a red plastic cup. His felt like the picador's lance had pierced his body, his heart. He slammed the cupboard door. Hung onto the cup, the Jack.

Audrey came into the room.

"Outta my way." He pushed her back against the kitchen table. "Stay away from me."

He went into the bedroom and slammed the door. A full cup of whiskey went down in two gulps. He savored the burn, the grimace it brought to his face. His eyes moistened, but not from the jolt of liquor. He squeezed his eyes closed, felt the tears escape. He poured another and sat on the edge of the bed. A long swallow followed by a shorter one. Then he swished a mouthful around against his teeth and let it slide down. He wiped the wetness away from his cheeks with the back of his hand.

Neville had planned to meet with Winston and have a little talk. They needed another man to store or run product—cocaine, marijuana, tech equipment—whatever was moving. Someone they could trust. Talk, that was all they were going to do. Just talk. How'd they get into a fight? Why couldn't Winston just get with the program?

His eyes narrowed. *That damn Maegan.* Audrey said *she* was there. Why? Maegan lived in L.A. He began to put it together. His boys probably had fought because of her. And that damned special account Neville wanted to get his hands on. If she hadn't been with Winston, this wouldn't have happened. Neville, his first son, would still be alive. And Audrey had muttered something else—about Roger Hemmings. How had he been found?

All at once, he felt out of the loop of his own business, in his own house. He held the Jack Daniels, ready to pour more, then dropped the cup and swigged from the bottle. Unsteady on his feet, he pushed himself up from the bed and flung the bedroom door open. Audrey was still on the couch, a tissue in her hand.

"What are you cryin' about? *Maegan? Roger Hemmings?*" He moved toward her.

Audrey jumped up, but he grabbed her arm before she could get to the front door.

"You all plottin' against me? Get my son out of the way and then you can run off with Maegan, Hemmings, and his money? Old Pearl in on this?"

"You're hurting me!" She pulled on his fingers to loosen his grip.

"Yeah?" And he twisted her arm as she squirmed and tried to move away.

"Listen to me," she pleaded. "Neville was trying to steal that account. For himself."

"Naw, he wouldn't do it just for him. Him and I are an *us*."

Again, the image of the strong black bull. The red cape waving in front of the animal's face. Red. Like Audrey's face in front of him. He swung at her with the back of his hand. She staggered back, lost her balance, and fell on her side. She tried to crawl to the kitchen doorway. He dropped the whiskey bottle and grabbed her ankle.

Chapter Forty-Five

Audrey Dupre

May 2008—San Bernardino, California

Audrey lay on the floor, between the couch and the front door, the darkness around her interrupted by hazy light from the kitchen. It cast a slice of cold whiteness into the living room. The TV, muted, boxing reruns flashing past, danced its figures into the half-light. How long had she been unconscious? She didn't know, but she could hear the neighbor's little terrier barking, like it did every night when they let it out around midnight. She opened her eyes. Or tried to.

Her hand went to her face and felt the puffiness. Her right eye. Swollen. She raised her head and lowered it slowly, feeling nauseated, the pounding in her skull and behind her eyes making her grimace. Then pain ricocheted from her jaw to the temple beside her right eye as she raised herself to her hands and knees. Every muscle screamed, like her body had been mauled by a lion, except her own husband had been the animal. He'd hit her before, but never like this.

She crawled over to the couch and leaned back against it, too shaky and unsteady to stand or tend to herself. Dixson would usually stay away for a few hours. That's what he always did after a "row," as he called it. Then he'd come back, all lovey, saying how sorry he was. How he didn't deal well with life's setbacks and putdowns. How he didn't know why, but he always took it out on her. Then for a few days he'd be the Dixson she remembered—the once-handsome baseball player, the gentle lover. For a few days.

But she wasn't sure what would happen this time with Neville dead. Would it tip Dixson even more? Her fingers and toes felt cold. Shock? Fear? Again, she wasn't sure. For the first time in a long while, she wanted her mother, Pearl. Someone to hold her and tell her everything would be all right. She hadn't been held like that in a long time. Everything hadn't been "all right" for years.

Was he gone or still somewhere in the doublewide? She turned onto her knees, steadying herself with her hands on the couch, and stood. She walked slowly to the bedroom. Maybe he'd passed out on the bed, but the room was empty, as was their bathroom. She looked in the kitchen, the washroom. Returning to the living room, she put her fingers on a metal slat of the Venetian blind, the dusty surface gritty beneath her fingers, pushed it down into a V, and peered out. The Honda wasn't in the carport.

Each step unsure, she walked back to the bedroom, into their bathroom and switched on the light. It glared into her eyes. No, into her eye. Her one-eyed stare reflecting from the mirror made her wince. She turned on the tap, letting the water run, wanting it ice cold, knowing it wouldn't be, and, with a soft washcloth, tapped the tepid water on her face. Once. Then again. She noticed the bruises on her arms.

She had to do something. This was more than just a drunken binge, a roughing up. She'd call Pearl. That's what she'd do. Now. Before she lost her nerve. Pearl would help her. The woman had been telling her to get out for years. Telling her. Begging her. "He's gonna hurt you real bad, baby," she'd say.

She made her way back into the living room. The telephone sat on the lamp table by the couch like a lottery ticket offering a last chance. She reached for the receiver. Then stopped. Maybe she should call the police right away and take out a restraining order. But she'd always heard it was just a piece of paper and didn't do much good. A small voice kept whispering, "Call your mother." She reached again for the phone and put it in her lap. Receiver to her ear, she punched in Pearl's number and began to count the rings. One, two, three. She hung up. What was she doing, calling an old lady in the middle of the night, upsetting her? And what could the woman do anyway?

Her growing anger jabbed through her numbness. At Dixson. At herself. But her anger always carried fear on its back. Fear for herself. An inner voice told her to leave. Now. She could go to their next-door neighbor Tom Silk's place, but that would be the first place he'd look. Dixson and Tom sometimes had a beer together. She could just hear Dixson. "Hey, you seen my wife?" There had to be someplace she could go. But she needed money.

Her flowered tote bag hung on a hook on the back of the bedroom door. She still had twenty-five dollars in the secret compartment of her wallet, left over from grocery shopping, along with a coffee coupon good the next week. Once in the bedroom, she quickly took the tote from its hook and fished out her wallet. She reached into the folded lining of the concealed compartment. The money was gone. She opened her dresser drawer. She had about fifteen dollars under a small pile of folded summer tees. Except the pile was no longer neat. He'd taken the money from there, too.

One more place to look. In the kitchen. She opened the cupboard where the cereal boxes stood in a row. But the boxes were tipped and turned. Cornflakes. Cheerios. Bran flakes. She had money stashed in the Bran flakes box. Between the plastic wrapper and the cardboard exterior. Before she looked, she knew it would be gone.

She had to call someone. Who? Winston was in the hospital. She didn't have any girlfriends. Dixson had seen to that. Not letting her use the car. Being nasty to anyone who called her on the phone. The only person she could think of was Maegan. Where was she? At Pearl's? No. Where had Maegan said she was staying? *Think. Think.* At the Hyatt in Palm Springs. *Yes, that was it.*

Audrey went to the phone on the table by the couch and called information, then punched the number for the Hyatt given by the operator. As the night clerk picked up on the second ring, Audrey sat slowly on the couch.

"It's a great evening at the Hyatt Palm Springs. This is Rosalind. How may I help you?"

Audrey took a deep breath and said, "I'd like to speak to a guest, Maegan Spence."

"I'm sorry, but we don't disturb our guests between 11 p.m. and 6 a.m."

"This is very important," Audrey insisted, urgency in her voice.

"Your name, please?"

"Audrey Dupre. I'm Maegan Spence's mother. This is a family emergency."

"One moment, please," Rosalind replied. "I'll see if Ms. Spence will accept the call."

Audrey waited, biting her lip, holding the telephone cord between her thumb and index finger, sliding them up and down the cord's smooth surface.

"I'm sorry, we have no guest by that name."

"What?"

"We have no guest by that name. If there's nothing else . . ."

"Wait!" Audrey slumped back, trying to think. She remembered something Maegan had said about Roger Hemmings being in Palm Springs. Could he be there, at the same hotel? Had the two of them somehow arranged a meeting? "Please try a Roger Hemmings."

"Is he also current guest?"

"Yes."

"One moment . . ."

Again, the wait. And then the call connected, and the phone rang. Instead of excitement for her good luck, Audrey felt a flush of blood to her battered face. What would she say? What made her make such a foolish call? About to hang up, she heard a ragged voice, sleep curling its edges. "Hello, Audrey."

"Roger?" She took a deep breath and exhaled years of heartache like fine champagne grapes neglected too long on the vine. She heard rustling. Roger cleared his throat. And then her heart pounded.

"Audrey," he said, his voice low, soft. "It's been a long time. How are you?"

She wanted to tell him about her life. How she'd never stopped loving him. She wanted to ask why he'd left her. Why he'd never called.

She wanted to tell him about the beating, about needing help. But she couldn't let him know her bad choices. Her shame. Not now. "I'm sorry to call at this hour," she said. "I'm looking for Maegan. She called earlier this evening to tell us about Neville, my husband's eldest son."

"Yes, an unfortunate accident."

Roger already knew? Why was he in Palm Springs? Had he come to find her after all these years? Or to find Maegan? Had Maegan found him? There was so much she didn't know. Would she ever know?

His gentle voice continued. "Audrey, this may not be the moment, but I would like to see you. And talk."

"I . . . Roger, it's so good to hear your voice. I want so much to see you." The image of her face, her bruises flashed into her mind. She couldn't see him now. Not like this. "Right now, I need to reach Maegan. Can you help me?"

"Yes, she's in 305."

"But the night clerk said they had no guest by that name."

"She's using a different name." Roger didn't offer an explanation or the name.

That's strange, Audrey thought. Maybe Pearl will know. Clinging to the sound of Roger's voice, to the memories, to the life that might have been, she said, "Thank you," and slowly settled the receiver into its cradle.

As she hung up, she heard, "Audrey, wait . . ."

Tears formed in the corners of her eyes, the swollen eye burning. She called the hotel again and asked for room 305. The same procedure as before and then the connection went through.

"Hello." A touch of irritation in the voice.

"Maegan?"

"Yes." A pause. "Audrey?" Another pause. "What do you want?"

"Please, Maegan, I need help. Can you come and get me?"

"What's happened?"

Audrey's floodgate opened, tumbling her words into the air space between them. "Dixson beat me. I know you hate me. I know I made a terrible choice. I'm sorrier than you will ever know. All I can tell you is, I want to get out. He's taken the car and all the cash I had hidden. Honey, I need help."

She could hear Maegan's breathing and a voice murmuring in the background.

"Just a minute," her daughter said.

Then more rustling. Muffled voices. Then, "Audrey, honey?"

Surprised by her mother's voice, she started to cry. "Mama, I want out of here."

"Finally, my baby's come to her senses. Where is Dixson?"

"I don't know."

"We'll be there just as quick as we can. Here's Maegan again. Give her the directions."

When Audrey hung up, she leaned back only to jolt upright. Oh God, hurry, she thought. Before he comes back. Before I lose my nerve.

Chapter Forty-Six

Pearl Spence

May 2008—Palm Springs, California

My blood pressure must have shot right up, the way I got so sweat-bothered hot after Audrey's phone call, what with that devil Dixson beatin' her up. I never been a violent woman, but I could have killed that no good scum right then and there. Forgive me, Lord.

Dixson seemed okay, at first. Ball player and all. Handsome. Had a decent job. But he was a man with a marriage gone bad and responsible for raising his two little boys, something Audrey didn't need back then. I wanted her to wait, grow up some more. She was a baby just learnin' to walk, with a baby just learnin' to walk—if you know what I mean. She wouldn't listen. I probably drove her away with all my badgering and preaching. Right into his ballplayer arms.

But then . . . something went terribly wrong with the wiring in his head, if you ask me. Folks have sad things or bad things come into their lives all the time. Like with Dixson and his wrecked knee and his wrecked pro ballplayer dreams. But they don't necessarily become bad people. I believe when you stumble on a bump, you haul yourself back up and keep walkin'. That man hit a bump and wandered right off the path into the muck.

After I hung up the phone, I started to pull off my cotton nightie and pull on my clothes so I could go with Maegan. Get Audrey outta that mess. But my granddaughter give me a real hard time about goin', telling me she could take care of it. That I might get hurt. Real feisty, she was. Part of me was proud she was so tough, but I didn't plan to stay in no hotel room, let me tell you. I might have failed Audrey when she was younger, but I wasn't gonna fail her now.

When Maegan said Audrey always made bad choices, that she should never have gone back to Dixson, I suddenly got real tired of that song. I grabbed the girl's arm and said, "That's enough. We all get an A-plus lookin' back at the 'shouldas' and 'couldas.' But listen here, Miss Lawyer, no one deserves to be treated bad, to be forsaken, to be abandoned. Everyone makes mistakes. We got some sorta cycle goin' on in this family, what with people leaving people and all. Roger Hemmings left you. He left Audrey. Then Audrey left you. *We're* not leavin' *her.* It's gonna stop right now, y'hear? That's three strikes. It takes a big person with a big heart to forgive a big wrong, and don't you forget that. And I'm convinced that just because a person leaves don't mean they carry away all their love, too."

Maegan never said nothin'. She just pursed her lips and got dressed. Maybe I'd been harder on her than I should. I wondered, if I'd worn Maegan's shoes, what would I have done? And my Audrey? Too stubborn all these years to admit she shouldn't have gone with Dixson after the rape attempt. And too proud to get out. I looked at the ceiling as if the answers might be written there, scrawled by some all-seeing hand.

Then there was a knock on the door. I almost jumped outta my old black shoes. My God, I thought, had that damn devil man found us somehow?

Chapter Forty-Seven

Maegan Spence

May 2008—Palm Springs, California

A quarrel with her grandmother was the last thing she wanted, especially in the middle of the night in a Palm Springs hotel room and Audrey over in San Bernardino somewhere crying out for help. She wanted to shout back at Pearl, "Audrey left me! But not before she'd tried to convince me to go with her. 'Oh, Dixson's sick,' she'd said. 'He's not a bad man. He was high on drugs. Come along now. He won't ever touch you again. Everything will be all right.'"

To go with Audrey to join Dixson on that night so long ago had been unthinkable. Maegan had chosen to stay with Pearl. Audrey's choice had burned with betrayal. Her own child should come first. Was Audrey afraid she'd never find another man? Afraid to stand on her own? Her mother's actions would always remain a mystery. The last few days had become a maudlin TV talk show. Except it was real and she was living it.

She felt a roiling in her stomach as she pulled on her black jogging pants with pink racing stripes down the legs and the white Nike logo nestled by the pant hem. She remembered something about Nike, from a long-ago mythology class. The goddess of strength and speed. And victory. I could use you tonight, she thought. Strange, the segues her mind could make in the middle of a mess like this.

But forgiveness for Audrey? *Forgiveness?* She'd read self-help books, talked to counselors, talked to her close friends, gone to church, searched inside her own mind, written in a journal. During one quest for answers, she'd even googled "forgiveness," finding quotes like, "You can forgive a person without forgetting what they've done." Another: "Forgiving is not forgetting. It's letting go of the hurt." Wonderful words—but how? How do you do this? After all her quest, she still believed some acts to be truly unforgiveable.

She slipped into her racer tee, the old internal debate again leaving her muddled. Just get your mother out of that mess, she thought. She knew she didn't want Audrey beaten or hurt. She pulled on her running shoes and tied them tight.

Pearl finished fastening her shoes. She had a steely look on her face. Hard. Immovable. Maegan remembered her grandmother's last encounter with Dixson. She'd struck him with a baseball bat. Now, older, and more unsteady, she often walked using a black cane with a silver grip.

Maegan readied to leave the room, waiting for her grandmother to gather her purse, when someone knocked on the door. Pearl looked at her, eyebrows raised, and whispered, "Who's that?"

With quick strides, Maegan was at the door, squinting through the peephole to see Roger Hemmings, in his wheelchair, alone, in his rumpled blue pajamas. She unhooked the safety chain and opened the door.

He glanced at her clothes, her keys, and the purse in her hand. "Audrey called me, looking for you. She sounded distracted, vague. Can I help?"

Maegan glanced at her grandmother who now stood beside her, then answered, "Her husband beat her up. We're on our way to get her before he gets back to their doublewide."

"Beat her up? My God. Does she live near here?"

Maegan nodded her head, showing him the directions, and Audrey's address and phone number. Roger removed a pad and pen from the side pocket on his wheelchair and jotted down the information.

"Did she call the police?"

"We don't know," Maegan replied.

Roger pulled his cell phone from the same side pocket. "I'm calling Hector. He'll meet you at the hotel entrance with the SUV." The call took mere seconds. "He'll go with you."

Before Maegan could reply, Pearl spoke up. "Thank you, Mr. Hemmings," she said.

Roger and her grandmother waited while she closed the hotel room door and then, together, the three of them made their way toward the elevator. The dim hallway pushed in around her, a garment shrunk too small, stretched around too many thoughts, unable to contain them.

A scattering of bronze wall sconces lit the passage, the dimness playing on their faces as they moved into light, into shadow, and into light again. During the elevator ride down, no one spoke. The doors slid open. The lobby was deserted except for the night clerk who glanced at them as they walked to the glass doors and outside. Within a few moments, Hector pulled up in the black GMC Savanna.

A clear desert night engulfed them; Palm Springs asleep, waiting for the sun to rise and bring shopkeepers and tourists awake. Maegan looked up at the black sky scattered with stars, at the silhouettes of palms reaching upward to meet them. She took a deep breath.

"You're going to bring Audrey here?" Roger asked.

"Oh, yes," Pearl said. "That girl is coming home."

He took Maegan's hand. "Call me when you get back."

Hector helped Pearl into the back seat and buckled her in. Maegan scrambled into the passenger side. She pulled her seatbelt around her and snapped it tight, wondering what to expect next.

"You be the navigator," Hector said, hopping into the driver's seat. "I'll get us there just as quick as I can."

Maegan nodded. "Head north to Interstate 10. We should make good time at this hour."

Roger watched them leave as Maegan pulled her cell phone from her purse and tapped in Audrey's number to tell her to be ready, that they were on their way. The phone rang . . . and rang. Why didn't she answer?

Chapter Forty-Eight

Roger Hemmings

May 2008—Palm Springs, California

The balmy night air did little to calm Roger's apprehension. He turned his chair and went back into the hotel. He could have ridden along with them, but that helpless feeling he had learned to hold at bay—despite the strength and skills he'd acquired during his thirty years of immobility—had settled over him. Hector would be better suited to the night's endeavor.

He moved himself to the elevator, the wheelchair's electric whir overly loud in the deserted lobby, its high ceiling an echo chamber. As the elevator rose to the penthouse, he watched the digital numbers flash by like the past three decades, the results of which now confronted him. He eased into the suite, pulled out his cell phone, and called Hector.

One ring. "Yes, Mr. Hemmings?"

"Is everyone all right?" Roger asked.

"Yes, sir. We're moving right along."

"Do whatever you have to do." Roger took a deep breath. "And don't hesitate to call the police. Let me know when you're on your way back."

"Yes, sir."

His phone back in the chair pocket, he decided to dress and be ready for their return. In the bathroom, he splashed water on his face and brushed his teeth. From the closet, he pulled beige slacks by the pant bottom until they came off the hanger. From the dresser came boxers and brown socks. He laid the clothing on the coverlet, removed his pajama top, and transferred himself onto the bed, moving well away from the mattress edge and as close to the center as he could get. On his back, his elbows bent, his arms and shoulders supplying the strength, he slowly backed his body toward the headboard and propped himself against it. Thus began the process he'd learned so long ago to remove his pajama bottoms and dress himself. A quick prayer always came to his lips, thanking God he'd been left with enough upper body mobility to be this independent.

Once in his trousers and socks, he transferred back to the chair and selected a pale blue golf shirt from the dresser, which he pulled on over his head, manipulated down over his chest, and tucked into his trousers. One at a time, he took his brown loafers from the low stool where Hector had placed them and set them on the chair's footrests. His hands around one thigh and then the other, he lifted each leg and eased his feet into the shoes. From another drawer in the dresser, he pulled a brown belt, slid it through the belt loops, and secured it. Tired from the exertion, he rested, wondering what he would say to Audrey.

From what he knew, Audrey fit the battered woman profile. How did she act now? Once so full of energy and life, had she become fearful? Was her confidence beaten down? The Stockholm Syndrome? PTSD? What did she look like? Her image as he last saw her so long ago remained vivid. A beautiful teenager, sweet and innocent. He remembered each moment they had been together. The day he'd first met her at Uncle Seb's souvenir shop, The Desert Tee, in downtown Palm Springs. The night at the disco, their meetings at Sandy's Coffee Shop. The final night in Hardy Park. Plans and dreams of how their lives would be. He closed his eyes, his thoughts wandering into the "what might have been."

But that memory road curved and angled into danger and depression. He'd learned to deal with reality long ago. He wondered what would be found tonight. Had Audrey been badly hurt physically? Certainly emotionally. Perhaps the words building in his heart would have to wait, but he pondered them as if preparing an opening statement for a court proceeding, seeking the words he would need to explain why he'd never returned. She would be his judge . . . and jury.

She would understand the accident, the difficult recovery, his need to adjust. She'd probably even understand his father's influence. But his never calling? Never seeing her again? That was something he wasn't sure he *could* explain—even to himself. He'd thought about coming back. But he always returned to the belief that she'd have been repulsed by his condition. That stopped him cold every time. Plus, his father forbade him to make contact, convinced him he had enough on his plate rebuilding his life as a paraplegic. After he'd learned she'd had their child, he made his father establish a special account for them.

Some might call it "conscience money." Was it? He hated that idea. Had he been a coward? A daddy's boy? A scared kid? Christ, after all this time, the same whirl of unanswered questions still assailed him. No matter the fancy words, justifications, and excuses, he couldn't explain. What could he say? He was dumb, stupid, and weak? No. A frightened kid whose life changed with a robber's gunshot? No. He'd say the one thing he felt so deeply he could cry. He was sorry; sorry he'd never called, never returned.

He sat for a moment buried by the tired replay of those past years and then went to the mini bar. *You sorry-assed bastard*, he thought. He wanted vodka, but the Ketel bottle was empty. Housekeeping hadn't replaced it. He opened the bar fridge and grabbed a small can of V-8. He hated waiting. Maybe he should have gone with them to get Audrey. With a snap of the aluminum tab, the can opened. He swallowed, the cold veggie blend settling into him. Waiting was no snap.

And what about his daughter? Maegan had become a trooper. He imagined living with Pearl would either make you tough as steel or hammer you into the ground. Pearl had stepped in where he should have been. He owed that woman more than he could ever repay. And then his daughter had found him, caused this meeting to happen— no, *these* meetings to happen—forcing him to confront what he'd run from all his adult years.

Despite the accomplishments in his life, his failures to the Spence women consumed him. At home in Arizona, time and life had gradually separated him from his past, allowing his daughter and Audrey to drift into the background like elevator music, playing *forte* on occasion and then becoming *pianissimo* on others. But here in Palm Springs, they were in his immediate thoughts every moment, forcing him to confront himself. *Fortissimo*.

He wanted them to return to the hotel, quickly. His hand went to his cellphone but stopped. If Hector did encounter a problem, he'd call. Instead, he reached for the remote; anything to kill time. Images came onto the flat screen. He flipped to Channel 36 reruns. The old series, *Law and Order*. He watched without caring or seeing. Waiting.

Chapter Forty-Nine

Pearl Spence

May 2008—Palm Springs, California

Only one thought ran back and forth in my head: *Why hadn't Audrey answered the phone when Maegan called to say we was on the way?* I squeezed the handles on my purse until the plastic was all sweaty and twisted like a dishcloth. I wanted to tell Hector to go faster, but when I leaned forward and saw that speedometer needle stuck on 85, I sat back and hung on to the armrest, prayin' we'd get to San Bernardino in one piece. I didn't want to get in no wreck tryin' to take my baby girl away from that Dixson.

I shook my head at the Almighty's plans, the way people turned out, and how He made things happen. Neville gone—stung to death, of all things. Dixson lurkin' around somewhere. A drunk and a wifebeater. And poor Winston, in the hospital after tryin' to save his brother. She wondered if Neville would have done that for Winston if the shoe had been on the other foot. How'd Winston turn out so good, with a father and brother straight from the devil himself? I was sorry for the day Audrey ever met that Mr. D. Dupre. What made God decide on a plan like that for Audrey?

And why didn't she answer the phone?

But I kept tellin' myself we'd have her back safe—and soon. Then I thought of somethin' else—made me sit up flagpole straight: Roger and Audrey hadn't laid eyes on each other in thirty years. My baby didn't know he was in a wheelchair. Didn't know about his accident. We was yankin' the girl away from a nightmare and throwin' her into a dream gone sour, what with Roger waitin' for us.

We'd tell her. On the way back to the hotel.

Oh, my stars. That new nettle would just have to get in line with my other worries. First, we had to make sure my Audrey was safe.

I looked into the night whizzin' by, into the headlights, and at buildings, all black except for windows lit here and there. And signs— them neon signs that never sleep. All I could think was hurry. Hurry.

Maegan turned and said over her shoulder, "You okay, Gramma?"

I pursed my lips and nodded. *Why hadn't Audrey answered the phone?*

Chapter Fifty

Audrey Dupre

May 2008—San Bernardino, California

Audrey hung up the phone. Maegan and Pearl were on their way. Her mind drummed in a one-two rhythm. *Hur*-ry. *Hur*-ry. How she wanted to sit on the couch and sob, letting all the regret and hurt leave every muscle, every joint, every thought. But urgency wired her nerves, telling her to stay on her feet and keep moving.

Into the bedroom. Audrey leaned her hand on the mattress and carefully lowered herself to her knees, her body aching, to retrieve a black carry-all from under the bed. She pulled it out and brushed her fingers along the closed silver zipper, across the cloth top. An absent-minded cleaning, leaving dusty grit on her fingertips. She rubbed her hand on her shorts, then swung the case onto the bed and unzipped it.

On her feet now, she pulled open a dresser drawer. Quickly she grabbed underwear, shorts, T-shirts. A sweater. Jeans and a pink sweatshirt. Two faded oversized sleep shirts, one with a palm tree and the words "Beautiful Palm Springs" scrawled on the front. The other with a picture of a gray kitten and the words "I Feel Purrty." She brushed hair from her face, feeling the puffiness of her cheek and eye.

Next, in the bathroom, her fingers flying, she grabbed a large cosmetics bag from a drawer next to the sink. Into it she tossed lipstick, soap, hairbrush, deodorant, and a toothbrush from the counter. She took everything from the drawer and medicine cabinet she thought she'd need. She zipped the small case and crammed it into the carryall. With a quick glance around the bedroom, she brought the still unzipped carryall into the living room and dropped it on the couch.

She headed to a built-in corner-cabinet and opened a drawer beneath the glass doors, again rubbing her sweaty palms on her shorts. From the bottom drawer she took a photo album called "Maegan's Book." No need to look inside. It chronicled Maegan's life. Baby pictures. Kindergarten. Third grade. Christmas Pageant. And so on through the years. She also grabbed a small box that once held note cards; again, knowing the contents. A napkin from Sandy's Coffee shop. Roger had signed it for fun. A disco flyer from Zelda's. A picture postcard of Hardy Park. A photo of Dixson in his Rancho Cucamonga Quakes baseball uniform, dirt on his knees, smudges on his handsome, grinning face after a big win. A photo of his little boys, their arms around each other's shoulders. Two pieces of life gone sour.

The carry-all bulged as she squeezed in the album and box, pulling the zipper tab in small jerks to close it. How long would it take them to come from Palm Springs? An hour? She sat on the couch, gripping the handles of the travel bag.

The doublewide began to feel like a prison. She stood and opened the venetian blinds enough to see outside. Nothing stirred. Then headlights came slowly down the narrow lane. Maegan and Pearl? No, too soon. Her heart stopped. What if it was Dixson? Usually, he'd stay away a few hours. But this wasn't the usual. His son had died; she'd received the worst beating of their marriage. Her body stiffened. Then the small pick-up drove on by and pulled into a carport three trailers down on the other side of the street.

What if Dixson got here before her family? She didn't want to be caught inside. If he found out she was trying to leave, his rage would escalate. Where could she wait? Outside would be best. She could hide in the neighbor's oleander bushes. Let him come back. She wouldn't be here. She'd be hidden. But . . .

The thought sent her into the bedroom once more. *Never again.* She dug in the corner of the clothes closet and pulled out a baseball bat. He'd never hit her again. With the bat clutched in her hand, she returned to the living room, and peeked through the window. Nothing. Taking a deep breath, she ran into the kitchen and grabbed her purse. Back in the living room, the bat and purse in one hand, she grabbed the carryall from the couch in the other hand, and let herself out of the front door, closing it with a soft click. She ran to a row of oleander bushes that separated their lot from the neighbor's. From there, she could see the lane and even her own kitchen window where the cat-shaped clock swung its black tail.

Across the street, she could see the flickering of a TV through sheer curtains—even at this hour—and hear a soft drone of sound. She sensed a heavy garbage smell. Melon rinds? Fish? The odor came from the neighbor's trashcans at the back of their carport. They were away for the week and missed the garbage pickup.

She heard the ring of a telephone. Where? Who called anyone at this hour? Then she realized the ringing sound came through her kitchen window. It was *her* phone. Dixson? She cringed and eased herself around the end of the row of oleanders and into the neighbor's carport where the garbage smell hovered in the humid air. From here she could see the road. From here she could run. From here people could hear her scream.

Two green plastic chairs sat in the carport near the neighbor's door. She placed her carry-all and purse on the carport floor, in the deep night shadows at the back of the structure, and up by the trash, and then she moved one of the chairs over next to her things. She sat, bat in hand, beside her belongings.

She prayed for headlights. That she'd see Maegan's car approach. Soon. She waited. A voice gnawed at her inside: *Why, Dixson? Why has it come to this?* Tears stung her eyes.

Chapter Fifty-One

Dixson Dupre

May 2008—San Bernardino, California

He eased the Honda down the lane, headlights off. No sense drawing attention to him and Audrey's latest dust-up. It'd blow over. Always did. After all, he'd lost his son. Man had a right to let go of the hurt any way he wanted, and this hurt was gonna be around a long time. Worst thing ever happened to him. He rubbed his eyes and peered into the night, the doublewides like rows of shipping containers, the kind you'd see down at the docks in San Pedro. Everything all in boxes—like Neville would be soon. The thought made him swallow hard. He pulled the Honda into their carport, a metal roof secured with rusty iron poles, and cut the engine.

He leaned back, feeling his eyes moisten, tears slowly rolling down his cheeks. He wiped them away with his fist. For a moment he saw himself playing with Neville, the kid dressed in his Little League uniform, trying to catch a fly ball. Then another picture of splashing around with the boy in a friend's pool.

He remembered the first time the two of them had broken the law—boosted some tech equipment and sold it. Then they made a drug connection with a guy in Coachella. Soon, Neville got big-headed, saying he didn't need his old man no more. Big shot-shit. Now he was gone. *But why?* Neville was the gutsy one, the one that made him proud. Not soft like Winston. What lousy goddamned breaks in this lousy goddamned life.

He needed a drink. Maybe a joint. He had some Acapulco Gold somewhere. Taped under the toilet tank lids in the johns or stuffed in a box in the closet. Had the hard stuff around too, but that was to sell. He just wanted a joint to mellow out, to get rid of the sadness hanging in his head. Add a little shot of booze.

He'd cozy up to Audrey. Promise to take her out for lasagna. Make nice. Woman wasn't all bad. Better than a stick in the eye. It always seemed that everything in his life eventually went south.

Slivers of dim light peeked through the Venetian blinds. Suppose she's sitting in there, he thought, ready to bring the guilts into his gut. Make him feel like shit. Well, she wouldn't succeed. He already felt as low as he could get. Lower than a flat tire. *Try losing a son, Audrey.*

He sighed and got out of the car, shutting the door with a slam, announcing himself. At the door in a couple of strides, he stepped in. Light from the kitchen angled its glow into the dark living room, everything graveyard quiet. He snapped on the table lamp and went for a glass and a bottle of Jack from the kitchen cabinet by the refrigerator. He carried the glass and bottle into the living room, poured a tall shot, and swallowed, looking around, wondering where Audrey was. *Probably in the bedroom, on the bed, cryin'.* After another swallow, he plopped the glass and bottle on the coffee table.

Scratching his chest, he returned to the kitchen and stepped into the washroom. The toilet tank lid felt cold. He lifted it and turned it over. No little bag. "Damn," he muttered. Then he remembered; he and three buddies had smoked up the stash during a poker game the other night.

At this moment, he wasn't interested in any words with Audrey, but to get to the Gold he'd have to go in the bathroom off the bedroom where she'd probably be lying awake or sitting in the chair. *Shit.* He walked in, not glancing toward the bed or chair, and flipped the light on in the bathroom. This time when he removed the tank lid, he smiled and untaped the plastic bag. He clanked the top back into position and shoved the bag in his pants pocket. When he turned, light flowing into the bedroom, he realized the bed was empty. So was the chair. *What the hell?* he thought and snapped on the room's overhead light.

"Audrey, where you hidin'? Come on out, honey. I'm sorry. Neville dyin' and all."

He stepped back in the bathroom and pushed aside the flowered shower curtain, expecting to see her cowering in the tub. He opened the sliding closet doors, first her side, then his. "Audrey? Where the hell are you?"

On his hands and knees, he looked under the bed. She wasn't there and neither was his carry-all. He always kept it at the ready in case he had to leave in a hurry. "What the—where are you?"

He moved through the trailer, looking behind furniture, behind doors, feeling his jaw get cement-hard, his guts boiling up with each door he slammed. Where was the bitch? He'd taken the car and all the cash from her dumb hiding places. Did she have more money hidden somewhere else? Did she call a cab and leave? *She ain't that smart.*

He went back into the bedroom. Some of her clothes were gone from the drawers. Next, into the bathroom. All her bottles and crap gone from the sink and drawer. One last look in the closet. Did she find his stash, thinking she could sell it? He dug in behind the hanging clothes and jumbled shoes and pulled out a box labeled "Baseball Cleats." It once held his lucky shoes—his homerun shoes. He opened it. Several bricks of coke—still there. Cash on the hoof. He stuck the box back in its place.

About to close the closet slider, he noticed something *not* in its place: the baseball bat from the last game he ever played. His homerun bat. He kept it in the corner of the closet by the sliding door where he could see it when he opened the door to get his clothes. It helped him get back the surge, the feeling when that ball had soared over the fence. He dug around in the closet, pushing clothes aside. Shirts and blouses slid off their hangers and onto the floor. That bitch was gonna get it if anything happened to that bat. He backed away from the closet, breathing hard.

He returned to the living room, poured three fingers of Jack, and downed it. He'd wait. The bitch'd be back. Probably chewing her nails over at a neighbor's place or hiding somewhere close. He'd check around outside. In a bit. He turned off the lights in the kitchen, bedroom, and bathroom. Then dropped onto the couch and snapped off the table lamp, wanting to just sit. He poured another shot and took a sip. A moment of quiet in the dark.

The sound of a car. He slipped a finger between two Venetian blind slats and looked out at the street. A vehicle cruised by, backed up, and stopped directly in front of the place. Was she back? *Not even the guts to stay gone?* Naw. It wasn't her. He didn't know anybody who drove a big black SUV like this one. Did a busybody neighbor call the police? Naw. That wasn't a police rig. Their undercovers were plain, unmarked sedans. Besides, their little scuffle hadn't been that loud. One of Neville's cronies?

The vehicle looked like a big GMC. A guy he didn't recognize got out and walked in front of it, surveying the doublewide. The passenger door opened, and a woman got out. Audrey? No. *Looks like . . . Maegan?* What the hell was going on? A guy can't even grieve for his son in peace.

Maegan had a lot of gall, coming here. Because of her, he'd gone to prison. Whatever game she wanted to play, he could play. Had Audrey called her? Summoned Maegan to the rescue? Had Audrey lost her nerve, changed her mind and disappeared? With deliberate, slow steps, careful not to make noise, he went into the kitchen and crawled out the back window. He dropped to the ground and slipped into the oleander bushes. Time to see what was going on.

Chapter Fifty-Two

Maegan Spence

May 2008—San Bernardino, California

Maegan quietly closed the passenger door of the SUV and turned to look at her mother's doublewide. A four-door Honda sat in the carport, the house dark, the venetian blinds closed. Tall California fan palms, queen palms and oleander bushes stood motionless in the windless night. In the distance, an air conditioner clanked and rumbled off. Open windows shared the sounds of people living too close to each other. A cough. Some talk. A thump. As an outside light came on across the lane, she sensed the connecting crush of people who knew each other's business.

She whispered through the open window of the SUV, "Gramma Pearl, does Audrey have more than one car?"

Pearl shook her head and pointed. She whispered back, "That car belongs to the no-good."

"He must be here," Hector said in a hushed tone as he joined Maegan.

Pearl unsnapped her seatbelt and opened the door.

"Shhh. No, Gramma. Stay in the car." Maegan pushed the door closed.

Pearl immediately shoved it back open. "Don't shush me. I'm not sittin' in the car with that man in there with my daughter. Who knows what he's up to?"

"Please, Mrs. Spence, do as your granddaughter asks," Hector whispered. "I'm here."

"Just because I'm old," Pearl grumbled, "don't mean I can't give that no-good a kick in the pants." But she pulled the door closed with a quiet thump.

Maegan and Hector started up the front walk when they heard an animal-like sound and muffled voices growing louder, followed by the scuffling of feet on concrete in the neighbor's carport to the left of Audrey's doublewide.

"You think you're gonna hit me?" A man spat the words. "Gimme that bat."

A woman cried, "You're hurting me."

"Gimme that, I said."

The woman's muffled scream broke in mid-cry.

Maegan ran toward the voices. "Audrey? Audrey!"

Hector followed. "Careful, Maegan. Careful."

As Maegan approached the front of the neighbor's carport, Dixson came forward from its shadows, gripping a baseball bat in one hand. "Get outta here."

"My mother's in there." She could see the form of a woman cowering near the back of the structure.

"Mind your own business," Dixson snarled.

Dixson stepped toward Maegan, bat up and readied. She felt herself shoved aside, just as Dixson swung. Hector dodged the blow and whirled around to face Dixson, who squared himself, the bat dangling. He looked from Hector to Maegan, eyes flashing. "I said, 'Mind your own business.'"

"Audrey," Maegan called. "It's all right."

"Stay where you are, woman," Dixson growled over his shoulder. He swayed from side to side, both hands now on the bat, intent on Maegan and Hector.

Suddenly, a bulging paper sack hit the back of Dixson's head. It split, scattering rinds, banana peels, and papers. An empty aluminum can clattered to the ground. A glass container broke into pieces. The bag's contents scattered, and with them, the smell. Dixson sputtered as he scrambled sideways, rubbing his head, brushing the damp, limp garbage from his face and neck, the bat still in one hand. Audrey backed away from him, clutching the shredded remains of the paper sack.

"You bitch!" He turned to swing at Audrey.

Hector grabbed the end of the bat and wrenched it from Dixson's hands. Dixson hesitated, then started running down the neighbor's driveway toward the road. As Maegan ran to her mother's side, Hector tossed the bat on the ground, gave chase, and tackled Dixson near the end of the drive. Dixson tried to kick free. Hector landed several punches, pulled the man to his feet, twisted one arm behind him, and shoved him toward the SUV. Dixson bumped into the side of the vehicle. Maegan saw the glint of metal as the silver tip of Pearl's cane rocketed through her open window and connected with Dixson's head.

"What the hell!" Dixson grabbed the side of his head and spotted Pearl. "You crazy old woman!"

Hector shoved Dixson to the ground, his knee square in the middle of the man's spine. He pushed Dixson's face into the gravel.

Audrey stood in the neighbor's carport, her shoulders shaking. Maegan took her hand, and they walked toward the SUV.

"Dixson won't hurt you," Maegan said.

Audrey looked at her with dull eyes and nodded. Maegan's anger flared, wondering how her mother could stay with the man. The old hurt bubbled up past the anger. Her inner child whispered, *You chose Dixson instead of me,* just as flashing red lights appeared at the end of the lane.

Hector called over his shoulder, "A neighbor must have alerted the police."

"A good thing, too," Pearl said, her voice erupting from inside the SUV.

Dixson tried to say something. Hector crammed his face in the dirt again.

"It's alright," Maegan assured Audrey as they approached the vehicle.

Audrey smoothed her hair away from her forehead and cheeks, away from the bruises and tears.

Dixson squirmed on the ground. Hector gave the man's arm another upward twist as Gramma Pearl emerged from the SUV, scowled at her son-in-law, and poked his shoulder hard with her cane.

"Get her away from me," Dixson sputtered.

Maegan steadied Audrey and helped her over to Pearl, who took her daughter in her arms. Maegan felt a surge of guilt. She could have embraced her mother, but what Audrey had done always held her back.

Maegan watched her mother and grandmother. Her stepfather and Hector. She thought about Roger Hemmings at the hotel. Winston in the hospital or now home in his apartment. Neville dead. For the first time in her life, they'd all come together. "Collided" would be the better word. This was her family. Like a Rubik's Cube, each part twisting and turning, something always askew, out of alignment. Except for Pearl.

"Glad you got here so fast," Hector said to the approaching police officers.

"We were nearby. Part of our patrol area," said the officer in charge, pulling out his pen and notepad. "Always something going on in this neighborhood. This isn't our first call on old Dixson here."

His voice surly, Dixson muttered, "Get lost."

The officer assessed the situation and took names. His partner secured Dixson's wrists in handcuffs and sat him in the back of the patrol car.

"Ma'am," the officer addressed Audrey as he closed his notebook, "are you ready to press charges?"

"Aw, come on, honey," Dixson's whiny voice called out. "I just lost my cool. Neville dyin' and all."

Audrey's body language softened as she looked at her bleeding and disheveled husband. Pearl's firm voice cut the air, her eyes on Audrey. "None of us is goin' through this again." Audrey flinched.

Maegan wanted to shake Audrey by the shoulders. Her mother seemed to waver, like a reed in the wind. Had they gone through all this for nothing? Everyone grew quiet, waiting.

"Well, ma'am?" the officer asked.

Audrey hesitated. She looked at Dixson who shook his head. At Pearl who nodded. Then at Maegan, where her eyes lingered. She touched her eye and cheek. "Yes," she murmured, "I'll press charges."

"You stupid cow." Dixson grunted.

Chapter Fifty-Three

Pearl Spence

May 2008—Palm Springs, California

On the way back to Palm Springs, transport trucks passed us, headin' east from Los Angeles across the desert toward Phoenix—just like my husband used to do when he drove one of them big semis. Every time a rig whooshed by, the SUV swayed.

I was glad Hector was takin' his time and that he'd found Audrey's carryall and purse in the neighbor's carport. The police kept the bat. Audrey rode in the backseat next to me, staring out the side window, wearing my sweater draped around her shoulders, holdin' a bottle of water Hector'd given her in a death grip. Now and then, I patted her arm. Once in a while she'd nod, look at me with a little smile, and then look back out the window with a blank stare. Everybody sat quiet with their own thoughts, nothin' to hear but the wind noise of passin' trucks and cars.

I waited for Maegan to tell Audrey about Roger Hemmings, but she'd gone into that dark, unforgivin' place of hers like she always did around her mother. I didn't think it up to me to spill the beans since it was Maegan got Roger out to California and all. But my patience was stretchin' thin. If my granddaughter didn't speak up soon, I was goin' to. My daughter'd had too many surprises already.

Maegan finally turned and looked at her mother as we was passin' the windmills on the outskirts of Palm Springs. "Audrey," she said, "there's something you should remember. Roger Hemmings is in Palm Springs, at our hotel."

"Wait, who?" Audrey turned away from the window, surprise jumpin' across her face. "What did you say?"

"Roger Hemmings is at the hotel," Maegan repeated. "He wants to see you."

"Oh. Right. He's here. Roger." Audrey chewed on this reminder for a bit. She looked out the window again and said, "Why, after all these years?"

Maegan told her mother about my note in her birthday card and how she'd found Roger. The short version. The girl could sure pack plenty of news into a few sentences.

Audrey closed her eyes and laid her head back. "Well, I rid my life of one man, and another wants to enter it. All in one night." She grew real still and quiet. "I don't want to see him."

A stone-cold silence dropped over all of us, except for Hector clearin' his throat. Felt like someone taped our mouths shut. Mine didn't stay taped long.

"Audrey, I can't tell you what to do," I began. "His comin' here is important to Maegan. Hope it's important to you. It'd sure mean a lot to your daughter if you two met up after all this time." I didn't add, it might help with healin' this family. I did say, "Know it's none of my business, but I'd be real happy to see all three of you talk, together." Guess I was likin' Roger Hemmings more than I might've guessed.

Maegan told Hector to take the next off ramp from Interstate 10 into Palm Springs. Still takin' her time, she finally blurted, "She can do what she wants. She always has."

Audrey glanced at the back of her daughter's head, then looked down. She placed the water bottle beside her. Her fingers clasped and unclasped in her lap, nervous-like.

Nearer the city, low rugged mountains edged one side of the road. Open desert stretched on the other. That old saying "Between a rock and a hard place" jumped into my mind. That's how I felt about my daughter and granddaughter. Audrey and Maegan were both stubborn, both actin' like they didn't care.

"Anyway, I couldn't see him," Audrey muttered, "looking like this."

I sat up. Did I just hear a crack open in the rocky night?

"Now, honey," I said, "We can do something about that. And there's one more thing you should know."

Maegan caught my eye in the rearview mirror. Maybe she read my mind and wanted me to shut up. I didn't. "Roger's in a wheelchair."

"What?" Audrey's hands froze. She looked up. "Why? What's the matter with him?"

The wheels in my head turned real quick. "Best if he tells you."

Maegan turned to scowl at me. But I figured tellin' my daughter about the wheelchair might be one way to get her to see the man. At least make her curious.

Audrey grew quiet again. The tires drummed along the pavement. Maybe a better word was pounded—at least, I know that's what my head was doin'. I heard Hector on his cell.

"Mr. Hemmings, sir, we'll be there in roughly twenty minutes."

"I don't know if I ever want to see him," Audrey murmured. "And certainly not in the middle of the night."

We rode quiet all the way back to the hotel. Was we makin' headway?

Fifty-Four

Audrey Duprey

May 2008—Palm Springs, California

Audrey smelled exhaust fumes as they stepped from their vehicle that sat idling under the portico of the Hyatt Hotel. Hector removed her carryall, handed the keys to the night valet, and the SUV disappeared into the building's underground parking garage. Maegan led the way toward the hotel entrance. Audrey walked beside her mother, followed by Hector, her carryall still in his grasp.

Stunned by the night's events, Audrey entered the hotel, her mother close on one side, Hector on the other. Like shields, they seemed ready to protect her from onlookers—except there weren't any, only a solitary night clerk and a man in hiking clothes, his backpack on the floor beside him, engaged in conversation at the registration desk.

Maegan strode ahead; Miss Independent, Miss Stubborn. Audrey followed the girl she hoped would allow her back into her life. Sometime. They neared the elevator, the bronze finished doors recently polished and freed of fingerprints by a night housekeeper who nodded and moved on to empty nearby trash containers.

Audrey caught her image in a wall mirror. She turned away. Dixson had wrenched the bat from her hands when she tried to hit him. He'd knocked her down and dragged her along the carport's concrete floor, leaving dirt and oil stains on her clothes and ripping her shorts. Nasty scrapes caked with blood throbbed on her arm and leg; the bruises on her face were tender to the touch, her hip, sore. Every bit of her ached, inside and out. She sensed Pearl looking at her, then felt her mother's arm slip around her waist. She wanted to put her head on Pearl's strong shoulder and cry. She didn't.

"We'll go to my room," Maegan said, as they entered the elevator. She pushed the button for the third floor.

Audrey couldn't remember the last time she'd been in a nice hotel. Her last away-from-home trip with Dixson landed her in a run-down Travelodge in San Diego, where she waited while he "took care of business." The elevator whirred upward. After it eased to a stop, Maegan and Pearl stepped into the hall. Audrey followed.

Hector handed Audrey's carry-all to Maegan. "When shall I tell Mr. Hemmings you'll be up?" he asked.

"Not tonight, if at all," Audrey murmured, ill-at-ease under the grilling stare of three pairs of eyes. She pulled her mother's sweater tight around her.

"We have to tend to my daughter, to her wounds," Pearl said.

Maegan exchanged a glance with Hector who nodded. He stepped back into the elevator, pressed the button, and the doors closed.

"Where's he going?" Audrey asked.

"Up to the executive penthouse suite," Maegan answered. She led the way down the hall.

Pearl took Audrey's hand. "Come along, honey."

Once in Maegan's room—and for the first time in quite a while—Audrey felt safe.

Pearl immediately dug through her suitcase and came up with a small tube of Polysporin, a box of Band-Aid® strips and a box of Band-Aid® gauze pads. "Good idea to always have first-aid stuff along. We'll get you cleaned up." She started for the bathroom.

As much as Audrey wanted her mother's touch, her shame grew stronger, her failures and self-loathing stronger still. "I'll be okay. I've done this before," Audrey said, and then added in a whispery voice, "I can take care of myself,"

"Oh, really?" Maegan tossed her head and dropped the soiled carry-all on the floor. "You fooled me."

"I'm not trying to fool anyone," Audrey answered in a low voice.

Pearl shook her head at her granddaughter and stepped toward Audrey. "Let me help you, honey."

Audrey repeated, "I can take care of myself."

Pearl hesitated, then carefully placed the first aid items in Audrey's extended hand.

"Honey," Pearl said, "you just go in that bathroom and shower. Wash your wounds. There's lots of hotel shampoo and sweet-smellin' soap. You'll feel better."

Audrey picked up her bag. "Thank you for coming, Maegan," she said quietly. Maegan didn't reply.

The bathroom door closed behind her, Audrey leaned against it, finally alone. Nothing else was left in her life. No home, no husband, no daughter. Nothing remained of her but a hollow shell. Tears slipped down her face.

She dropped down onto the side of the tub, bag and first-aid items slipping from her hands, and sobbed. Sadness, regret, and loneliness tumbled through her like water over rocks in a stream. She wrapped her arms around herself and rocked back and forth. Could she find and hold together the pieces of the girl she once knew named Audrey? A rap on the door startled her. She wiped her eyes.

Pearl asked, "You okay, honey?"

"Yes," Audrey replied.

"Just checkin'. Didn't hear nothin'."

"I'm okay." Audrey brushed her cheeks with her fingers, searching for the strength to move. She removed her clothing gingerly to avoid hitting her wounds, each piece a layer of life she never wanted again. The soiled clothes dropped onto the floor, stained with her so-called existence.

She avoided the mirror and turned on the shower, stepping in under the spray, easing it onto her body. Despite a stinging sensation in some of the wounds, the water calmed her. She cleansed the abrasions; if only soap and water could wash away the wounds buried inside. Steam rose around her. She threw her head back, felt fine spray on her face, then turned around, the water soothing the nape of her neck.

A small bottle of lavender-scented shampoo sat in the shower on a corner shelf. She washed her hair, lather slipping into her ears and over the ugly bruises on her face. She squinted to keep soap from her eyes, but not too hard; it hurt.

Wash. Rinse. Breathe.

She stepped from the shower and gently toweled her body, her mind trying to blot away Dixson's last words. They'd cut into her, knives of shame and embarrassment. Unlike her scrapes that would heal, those words would embed for life.

"You stupid cow, you stupid cow," he'd cried.

She grabbed a blow dryer from its wall bracket, turned it on high, the sound filling the room. For the moment, at least, she couldn't hear her thoughts. She finger-fluffed her hair, avoiding her facial wounds. When her hair felt dry enough, she secured it into a ponytail with a pink scrunchie from her bag. Wounds on her calf, thigh, and elbow received gentle dabs of Polysporin. She covered the wounds with gauze pads or adhesive strips. Her hip had a large bruise.

Warm and clean in a white terry cloth robe from the hotel, she opened the door, girding herself to get through whatever came next.

"Aw, honey," Pearl said with a gentle smile, "you look better. How do you feel?"

"Not so good. Do either of you have any Tylenol?"

Maegan nodded and dug in her purse. She handed Audrey the pill container, along with a bottle of water from the minibar. Her daughter watched her open the medication, shake two pills into her hand, and swallow them with several gulps of water. It felt like a judgmental stare, digging deeper into Audrey.

"Thank you." she said and returned the Tylenol bottle to Maegan, who placed the pill container on a bedside stand and said nothing.

"Here, Audrey, honey, sit over here with me," Pearl said.

Audrey joined her at a small round table by the sliding doors. The water bottle had beads of condensation on it. She absently wiped them away with her fingers. Maegan sat on one of two queen-size beds.

"Thank you again for coming to get me. Dixson never beat me this bad before."

"Really? Hard to believe," Maegan said as she studied her mother. "You know it'll only keep getting worse, don't you?" Her voice hardened. "I hope you aren't changing your mind. About pressing charges."

The room grew quiet.

Audrey's mind whirled. Her stomach tightened. Two men had entered her life and changed it forever. Roger, who'd never returned, and Dixson, who'd done the unthinkable. Through it all, she'd clung to the dream of having a family and keeping that family whole. To be alone, to feel unwanted, required strength she couldn't find or didn't have.

She wanted to say how she regretted having chosen to stay with her husband, that mistakes happened in a family. Maegan had refused to live with her and Dixson and chose to stay with Pearl. Now Audrey wondered how she could have ever imagined that Maegan would want to live with her in a home with Dixson. An attempted rape is more than a mistake.

Audrey replied through the emotional wounds hanging in the air between them, "No, I'm not changing my mind."

The telephone on the bedside table rang. Maegan answered. She covered the receiver with her hand and looked at Audrey. "It's Roger. He wants to know if we're coming up."

"I don't think so," Audrey began.

"We just thought . . ." Pearl paused. "We thought you might want to, even if it's just for a few minutes."

Audrey knew in her heart the meeting would happen. But why hurry? In the morning they'd all be clear-headed. She'd have time to gather the words she'd rehearsed over and over through the years in case she ever did see Roger again. What he'd done to her. She'd have her satisfaction.

Maegan, Pearl, and Roger were pushing for the meeting. *But what about me?* She was tired, aching, the night's events jamming in on her. *Let him wait. I've waited thirty years.* But the desire to see the man she'd loved unconditionally, who'd fathered her child, grew stronger, mixing with a strange combination of dread, curiosity, and desire.

The urge overwhelmed her. "All right, but only for a moment," she finally replied.

"We'll be up in a few minutes," Maegan said and hung up.

Audrey returned to the bathroom. With care in each movement, she put on a bra and panties, clean, loose cotton slacks, and a blue tee from her bag. Lipstick. Flip-flops. Her hair, at least, was clean. She looked at herself in the full-length mirror on the back of the bathroom door.

This wasn't the way she'd envisioned a meeting with Roger. Pulled from a drunken, doper husband. Covered in battle scars. Twenty pounds overweight. Numb to life. Her very soul locked in a box with guilt, shame and hurt. An angry daughter who couldn't stand her. Audrey wished she could lie down and bury herself under warm blankets. But the night wasn't over. Along with an increasing unease about seeing this man, her nerves also tingled with a hint of anticipation and excitement. She opened the bathroom door.

"One thing before we go," Audrey said. "You told me Roger was in a wheelchair."

An image flashed in Audrey's mind of the strong, young man, twisting and turning as they danced at Zelda's Night Club so long ago.

"What happened to him?" she asked.

Pearl started to reply but Maegan held up her hand. "Let's get our things and go. Let him tell you."

The three made their way down the hall to the elevator. Audrey's heart rate increased. What would he be like? What would they say to each other? What happened to him? What would he think of what happened to her?

The elevator door opened on the penthouse floor, and there stood Hector. He smiled kindly at Audrey. The three women stepped into the small vestibule, the door to the executive suite ahead of them. Hector knocked once, opened the door, and stood aside. Maegan led the way into the room. Pearl cleared her throat and went in next. They moved aside. Audrey entered.

No one spoke.

Before her sat the man who had abandoned her. Audrey took him in slowly. He had the same full head of hair, now grayed, framing the lines on his once-youthful face. The same eager eyes brought a catch in her throat, even though dark pouches now circled beneath them. She took in his muscular upper body, the motionless, angular knees, and the withered legs beneath his slacks.

After thirty years, neither she nor Roger could hide their physical wounds. They were visible to everyone. Was he as wounded inside as she? Her remorse for what could have been collided with her actual life, battling the feelings for him she'd never lost.

She brushed at her forehead as if to cover her black eye and bruised cheek. Her fingertips slid down her face to her neck to her breast. A moment of tenderness slid away. Her body stiffened.

"Audrey." Roger's soft voice rippled through the room. There were no other sounds.

Fifty-Five

Roger Hemmings

May 2008—Palm Springs, California

Roger's breath seized in his throat as Audrey entered the room. She stood motionless. For an instant, time traveled to a long-ago spring break, when he nonchalantly walked into a souvenir shop and saw her for the first time. Just as rapidly, the urgency of the moment pushed aside the image, and a kaleidoscope of memories flooded his mind.

Time reverted to the present, solid and real. Bruises on Audrey's face and the nervous twitching of her fingers jumped to the foreground. His neck flushed in the awkward silence, aided by the steely look on her face.

"It's good to see you," he said, his voice soft and raspy. He swallowed; his mouth suddenly dry. "I have so many things to say."

Audrey's eyes—one slightly swollen—glinted in the light cast by a table lamp beside the couch. Her body stiffened. For a moment, the air taut between them, he thought she might turn and leave. They had to talk tonight, or he might never have another chance. They had to be alone.

Before he could speak, Pearl said to Audrey, "Honey, we'll only stay a minute or two. When you're ready, I'm sure Hector won't mind bringing you back to our room."

"You don't have to go at all. This won't take long," Audrey said, a sharp edge in her voice.

Roger's chest tightened. "Audrey, I hope you'll hear me out."

Her eyes roamed over his face. His body. The chair. Back to his eyes. The room seemed to close in around him, pushing him deeper into the wheelchair.

Audrey punched her words. "As I said, this won't take long. It's almost three in the morning."

"Then, may we have a few moments?" Roger said, looking from Pearl to Maegan to Hector. The three stood transfixed, knowing they should go but not quite able to leave, knowing they were witnesses to a meeting thirty years in the making.

Hector cleared his throat, nodded, and excused himself, discreetly retreating to his room. Pearl and Maegan said their goodnights. Maegan's voice seemed to catch in her throat.

And then Roger and Audrey were alone.

As the door closed, her words erupted into the room, cutting into him. "I waited for your call. It never came. I waited for you. You never came. Then you tried to buy us off with your money." The harshness in her voice cracked. Little rivulets of tears found their way down her cheeks. She clasped her arms around her body, hugging herself. "All I ever wanted was . . ."

"Audrey, I . . ."

"I needed you! Maegan needed you." She fumbled in her pocket, pulling out a tissue. "Nothing but problems. Being a mother. Raising a child. Trying to have a life. I hate you!" She covered her face with her hands. "I was nothing but a stupid kid to think you loved me."

Each sob stabbed him, his own eyes moistening.

"I have no excuses," he whispered. "Please, please sit down so we can talk."

"I'm just about done talking." Audrey wiped her eyes, her nose. "Do you know what it feels like to live your life numb?"

He nodded. "In a way."

"You're the lowest snake in the desert!"

The venom in her voice cut deep. He rubbed his useless knees. "I have no excuses. When I became paralyzed, everything changed."

"Well, poor you!" Her hand flew to her chest. "I was paralyzed, too. You crippled me."

Each accusation scraped across his mind, leaving welts.

"Well?" she demanded. "Are you going to tell me? No one else would. How did you get in that wheelchair?"

"I was shot," he said softly. "During a robbery."

"Shot?" Audrey's face couldn't hide her surprise. "When I saw you, I thought you were sick or something."

"Please, won't you sit?" he begged.

"For a minute. I'm not staying very long." She lowered herself onto the couch.

He moved his chair closer to her, his elbows on the armrests, and began to talk. Slowly, he told her about the shooting at the convenience mart. About the injury to his spinal cord. That he was lucky the damage hadn't been worse, that he hadn't been totally paralyzed.

"When did that happen?" she asked.

His voice became a whisper. "The day after I left Palm Springs. And you."

Her hand flew to her lips, her eyes on his. "My God, that's why you never called?"

"Audrey, I was a scared kid, full of self-pity. I rejected myself, and I was certain you'd reject me, too. My parents discouraged my reaching out to you. I couldn't find the courage to risk a phone call to you. But because I talked so much about you, my father hired a private investigator."

"You spied on me?"

He hurried on. "When we learned about the baby, I insisted on a special bank account. My father agreed—on one condition. You and I could never have any contact."

Audrey leaned back on the couch, unable to control her tears. "Couldn't *someone* have called me?" She wiped her eyes. "I guess I wasn't good enough for your family."

"I wasn't supposed to fall in love on spring break."

"Love?" she murmured. "That's what it was? Not just a fling?"

"Yes," he said. "I was a determined kid. I knew what I wanted even then and that was *you*."

"I don't know what to believe anymore." She turned her head away. "I decided you were just a spoiled rich kid. You went home, found a pretty college girl, and had a life. After ruining mine. My mother made me take the money—for the baby." She studied the back of her hand, palm pressed into the couch cushion. "I don't know what I would have done back then, learning you were in a wheelchair and all. But you should have told me. Someone should have told me."

"I am so sorry." He didn't tell her the number of times he'd reached for the phone. How he'd wanted to hear her voice. But the decision had been made. Since he couldn't be there as a whole person, the money could.

"Roger, for thirty years, I've believed you to be a liar and that you never loved me."

"I hope you know neither is true." He wished he could sit beside her, take her in his arms. "I thought you'd be better off without me."

Audrey rose, walked past him, and stood looking through the balcony slider at the intermittent lights of a sleeping Palm Springs. He turned his wheelchair toward her. She kept her back to him.

"After a while," she said, "I thought I'd be okay. I met Dixson Dupre. He was good looking and nice. Divorced. A good job. Two little boys. Not every guy I met, especially if he already had kids, was ready to take on a woman with a little girl. We got married."

He wanted to ask why she'd stayed with a man who abused her, but he said, "What happened?"

"He played minor league ball. Scouts had their eyes on him. One night, he was in a terrible collision at home plate. It destroyed his knee. Left him with a limp and no future in baseball." She placed her forearm on the window, leaned her head against it. "After that, job problems. Money problems. He looked for easy ways—gambling, stealing, drugs. And always trying to get at Maegan's special bank account."

"Did he lay his hands on any of it?"

"No. My mother saw to that." She turned from the window. "Dixson tried to rape Maegan."

He opened his mouth to speak, but Audrey put up her hand. A stop sign.

"That's when I made a terrible choice, too." She shook her head. "I stayed with Dixson. Thought I loved him. That he could be 'fixed.' Rehabilitated. That everyone could forgive and forget. And we'd all be a family again."

He moved his wheelchair closer, reached for her hand.

Audrey pulled away. "And, truthfully, I stayed because I thought no man out there would be interested in me and my baggage."

"I was always interested."

She gave him a small smile and returned to the couch. "In my delusion, I wanted Maegan to have a father. Every girl should have a father."

The word bored into him. *Father.* His heart beat like a tympani in his chest. He exhaled from deep within his lungs. "I think we could both use a drink."

She rubbed her forehead with her fingertips. "Sure."

He turned himself toward the bar, the wheelchair's whir the only sound in the room. Light reflected from the glasses. From the bottles. Maker's Mark, Blue Sapphire. He selected a bottle of Booker's and poured them each a drink.

"Ice?"

She nodded. The cubes plinked into the glasses.

With both glasses held in one hand, flicking the switch on his chair with the other, he returned to Audrey and gave her the drink. He held up his glass.

"To what?" he asked. "The future?"

She hesitated and then shrugged. "The future?" She brought her glass to his with a soft click. "Sure. Why not."

They each took their time. One sip. Another. A balloon that had filled up with regret for thirty years, that seemed about to burst, slowly released pressure with each word. Could they find a way?

She gently swirled the liquor in her glass. "Now that I know, thank you for the money. It gave Maegan a chance in life."

"Money was a poor substitute for a husband and father." Regret hung on his words.

"Yes, it was." She agreed, her sigh pushing into the weighted air hanging heavily in the room. "I felt abandoned when I never heard from you again. Then I cast that same hurt on my daughter by staying with Dixson." She finished her drink. "All I ever wanted was my family around me."

Roger took a final swallow of bourbon and cleared his throat. "In a way, you know, we're lucky."

"Lucky?" She set her glass on the coffee table and leaned back, looking at him, her eyebrows arched. "How can you say we're 'lucky'?"

"Think about it." He inched his wheelchair forward. "I know we can't 'do over' the lost years. But we have a daughter. We can start from now, this moment. Be a part of each other's lives."

Audrey turned away. "Everything's too broken."

"I don't think so," he said quickly.

Audrey turned back to him. "Look, Roger, Maegan has shut me out of her life." She paused. "And, quite honestly, I don't know if I want you back in mine. Whatever we thought we had, we were kids. And now we're strangers. With a lot of years of unhappiness between us." She stood. "I'd better go."

"Audrey, I believe, for whatever reason, we've been given an opportunity."

She walked toward the door. The wheelchair purred across the carpeted floor as he followed her. He caught her hand. "Think about it. Please."

For a moment she looked at him, didn't pull away. "I'm just too tired now."

He couldn't tell if she'd cocked her head, shaken it, or nodded, the movement was so slight.

"Please think about what I said." He squeezed her hand and called to Hector.

She murmured, "Good night," as Hector stepped out of his room.

The penthouse door closed behind them as Hector saw Audrey to her room. Roger turned his wheelchair to the expanse of windows and moved toward the dim light. The sky glowed in the distance behind the hazy mountains of the eastern valley, the sun preparing to make its entrance. But the coming brightness of a new day eluded him. His shoulders heaved as he lowered his face to his hands and sobbed.

Chapter Fifty-Six

Pearl Spence

May 2008—Palm Springs, California

I hoped Audrey and Roger were havin' a good talk. My poor girl'd been through the quagmires that night. Made me realize somethin' about her that musta been there all along. The girl was tough. She'd been beaten down by that no-good Dixson, then bitten by the "stubborn" bug, and vaccinated with a good dose of pride. But gumption from somewhere made her make that telephone call to Maegan. Get herself out of that mess. Go up to see Roger, stay and talk to him. She still carried a hint of a spark inside her. Made me kinda happy.

While we waited in our room, Maegan didn't say much. Musta been quite a shock to meet her real father. Then to start talkin' to her mother again after so many years. On top of that, to see her parents together after they hadn't seen or heard from each other for thirty years.

I know I was near bustin'. Couldn't stay quiet.

"Wonder what they're sayin' to each other," I ventured. I sat at the little table in a straight back chair, cushy-soft chairs too hard to get out of.

"If they're saying anything," she answered. She had the TV on, no sound. Some movie, in color it was, somethin' with a man dancin' around in the rain.

"Maegan, honey, could you turn off the TV? Nobody's dancin' here." Then I tiptoed into prickly territory. "I'd like to talk a little."

She looked at the remote restin' in her hand and slightly moved her thumb onto a button. The TV clicked off. "What, Gramma?"

"How are you doin' with all of this? One part of your family fallin' away—guess you could call that the bad part. Another part maybe comin' together." I held my breath, hopin' I could talk with my granddaughter's sweet side and not her lawyer side. That side could be all business and cold to the touch, or kinda smug and flip. When she'd come visit from Los Angeles, I'd hear her on her cell phone, talkin' tough turkey to some poor soul.

She stood and resettled herself on the couch, one knee tucked under her. "Oh, Gramma, I don't know." A shrug of her shoulder.

I heaved a sigh inside. At least she hadn't shut the door on talk. I pursed my lips. This was a time to just listen. Maybe.

Maegan put her hand on her thigh, studied her fingers. "Some things I do know. Neville is dead. I hate Dixson." She moved her hand toward her hair, wrapped a strand of auburn around her finger like when she was five. Reminded me of the time she told me a boy in kindergarten had pulled her hair. "But with Audrey and Roger? I'm not sure I'm the forgiving type."

My old gut clenched a little. I put my hands in my lap. But she went on quiet-like.

"Winston and I have always been close. I promised I'd help him with his music career if I could, and I'll make good on that. Introduce him to the right people if I can."

"He's a good boy," I added. "Don't know how he turned out so good with that brother and father of his." It got quiet between us. Then she ran right into what I was thinkin'.

"Gramma, I know you want to know about Audrey and me."

Sure would have been nice if she could say *Mother*.

"I know that's been hurtful to you," she went on. "It's not pleasant in any family when a mother and daughter grow apart."

I was amazed at how calm she was bein'. Usually, she just flared all over the place when the subject of her and Audrey come up. I stayed mum.

"I still feel betrayed," she continued. "I've tried to be objective, understand her side. But every time I see her, even if I think I might be able to be civil, an emotional dam breaks."

She stiffened. Neither of us spoke. She straightened her legs out along the seat cushions, scooted down, and settled her head on the arm of the couch. Then her eyes closed. Guessed that was the end of the conversation, so I decided to get myself ready for bed. Least I knew she was tryin' to find a path, even if it kept twistin' on her.

My comfortable old nightie felt good after bein' dressed all the long day. I got between the sheets and pulled up the light covers. As I wondered how Audrey and Roger was doin', I felt my eyes start to slip shut. Maybe just doze a little.

Next thing I know, I'm swimmin' up through a tunnel of sleep to hear the low murmur of voices. For a minute, I didn't know where I was or who was talkin'. Then I realized I was in the hotel room, and it was Maegan and Audrey talkin'. I kept my eyes closed, but my ears was wide open.

"Audrey," Maegan was saying in a half-whisper, "take my bed. I'll sleep on the couch."

"Are you sure? I'm so tired my insides are collapsing."

They rustled around with clothes, goin' in and out of the bathroom. Then I heard the lights click off. First the bathroom light. Then the lamp by the couch. I peeked. Audrey was in the other queen bed. Maegan lay on the sofa, covered with an extra blanket from the closet.

Audrey spoke in the darkness. "I know I'm repeating myself but thank you for coming to get me. I made a terrible mistake."

Maegan stayed quiet, then said, "Pearl insisted."

There was that hard side of Maegan. *Oh,* I thought, *please soften, even if it's just a little.*

"I've always loved you," Audrey added. Silence. "Good night, honey," Audrey murmured. Her voice had a catch in it.

"Good night, Audrey."

Maegan just couldn't say that word *Mother.* At least they was talkin'. I opened my eyes. I could see daylight through the crack in the drapes, but I wasn't gettin' up yet.

Chapter Fifty-Seven

Maegan Spence

May 2008—Palm Springs, California

Maegan's back muscles cramped. She turned onto her side. The cushions on the hotel sofa resembled an old, lumpy mattress. A ridge here. A hollow there. With a groan, she kicked the blanket aside and glanced over at the two queen beds. On one, Pearl snored lightly, with an occasional mumble, the blanket pulled up under her chin. Audrey lay curled on her side on the other bed, covers pushed away in a jumbled mound, pajama bottom twisted around her legs. The soft light seeping in around the edges of the drapes helped Maegan see the time on her watch. A few minutes past seven.

She hadn't noted the time when her mother had returned from Roger's room. The two must have talked quite a while. She wondered what had made Audrey stay. Anger? A chance to have her say? Curiosity? Finally finding answers to a lifetime of questions?

Maegan gave up on sleep and slipped from the makeshift bed. Too many thoughts about Roger. Audrey. Pearl. Winston. In the semi-dark, she fumbled through her suitcase and pulled out a pink shell, socks, and black crop pants. She dressed and sat on the couch to put on her running shoes. She needed some alone time, some think time.

Pearl's whisper surprised her. "Where're you goin'?"

She should have known Pearl would wake at the least little movement. "The exercise room. Won't be long."

"You ain't had much sleep."

Maegan walked over to her grandmother's bed, patted Pearl's hip, a curve beneath the covers, and said, "I'll be okay."

She left the room, keycard in hand, and took the elevator down to the second floor. The elevator doors opened to an empty hall. A sign on the opposite wall had the words "Exercise Room" on it with an arrow pointing to the right. She followed the arrow. At the workout room door, she slid the card in the slot and the green light flashed, allowing her to enter.

The place held fitness machines, weights, a stair stepper, and a treadmill. Maegan stepped onto the treadmill, pressed "Start" and hit number two on the speed button. Moving her body felt good. She walked slowly to loosen up after the fretful night, then increased the pace to three. The incline button, set at zero, she pushed to two. Nothing strenuous. She just wanted to move, give herself some energy for the day.

Thoughts whirred and circled in her head like a roller-derby marathon. Her father's bad luck—and a decision he wished he could undo. Her mother's unhappy life—and a choice she wished she'd never made. Maegan wondered about her own future, the pivotal decisions she now faced. She had to choose carefully, or end up the same as her parents, living a life filled with regret.

She notched up the treadmill's speed. With a sudden urge, she punched the button again. Her feet moved faster. And faster. The sound of her footfalls thumped in the room. She wanted to run away—from everyone. Perspiration beaded in the small of her back and on her forehead. No matter how fast she ran, she couldn't outrun her edginess, her fear of what to do next. She'd brought Roger back into her life. Did she wish she hadn't? She'd brought Audrey back into her life. Did she wish she hadn't?

Each thought pressed for an answer. Options emerged from the emotional maelstrom.

Maegan's heart raced, her breath coming in gasps. She hit a button, and the treadmill began to slow. She pushed another button, the treadmill stopped. Her feet tingled from the pounding as she turned and stepped off the exercise machine. For a moment, she stared back at the black track, reminding her of the way her family's path had been blackened by stubbornness, pride, and bad luck.

Now what?

She could tell Roger and Audrey how she felt instead of carrying around her silent anger. Catharsis. Might it be good for her soul?

Or she could walk away. After Gramma Pearl's note, she'd found her father, and fate had brought her parents together. Enough baggage existed between them to last two lifetimes. Let them have it. She had her own life to live.

Or she could forget the past. Before her lay a chance at a relationship with both her father and mother. Was she ready? Could she accept them as they were? Accept herself? Just *accept*? Her chest tightened.

Goddammit. She jumped back on the treadmill and punched up the speed again. Her heart once more pounded along with her feet.

When her leg muscles began to burn and she felt she would burst, she slowed for a cool down, and then pressed stop. She stood—chest heaving, catching her breath—and stepped away from the treadmill, thankful to be alone in the room. On a counter near the door were stacks of white towels. She grabbed one, wiped her face and neck, and threw it in a container marked "Soiled Towels." A floor-length mirror, hanging on the wall next to the door, gave her pause. She faced it, assessing herself.

"Well, what are you going to do?" she asked her image. Her tone sounded odd, between a plea and a whine, neither of which she liked.

She knew Pearl would tell her, "Honey, having a father and mother is something you've wished for all your life."

She pulled a paper cup from the dispenser hanging on the water-cooler near the door and filled it. Her tongue tingled from the cold water. She drank the cup empty, then another. Maybe coffee would help, too. In the pocket of her crops, she always kept a ten-dollar bill. She left the exercise room behind and took the elevator down to the lobby, hoping to get some coffee at the kiosk. A long line of waiting coffee drinkers turned her away. A Starbuck's just down the street might be quicker.

She left the hotel, jogged past early morning pedestrians and the Blue Coyote nightclub and bar. In the bar window, a flyer advertised Win Spence and The Blasts. If she'd had her cell phone, she would have called Winston right then, even though he'd always told her, "Don't call me before noon." What would his advice be? She felt a pang of guilt. He'd been left with the arrangements for Neville's funeral.

Starbuck's bustled with people on the way to work, other joggers, and tourists getting an early start. She jumped in line, ordered, and, with a strong latte in hand, returned to the hotel. When she entered the room, she found Pearl sitting at the table by the windows. Fresh coffee brewed on the room's coffee maker, the aroma warm and comforting. Soft light from a floor lamp outlined her grandmother, who, wrapped in her melon-colored chenille robe, waited for her.

"Come sit with me," Pearl whispered. Audrey appeared to be asleep.

Maegan set her cup on the lamp table. "In a minute. I better hop in the shower," she murmured. "All sweaty." She took clothes from her suitcase, grabbed her coffee, and entered the bathroom.

In the shower, as water pulsed down on her, she thought about what Winston would say: "Do your own thing, sis. You gotta be true to yourself."

The problem was which "self." She had many from which to choose. The daughter self. The granddaughter self. The hurt, abandoned, betrayed self. The educated, objective self. She paused. A newborn self with a fresh beginning?

What was the rush? It took thirty years for her life to get to this point. She shut the water off only to hear the phone ringing. Was it Roger, wanting them all to come to his suite? Again? She stepped from the shower and grabbed a towel, drying herself slowly, wondering if she was ready for a day with her father. And mother. She wrapped the towel around her and leaned against the sink.

A sip of now-lukewarm latte slipped down her throat as the room phone stopped ringing. She heard Pearl say, "My Audrey needs some sleep. We'll be up in a while."

Chapter Fifty-Eight

Pearl Spence

May 2008—Palm Springs, California

Roger called that day for us to come up to his room for what turned
out to be lunch—or "brunch," as they call it. Audrey and me fussed
gettin' ready. I pulled out a flowered skirt and a long, white top made
of wrinkly, gauzy material, kinda clothes that hide an old lady's shape.
Put on my Eva Gabor wig. Noticed Audrey had brought nice, navy-blue
capris and a powder-blue top. She looked good, heavier than she used
to be, but her curves looked nice, not lumpy. She'd used make-up to
disguise her bruised cheek. Guess she'd had practice doin' that.

Maegan owned nice clothes. She had on a mint green sleeveless
top. Made her auburn hair and brown eyes stand out like they was
neon. Her white slacks ended just above the ankle. Looked like what
we used to call "high-water pants." Now they call them "ankle pants"
or some such. My daughter and granddaughter looked nice, and I felt
proud of them.

I also felt hungry. I ate when I was worried. 'Course, I ate when
I was happy, too. Didn't help the figure. I had mixed-up feelings that
day 'cause I just didn't know what was gonna happen. Maegan bein'

so independent and Audrey maybe tryin' to be. No, I'd say she was more like a deer standin' in the headlights, confused-like, frightened and maybe thinkin' on runnin', but not sure why, where, or if. And that Roger, wearin' his heart on his sleeve.

I was confused, too, about what everyone wanted from all this meetin' up. Maybe they all was just curious to see what everyone looked like and how each one had turned out. Maegan had been around her father a bit, learnin' about him. Audrey was double-whammied by meeting Roger and reconnecting with her angry daughter. I knew what I thought: everyone oughta try to come together, try to know each other, and try to understand each other. Maybe even be a family. After all, that's what we really was, no matter how you sliced the cabbage—a family. Sure would make me happy.

Maegan spoke up and broke into my heavy thinkin'. "Everyone ready?" she asked.

We left the room, Audrey brushin' at her capris, Maegan walkin' ahead. I couldn't tell what that girl was thinkin'. Couldn't get much out of her. She just wasn't talkin'. Poker face? Lawyer's face? Didn't know what to call it. The elevator droned us up to Roger's floor and then we was at his door. Maegan knocked and Hector answered, all smiles.

The room smelled like Pearl's Place used to at breakfast rush. Took me a minute to understand. A man in a white coat and cook's hat—guess they called it a "chef's hat"—stood behind a table covered with a white cloth. And on that table? Oh, my stars. An omelet pan on a hot plate, a dish of eggs, little dishes of tomatoes, mushrooms, green onions, shredded cheese, spinach leaves, chilies, peppers. A toaster. Jams and jellies. A pitcher of orange juice. A small coffee urn. Real nice. But how was we gonna talk? Maybe that was the point. We weren't gonna.

"What's all this?" Maegan asked, arms spread. She threw her purse on the couch.

"I thought we'd all enjoy a good brunch," Roger answered from his chair by the round hotel room table. "It is a celebration."

Audrey looked overcome. Don't imagine anyone waited on her in that doublewide. Me? I was ready to eat.

"Come on, Mrs. Spence, don't be shy." Roger held his hand toward a small stack of white plates. "Take a plate. Ernesto is ready to make you an omelet."

"Well, you know what?" Maegan stepped forward, hands on her hips. "I don't feel like it's old home week. I came here to talk. Making merry is a little contrived at this point and I don't like being manipulated."

"Oh, Maegan, it's all right," Audrey interjected. "We can talk afterward."

"No, it isn't all right," Maegan said, eyes flashing. She reached for her purse.

Roger looked like he'd been hit in the head with a ketchup bottle. "Maegan, I thought we were doing fine. We're all together, with time to get to know each other."

Oh, boy. I could see Maegan and her father both liked to be the boss. The acorn sure didn't plop on the ground far from that tree.

"How about we talk *and* eat," I said.

"No, Gramma, not today. I need to get back to Los Angeles." Maegan walked toward the door. "You know what, everyone? This is a little too much for me today, a little too fast." She paused. "Could Hector drive Pearl and Audrey back home to Beaumont Valley?"

Roger nodded, but added, "I wish you'd stay."

Maegan shook her head. She came over and gave me a kiss on the cheek. Whispered in my ear, nodded to everyone, and left.

The room grew cemetery quiet. Somethin' set Maegan off. I thought she was dealin' okay with her father and mother. But Audrey had another idea. She wiped her cheek with the back of her hand. "She's never going to accept me."

Ernesto didn't know what to do—cook or leave. Hector looked out the window. Roger had his hands on his knees, studyin' the rug. Audrey looked at me.

"Well, all I can say is you both know about livin' with years of wishin' things was different," I said. "Maegan just got sort of a double helpin'. A father she never had but wanted and is here. A mother she's had, but pushed away, and is back."

Roger and Audrey nodded, glanced at each other.

Made me wonder. Was Maegan's plate so full of bad feelin's she couldn't never put anythin' good in it? What a day. I picked up a plate and stood in front of Chef Ernesto. "Sad as I am, I'm gonna try myself a omelet. Calm myself down."

Hector joined me, then Audrey, and finally Roger. Bit of a sad-sack group. We talked, but not about what was heavy in our hearts. Maybe it was good just takin' the time to get a sense of each other. Trust builds real slow when the building blocks is damaged. I wished my Maegan had stayed. I didn't tell them what she'd whispered in my ear.

I tried, Gramma, but I just can't. It's too much for me.

Chapter Fifty-Nine

Maegan Spence

May 2008—Los Angeles, California

Maegan closed the door to Roger's room and stepped across the hall into the waiting elevator. Contacting her father and taking Audrey out of Dixson's hellhole had seemed right at the time. But now her father and mother existed in her life in real time, no longer remote beings to serve as mental punching bags.

Filled with resentment, she could only seem to confront and lash out. She was used to confrontation. She often represented difficult clients or interacted with opposing counsel. But taking on a father after thirty years and a mother for the first time in what was really fifteen years were not the same. Emotional connections clouded her judgment. With Neville's death and Winston's trauma, she felt like she'd sunk into a bog that was pulling her down fast. Her shoulders ached. Her eyes looked tired and dark as caves. She believed herself to be strong, but now she needed rest. And space. And time.

Once in her hotel room, Maegan tossed her things into her suitcase. She called the reception desk to explain she was leaving, but the room would be occupied a few more nights by a Pearl Spence.

"Just put the additional charges on my card," Maegan said.

After a moment of clicking computer keys, the young man replied, "The room is all paid up, Miss Spence, with arrangements for two more nights."

Maegan cleared her throat. "Can you tell me who paid it?"

"Yes, ma'am. Roger Hemmings. Said it was a family reunion."

Maegan hung up. The man was a control freak. This would be the first and last so-called reunion. She grabbed her things and glanced around the room. Her eyes assessed Audrey's belongings by the one bed and moved on. She felt a little pang, a wave of guilt seeing Gramma Pearl's robe on her bed, her old slippers nearby. She'd call Pearl when she returned to Los Angeles. Right now, she needed to get away.

She hurried to the elevator and pushed the button. The doors opened and she stepped into the enclosed, claustrophobic space. At the next floor, the elevator stopped for a couple with three small, wiggling children. They were from Iowa the man declared, in Palm Springs to enjoy the sun and visit the grandparents. Maegan smiled, knowing she'd ventured into a long winter with no thaw in sight, weather of her own choosing. She looked at the family with a tinge of sadness, her eyes moistening, and dug in her purse for her car keys.

On the drive from the hotel to the interstate, she barely noticed the change from high-end urban art galleries, restaurants, and shops to bleak, unforgiving desert, edged by brooding brown mountains and lowlands dotted with windmills. On I-10, she pushed the accelerator of her small BMW, racing to get back to her own life. Anger worked up her spine. First, at her father for acting so blithely, like nothing had happened. Then at her mother. Audrey hadn't left Dixson because she wanted to reunite with her daughter; she'd left to save her own hide.

Maegan gripped the steering wheel until her hands hurt. She glanced at her speed and checked her rearview mirror for the highway patrol. She was doing eighty-five miles per hour.

Transport trucks hogged the two slow lanes as she neared the San Bernardino Freeway. San Bernardino. She'd never forget her night there, rescuing Audrey. Before her thoughts went down that path, a green jumble of freeway signs appeared. She merged onto I-5 North, exited at Los Feliz Boulevard, and made a left onto Hillhurst—or was it Franklin? God, it felt good to be in her own territory where there'd be no more surprises. Powering down the windows, she was greeted with car noise, voices of children, and the sound of an ambulance. The city had planted trees along the avenue to soften the surroundings. But with cars lining the busy city street, making a parking spot hard to find, the trees seemed anticlimactic.

She drove slowly. A silver Jaguar sedan pulled away from the curb and she eased her car into the spot. Across the street the balcony and windows of her apartment beckoned.

Once inside her living room, the weight of the past hours slowly began to lift from her shoulders. She dropped her purse and bag on the couch, noticing dust on the coffee table, and opened the balcony slider, allowing dead, stale air inside the apartment to escape. She stood in the open doorway, feeling the sights and sounds of the neighborhood settle around her. A sense of renewed control over her life seemed to arrive with them. For the moment, she no longer felt like a disjointed marionette, with too many people trying to pull at her strings.

Roger's breakfast hadn't been on her menu and now hunger gnawed at her. She went to the kitchen, rummaged around in the cupboard and refrigerator, and found a half-loaf of bread, a jar of Skippy's Creamy and an open container of milk, still good according to the carton's date. With a peanut butter sandwich in one hand and a glass of milk in the other, she returned to the living room, shoved her bag onto the floor with her foot, and dropped down onto the couch with a heavy sigh.

God, what a few days had just passed. She took a bite of sandwich, chewing on it along with her thoughts. She finally had her answer. She now knew why Roger had stayed away, why he hadn't contacted her mother or sought to be her father. Maybe that was enough. Move on. End of story.

But was it really the end? She wished she felt more certain.

Her father and mother were knocking on the door of her life, and, truth be told, she didn't know whether to open it or not.

Roger seemed to think everything and everyone would just slide into place. *Voila!* Instant family. Father and daughter and mother united. True, Roger couldn't be blamed for the shooting. But after that? Throwing money he'd never miss into a special account for a daughter he'd chosen to never meet wasn't the answer. And now, trying to rush feelings she could not rush wasn't working either.

Audrey knew staying with Dixson had been a mistake. Had she finally realized how betrayed Maegan felt? The woman also had to make the decision whether to accept Roger or not. She also must have realized her daughter might or might not accept her back into her life.

Maegan swirled the cold milk in the glass, slowly raised it to her lips and swallowed. The glass felt cool in her hand, the milk soothing.

The issue with Audrey began to put a knot in her stomach. Her first instinct was to continue as before. Ignore her and what she had done. But this might be difficult to do, now that Audrey would be staying with Pearl, at least for the immediate future. Could she at least manage to be polite?

Maegan reflected on Roger's breakfast extravaganza. Her ability to be polite had disappeared with the first whiff of bacon.

She chomped on another bite of sandwich. The peanut butter clung to the roof of her mouth, like the thoughts clinging in her head. She chewed and washed it down with another swallow of milk.

Were Roger and Audrey actually such terrible people? Or was she the awful one? The unreasonable one?

She put her food on the coffee table, reached for her purse, and took out her cell phone. She scrolled to the name "Jennifer Bivens" and hit "call."

"Hello?" Jennifer said.

"Jennifer? This is Maegan."

"Hey, you're back." Jennifer paused. "Well, how did it go?"

"It was a real bitch, from start to finish."

"I'll be over as soon as I'm done here at work. About an hour?"

"Great," Maegan replied and dropped her cell phone on the couch.

Maegan busied herself putting her clothes and make-up away. Just as she closed the drawer in the bathroom vanity, her cell phone rang. She walked back to the living room, picked up her phone from the sofa and said, "Hello, this is Maegan."

"Just wanted to make sure you got home okay, honey," Pearl replied. "I'm worried about you."

"Don't be. I'm okay."

"Just know I love you."

"I know."

"Well, you probably got things to do. You take care." Pearl hung up. Never any judgment, always unconditional. God, she loved that old woman.

She left the apartment, keys in hand, and went down the stairs to pick up her mail, reminded of the day the card arrived for her thirtieth birthday. Sometimes she wished Pearl had never broken her silence, had never sent that card containing the note about Roger. But her grandmother couldn't be blamed for this mess. She'd badgered Gramma Pearl for years to talk about the boy Audrey had met at spring break so long ago.

The row of tarnished brass mailboxes stretched along one side of the entry hall. She opened her box, finding it stuffed with advertising flyers, bills, and catalogs. Back in her apartment, she tossed the mail on the coffee table, except for a J. Jill catalog. She slumped onto the couch, paging through pictures of the latest fashions. It was so good to do something normal, mundane.

A knock on the door interrupted the quiet. She opened it to find Jennifer holding a bottle of Moet and Chandon Champagne. "Well, is it a celebration or a wake?" her best friend asked.

"I'm not sure. I don't know if I'm mad at you or not."

"What did I do?" Jennifer said, eyebrows raised. She entered and placed the champagne on the coffee table.

"You called a damned private detective. I told you not to tell anyone."

"Wow, you came back in a real snit. I was worried about you, what might happen to endanger you." Jennifer put her purse on the coffee table next to the champagne. "Sorry. I couldn't help myself."

Maegan glared at Jennifer for a moment, then softened her hard look. "Oh, just sit down and listen. I'm more of a mess now than before I went to Palm Springs."

Maegan related each step of her trip, each meeting. Jennifer interrupted periodically with questions.

"Wow, a real baptism of fire," Jennifer said when Maegan had finished. "What are you going to do? I'm thinking of that adage, 'Be careful what you wish for.'"

"I don't know whether to continue or just cut everything off," Maegan said. "It got complicated real fast." She ran her index finger across the nap of the couch fabric causing a change of color from light green to dark. Then she took her palm and brushed it smooth again.

"You have to do what you think is right—for you." Jennifer studied her friend. "Dealing with people doesn't come with black and white answers. There're more shades of gray than you can count."

Maegan nodded. "I'm at a real crossroads."

Jennifer stood. "For once I'm not offering advice or answers. I'm with you whatever you do." She picked up her purse. "Since we don't know if we're celebrating or not, hang on to the bubbly. Do you want to go get something to eat or be alone?"

"I haven't called Jack yet. I'd better do that."

"I guess that means alone. Call me, girlfriend." Jennifer gave her a quick hug. "Put the bubbly in the fridge."

She saw her friend to the door, closed it, and leaned against its painted surface. Her thoughts turned to Jack. He was the only other person who knew about her struggle, her quest, besides Jennifer. *Jennifer.* Maegan walked the bottle of champagne to the refrigerator.

Jack. They seldom called each other anymore. The last break-up had seemed more final, unlike the others before it. She hadn't called him the entire time she was in Palm Springs. He knew why she'd gone. He saw things differently, wanting her to leave the past in the past. Walk away. Make a new life and memories. With him. Would that have been the wisest course?

Chapter Sixty

Maegan Spence

May 2008—Los Angeles, California

Maegan sat on the couch, staring straight ahead, trying to decide. Slowly, she picked up her cell phone from the lamp table beside the couch, scrolled through her contacts and placed the call. After three rings, voicemail picked up. "Jack here. Leave a message."

"Jack," she began. "This is Maegan. I just wanted . . ."

Before she could continue, his live voice interrupted. "Maegan?"

"I know you're probably busy and I know our last meeting was supposedly our last, but I have something to tell you."

"Okay" he said. "I'm listening."

"I've met my father."

After a pause, Jack said, "I sense there's plenty to tell. Should I come over after work? First, I need to finish up some papers for a case."

"Please."

Maegan disconnected and put her phone down, knowing her family had always been a delicate subject with Jack, often becoming the opening salvos for their quarrels. But she wanted him to know. It would be a small gloat because her tenacity had paid off. He'd always said it was a hopeless quest, that little of value would be accomplished after all these years, even if she found her father. The fence had been broken for too long.

Mostly it was the desire to share the events and revelations of the last few days in Palm Springs. Her obsession with her family had often affected their relationship and he had the right to know the outcome. Deep down, she wanted his thoughts.

And another reason knocked on her inner wall of feelings. Was her relationship with Jack meant to be over?

She busied herself doing her own case work remotely after being gone a few days from work, supposedly ill with "the flu." A return to normal routine after the onslaught of what happened in Palm Springs felt good. Her mind welcomed the structure, the use of rational thinking, the lack of emotional turmoil. At some point in the late afternoon, she showered and slipped on a tunic blouse and jeans.

Around seven o'clock, she heard a light rap on the door and opened it to find Jack holding a bottle of wine and a large pizza box, the aroma hitting her hard. Her only food all day had been a peanut butter sandwich. His brown eyes smiled.

"I know I haven't eaten yet. Thought we maybe could use this," he said and kissed her lightly on the cheek.

She enjoyed seeing his face, his dark unruly hair, his tallness hovering in the doorway; happy to feel his confident manner as her own floundered. She opened the door wider, and he came in, his presence filling the room like always. Neither spoke.

Jack placed the box on the coffee table and opened it, revealing a salami, cheese, and mushroom pizza. As he laid out the restaurant napkins in readiness and began to uncork the bottle, he asked, "Glasses?"

"Guess we need them." She laughed lightly and went into the kitchen. She returned with two stemmed wine glasses. This was a routine they'd often done before, when they were too tired to cook or go out, when there were no elephants in the room.

He poured wine for each of them. After they'd raised a glass to each other and taken a sip, Jack put his back down on the table. "Tell me what happened." He sat on the edge of the chair, picked up a piece of pizza, took a bite, his chewing slow, his eyes on her. He reached for a napkin. He continued to eat.

Maegan nodded, settling across from him on the couch and taking a slice. Buying time, she said, "I haven't eaten all day." After a few bites in silence, she placed the unfinished slice on a napkin, took a fresh napkin to wipe her mouth and hands. Jack followed suit.

Like old confidantes, she told Jack about Roger and the shooting, about Neville's bizarre death, about Audrey's abuse, about Dixson's arrest for domestic violence.

"Wow." Jack exhaled loudly, shaking his head. "You had quite a trip. And Pearl?"

"A rock, like always."

"With so many questions answered," Jack paused, then asked, "how do you feel about all of this? What comes next?" He sat back in the chair.

Maegan knew the conversation approached the crux of their differences. Now that she knew about her family, what *was* the next step? Would the obsession continue to consume her if she tried to build a relationship with her father? And address the relationship with her mother? Like an unwelcome incoming fog, tension settled between them.

"I'm not sure." She crumpled the napkin in her hand. "How do you feel about it, Jack?"

"How do I feel?" He clasped his hands in his lap. "You know I wanted you to leave the past in the past. I never felt our relationship was as strong as the strength of your quest. A hurdle we couldn't quite leap over. I didn't feel you were fully invested in, well, us."

Maegan took a deep breath, remaining silent for a moment. Finally, she said, "That's fair, and to be honest, I wasn't."

"And now," Jack continued, "with the building of this new relationship with your father, and if you decide to reconnect with your mother, we'll still have hurdles and a quest that probably will continue to consume you, just a different slant on the same old story."

"I wanted you to know what happened." Maegan paused, feeling the start of the same old friction. Before she could stop herself, she blurted, "I didn't call to discuss getting back together."

"Ah, okay, then." Jack cleared his throat. "I'm happy for you and glad you called."

They sat in silence, the pizza and wine unfinished. Stalemate.

Jack placed his hands on his knees. "I guess I'd better be going." He heaved a big sigh and stood. "I want to love you, Maegan. I *do* love you, but, like I've said before, there are always too many people in the room." He looked at her with sadness in his eyes. "I'll show myself out."

Chapter Sixty-One

Pearl Spence

September 2008—Beaumont Valley, California

Maegan left that last morning we was all together and drove back to Los Angeles. I called her, makin' sure she got home okay. After that, I never heard a word. She came whisker-close to gettin' to know Roger and bein' around Audrey again.

I wondered what she was doin'. I knew she had a boyfriend. Or used to, at least. Jack was his name. Maybe she was spendin' all her time with him. I only met him once when she come for a visit and brought him along. Seemed nice enough. Handsome, too. Or maybe she was with her girlfriend Jennifer. Or worse yet, workin' her heart out. I didn't know which. I called and left messages on that answering machine of hers.

Upset me terrible that Maegan didn't answer or call me back. I'd get mad at her, then worried. And I'd end up sad. First time I ever really fussed in my head like that toward her. Now seemed like I didn't have a granddaughter anymore, but I *did* have a daughter again. I talked to God. Explained how it would be nice to have both my girls together. He didn't answer, either. Maybe it wasn't meant to be—everyone together.

Well, what will be, will be, I guessed. Maybe it was just me playin' with old-fashioned ideas. People was more independent now, goin' all which ways.

Audrey moped around the house. Reminded me of when she was a teenager, waitin' for Roger to call. But after a bit, he began callin' every once-in-a-while, and the two of them would talk. Winston took to callin' and stoppin' by again. Him and Audrey was always close. She even helped at a couple of church potlucks. Kinda cheered her up. The new preacher seemed able to get her to talk and even get her to laugh.

But when Audrey and me talked about Maegan, my daughter hung her head. I knew she felt ashamed about goin' back to Dixson the way she had.

"Honey," I said, "you got to stop beatin' yourself up. We all make choices. We all make mistakes. All we can do is learn from them. I know you never stopped lovin' Maegan. We just got to keep prayin' she'll figure things out for herself. And you got to get on with the life you still got, no matter what." We kept talkin' every day. I kept tryin' to build her up. Get her goin' again.

One morning she come out of her room lookin' real nice. Brown slacks and sandals. Aqua blouse, all starched and ironed.

"I'm going to Walmart," she said, "to apply for a job."

And away she went in the car. Made me feel so good. And she got a job, stockin' shelves while she trained to be a checker.

Life had become like a kid's trampoline. Up and down. Up and down. Audrey found—up I went. Maegan lost—down I went. My old knees ached along with my heart. Roger and me talked every now and then. He hadn't heard from Maegan neither and hadn't been able to reach her. We both prayed time might help; just give her time. But time was something I didn't have a lot of. I was an old lady.

I remember seein' a card at Walmart. Showed a beautiful butterfly flyin' off into the sky, its wings sheer like fine silk stockings. Inside, words said somethin' like, "If you chase after it, it'll fly farther away. But if you don't go lookin' for it or fussin' after it, it'll come and sit on your shoulder." Did that really happen, or was it just a pretty thought? Maybe Maegan was our butterfly. Our shoulders was waitin'.

One good thing happened pretty quick. That Dixson? Let me tell you, he got a good kick in the pants. Not only was the no-good found guilty of beating my Audrey, but they also got him for drugs. Usin' *and* sellin'. The officers found a plastic wrapper filled with cocaine in the doublewide, stuffed in a shoebox of all things. He's gonna have free room and board at the Chino Men's Prison again or wherever they send him.

That man was out of our lives for good. Now I needed to get Maegan back. And I did ever so slow. It began with phone calls she finally answered. Then she started callin' me once in a while like she used to. An occasional quick visit. I let her talk about whatever she wanted.

I know from all my years on earth that people don't change fast if they're gonna change at all. Takes time to make changes. And the time passed.

Chapter Sixty-Two

Audrey Spence

September 2009—Beaumont Valley, California

Audrey hung up Pearl's landline with a dull click after the early morning call. Streaming through the kitchen window, sunlight shone on the receiver's blackness, making it ebony-like and precious. Her fingertips brushed over the sleek surface. As she leaned her hip against the worn, Formica-topped counter in Pearl's kitchen, she realized how much Roger's calls meant to her after he'd returned to Arizona. She thought after a month or two he'd lose interest in what she had to say, their lives farther apart than the North and South Poles. Whatever spirit guided him, he called once a week like he said he would. And the time passed.

The memory of waiting by the phone so many years ago slipped into her mind and for a moment hung heavy weights in her chest. She pushed away from the counter. Each time Roger's call ended, after the emotional high ebbed away into low tide, a faint sadness would drift into her mind, a foreboding he might not call again. She hugged herself, rubbing her upper arms, looking out into the backyard, knowing the hard-won answer. If he didn't call, it would make her sad, but it wouldn't be the end of the world, not this time. She'd survived both Roger and Dixson. It hadn't been easy. If only her daughter . . .

Pearl called from the front room. "Come see Regis and Kelly on the TV. They got Tom Selleck on. My, my, what a nice-lookin' man. And he's no kid neither."

Audrey took the few steps into the small living room where her mother, in flowered housedress and scuffed slippers, rested in a La-Z-Boy recliner watching her favorite morning talk show. She perched on the edge of the couch near Pearl, hands clasped around her knees.

"Remember how we used to watch *Magnum P.I.*?" Audrey smiled at her mother.

Pearl nodded. "Sure do."

For a moment, they were just another mother and daughter safely cocooned with a TV and each other in a small living room. A carefree Monday morning. That was the problem. It was Monday. Pressure built inside Audrey, knit across her shoulders, purled along from nerve to nerve. She had Mondays and Tuesdays off, her supposed weekend, with errands to run, the week's grocery shopping to do. The car needed an oil change. She sighed. Her mother only asked for a few moments of her time. She tamped down the floodwaters of stress and made herself sit with her mother.

Audrey chewed her lower lip as Regis Philbin spun a big prize wheel for a viewer waiting by the phone somewhere in Baltimore. The wheel slowed to a stop, its arrow pointing to a trip to Antigua. Pearl clapped along with the audience.

"We shoulda sent in some postcards with our telephone number," Pearl said. "Never have done that. Maybe could have won us a trip."

Pearl's words made Audrey wonder: Did her mother have any regrets? Not the everyday stuff, like not sending postcards to a talk show. Real big-time regrets. Like Roger's. Like hers. She'd never asked, and her mother had never confided in her. She knew Pearl's favorite saying: "Just keep puttin' one foot in front of the other." And Pearl had. Regrets or no. All these years. She'd never had a meltdown.

Put one foot in front of the other. Audrey realized how much she'd been wallowing in self-pity all these years. It's hard to love someone doing that, someone like her, but Pearl had never stopped. She felt an overwhelming desire to do something special for her mother. To give instead of always taking. The hint of an idea nudged into her head. She unclasped her hands, put her feet firmly on the floor, and stood. Pearl's birthday was in October. She'd make it a big one. "Mom, sorry, but I have to go now. I'll be gone a couple of hours."

Kissing her mother on the forehead, she returned to the kitchen, and, about to pick up her purse and car keys, stopped. The plan, which had blossomed in her head like a fresh-cut bouquet, began to open. A birthday party. Cake. Ice cream. Would Roger come? His parents? No, wait. He'd said his mother had died a few years ago. What about his father? He must be curious after all these years. About Maegan. About his only granddaughter. Who else? Hector of course. Winston. Did he have a steady girl? She didn't even know. A few girls she cashiered with. The Ladies' Auxiliary from Pearl's church. The pastor. She stopped. *And Maegan?* Would she come? Even Pearl seldom heard from her like she used to. *I know Maegan can't stand to be in the same room with me. But she wouldn't miss her grandmother's birthday party, would she?*

Audrey took the calendar from its wall hook and turned to October. The seventeenth fell on a Saturday. The party could be on

Sunday afternoon. She'd switch with another cashier to get the day off. A potluck. The church ladies loved to show off their cooking. Dessert. Decorations from Walmart. Paper plates, napkins, cups. She'd save money with her discount. Roger would have to be the one to invite his father. He was a widower, possibly close to Pearl's age. Audrey's final thought. She'd leave a message on Maegan's answering machine and hope for the best.

The sore feeling in her back and legs disappeared like an eclipsed moon. She jotted a list of the items she would need, grabbed her purse and car keys, and called another goodbye to Pearl. How happy she felt, making plans.

Chapter Sixty-Three

Pearl Spence

October 2009—Beaumont Valley, California

The air is movin' around a little and pushin' coolness onto the porch. Feels real good. Nice when a little breeze visits in the late afternoon and stays while the sun is goin' to bed. Best time to sit outside.

Still lots of commotion. People talkin' and carryin' on in the house and out in the yard. That Audrey. Got this whole birthday thing for me together. Sure pleases me plenty, but can't say the birthday party was a surprise like it was supposed to be. Overheard Lydia Folsom askin' the head of the Ladies' Auxiliary about bringin' a three-bean salad to Pearl's party. My ears got real long but I didn't let on I heard 'em. Did set me wonderin' though. Didn't take me long to put party and birthday together.

Winston and his girl, a tiny little thing, stand out under the front-yard elm by the old swing, holdin' hands, talkin' close. Understand she works at the Hyatt Hotel, near where Winston and his band play.

Audrey bustles about like she's queen of the world. Good to see. Some of her friends from Walmart come over, too. And a lot of people from the church. Been a member for years. We kinda grew old together. Even that miserable Edna Smythe—who thought I stole money from the bake sale years ago—is here. Guess you forget and forgive, like they say. Pastor and his wife sure do like the cake. And Roger gets around, talkin' to everyone, introducin' himself. His wheelchair don't seem to get in the way. Hector knows when to be close to help him and when to hang back. Every now and then, I see Roger and Audrey pass each other, say somethin', and laugh.

Only one thing makes me sad. Maegan didn't come. Audrey said she'd called. Said she'd tried. But it's kinda late now on a Sunday to be comin' from Los Angeles. Audrey even told her that her grandfather, Roger Hemmings, Senior, might be here. Thought that would make the girl want to come. You know, curiosity and the cat. But I guess it didn't work.

RJ, Roger's father, is sittin' right here on the porch with me. In the other rocker. Two old coots we are, gabbin' all afternoon until time to eat. Then me openin' presents. Then cake and ice cream. Wonder if the man's still hungry? Audrey heaped his dessert plate with chocolate cake and strawberry ice cream, and he's been busy at it.

"Get enough to eat?" I ask. I already set my paper plate on the little table between us.

"Stuffed," RJ says, swallowing the last bit of cake and setting his plate on the table, too, over mine. He leans back in the rocker and sighs, the way a man with a full stomach sittin' in a comfortable chair will do.

R. J. Hemmings. Roger Joseph. Tall man, thick gray hair, eyes that can dance or bore a hole right through you. Wouldn't like to cross him. Keeps a gray beard, trimmed up nice and clean. Seems to me it would be awful hot to wear somethin' like that over there in Phoenix or here in California, but I guess he thinks it makes him look distinguished.

Nice hands. I can tell he never worked outside or fixed a truck engine like my Hank did. I know he's rich. But he seems nice.

"Hope I didn't wear out your ears, tellin' you all about my family." I rubbed my right forearm, then glanced over at him. "Actually, it's your family, too."

He'd wanted to know about us, what had happened through the years, so I'd told him, from beginning to end. Things you thought you forgot pop right up when you start diggin' in your head. Maybe, too, it's like they say: The older you get, the further back you remember, but you don't know what you did yesterday. I thought his ears might fall off, listening to me all day.

"I'm happy to know," RJ said. "I was protecting my only child. My son. All I could think about? How his life changed in an instant. I didn't have room for thoughts about anyone else. I'm sorry, Pearl. I—*we*—could have helped much more. My advice to my son was selfish and short-sighted." He slowly runs his palms back and forth on the armrests of the rocker.

I feel the hackles rise on my neck. "We done just fine."

"Yes, you did. I admire you." He looks out at the street, into the night. "I guess I'll miss meeting Maegan, my only grandchild." His voice sounds a little raspy. "Something must have come up, she couldn't be here."

Audrey comes by and asks if we want anythin', then goes back in the house just as an expensive-lookin' white car pulls into the driveway behind Roger's big GMC. The headlights go off, the driver's side door opens, and there she is. Maegan. I thought that Jack person might be with her. She carries a present. Package looks too small for a new robe, which I could use. I push myself to my feet, kinda bent over, and slowly stand up. So does RJ.

"Hi, Gramma," she says like we just talked yesterday. She comes up the steps, gives me a hug and a kiss on the cheek. "Happy Birthday."

She glances at RJ., then pushes the box toward me. I take it.

"You make me a happy old lady, comin' and all," I say and shake the box by my ear. Somethin' inside rattles. But somethin' else is more important. "I want you to meet your grandpa, R.J. Hemmings."

Maegan takes a quick breath and studies the man. No one says nothin'. Then she says, "My father has your eyes."

"And I see his eyes in yours." He takes her hand and grasps it between his. "I understand you've become a successful attorney."

"I'm trying," she says, withdrawing her hand, looking around, a little flustered. "Gramma, when are you going to open your present?"

"Right now," I say. I untie the bow and peel away the yellow flowered paper. I hand them to Maegan. Inside's a small gift box. When I take off the lid, I see a little blue jeweler's case. I slip it out of the gift box into my hand. Maegan takes the box. I open the blue-hinged lid to find a gold heart on a chain.

"Oh, honey," I say. "That's just real pretty." I hold it up for R.J. to see.

Before I can say more, Audrey appears in the doorway, but she don't come no closer. She sees there's a gift. I hope it don't light the jealousy fires. I know with me helpin' to raise Maegan, it was hard on Audrey at times. I slip the necklace back into its case and put it in my dress pocket. I'll show it to her later.

"Hello, Audrey," Maegan says. "It took me a long time to decide. To come."

Maegan could have gone all day and not said that. I hold my breath in case Audrey says somethin' snippy or pouty. But she don't.

She clasps her hands together. For a moment she just stands there, takin' in the bulge in my dress pocket, the wrappin' paper. But then she smiles—a real smile—with real happy eyes. "I'm glad you're here. Can I fix you a plate?"

"All right," Maegan says, then adds like she just remembered her manners, "Yes. Thank you."

Audrey disappears into the house. Good. My girls will have to take it slow, real slow. Otherwise, things'll burst like one of them balloon decorations in the house that Edna Smythe backed into. Scared the livin' daylights out of her.

Maegan leans against the wood railing, talking about all the cars on the freeway. Moments later Hector helps Roger get his chair out onto the porch. Roger holds a paper plate full of potato salad, fried chicken, and coleslaw. Audrey is right behind him and stops in the doorway, still a real happy look on her face. She's not pastin' on any fakeness. I'm proud of her.

"This is for you," Roger says to Maegan. "You must be hungry after that long drive."

Maegan nods, takes the plate and plastic fork and leans against the railing. Winston walks his girl up the porch steps and gives Maegan a one-armed hug.

I feel the tight air loosen around me, like a rubber band losin' its snap. Or maybe all the tightness was inside me. We're all here. It's up to them now. Sure do wish my Hank coulda been here to see every-body all together.

Chapter Sixty Four

Maegan Spence

October 2009—Beaumont Valley, California

Maegan looked from Audrey to Roger. To RJ., to Pearl, to Winston. The bittersweet day was not lost on her. This was it, what she'd wanted as long as she could remember. She had a father if she wanted. She had a mother if she wanted. And a brother. She always had her grandmother, and now even a grandfather if she wanted. When she'd called Jack to tell him about the party and asked him to come and meet the family that had been "the too many people in the room between them," he'd said it was probably best for her to absorb that first meeting without him.

Being in the Spence family was complicated. Like being an acrobat on a trapeze who learns to leave the security of the platform, even when it's a leap of faith. Who learns to catch the moving horizontal bar, even when it's scary. Over time, she'd been grasping that bar with her fingertips, the prospect of slipping off ever present. She knew this was the moment to either tighten her grip or freefall into her own safety net and hope it was strong enough and she was strong enough to go it alone. If she stayed, she knew she couldn't expect miracles. All she could do was choose to hang on . . . or let go.

As the evening moved along, she listened. Winston had just auditioned a new singer to join Win Spence and the Blasts. R. J., laughing, told them about the time Roger, then a high school junior, dented the fender of their new Cadillac. Roger commented that no one found it funny at the time. Audrey told about a fight that broke out between two women in her check-out line at Walmart. Over a pair of socks. Roger demonstrated how he ran over the opposing counsel's toes the first time he wheeled into a courtroom. Pearl clapped with delight at each of their tales, her eyes bright.

Maegan listened to their stories. They were just people, living their lives, doing the best they could. Making choices. Making mistakes.

But she knew they were much more than that. They were *her* people, *her* family. Their stories intertwined with hers and shaped her life. And as she absorbed the evening, a car came slowly down the road. The driver parked it across the street. The door opened, and Jack emerged. He strode up the walk. She walked down the porch steps to meet him. He stopped, smiled, and opened his arms to her. She ran into his embrace. He whispered, "I'm ready, if you are." Together they walked to the porch, to the party.

After all the chaos and indecision, she wasn't going to turn away from the people who'd influenced who she'd become. She had her answers. There was work to be done, but getting to know someone and being around them were better choices than carrying anger and hurt or harboring regret for the rest of her life. And if relationships faltered? It takes time for people to adjust, change attitudes and behaviors. She was a prime example.

Pearl's mantra rang in her ears: *Just put one foot in front of the other and hang on.*

END

www.ingramcontent.com/pod-product-compliance
Lightning Source LLC
Chambersburg PA
CBHW030632020726
47493CB00006B/1671